STEVEN E. WILDE

BOOK 6 OF THE *GEMINI GATE* SERIES

HERITAGE OF ASPEN VALLEY

Heritage of Aspen Valley (The Gemini Gate series, Book 6)
Steven E. Wilde
Hardcover edition 978-1-77342-111-7
Paperback edition 978-1-77342-110-0
Ebook edition 978-1-77342-109-4

Produced by IndieBookLauncher.com
www.IndieBookLauncher.com
Interior Design and Typesetting: Saul Bottcher

The body text of this book is set in Adobe Caslon.

Dedicated to my reviewers. You helped me get to the end of the story. Thanks for your support.

3. And it came to pass that while they were thus conversing one with another, they heard a voice as if it came out of heaven; and they cast their eyes round about, for they understood not the voice which they heard; and it was not a harsh voice, neither was it a loud voice; nevertheless, and notwithstanding it being a small voice, it did pierce them to the very soul, and did cause their hearts to burn.

—*Book of Mormon, Another Testament of Jesus Christ,*
3 Nephi 11:3

Prologue

The Old World—Ft. Laramie, Wyoming, four months after the war

"Lisa, don't leave me!" Kerri bawled as she realized Lisa was freezing to death. The Outcasts had arrived in Ft. Laramie in the middle of a freak blizzard and Lisa was the only one who's core body temperature they could not raise sufficiently, using warm baths, warm soup and shared body heat, that first night.

"What did you mean when you told Lisa to come back and not leave you," Callie asked Kerri as they sat side-by-side, near the fire, under blankets they had wrapped around their bodies.

"She . . . she told me she was leaving me," Kerri said, choking on her words, "and not to worry about her. That's what woke me."

"I didn't hear anything," Callie said apologetically.

"You wouldn't. Her voice was in my head. She said she was happy."

Later, when Lisa had recovered, Callie had asked Kerri about her relationship with Lisa. "What did you say about hearing things in your head? Is it telepathy? Does it happen often and how long has it been going on?"

"We first realized that we could communicate mind-to-mind—call it telepathy if you want—when we were working for Ambassador Daniel Porter at the UN. We were watching the ambassador giving directions to a group of foreign diplomats and I thought I heard Lisa say 'He's magnificent. I wouldn't mind spending time with him away from the office.'"

"What did you say?" I asked.

"I didn't say anything." she said.

I told her what I'd heard and she said she hadn't said that, out loud, anyway. She admitted that she'd thought it, so we started testing our ability to communicate telepathically, we called it 'sending'. It turned out to be a lot of fun, talking about people; the male interns, the foreign diplomats, and others. But we had to be careful to not accidentally say what we thought, out loud."

"Did you? Share your thoughts out loud, I mean?"

"We did, on occasion, then had to make excuses or outright lie about it. Even that was fun, trying to cover for our mistakes."

"So, you actually heard Lisa tell you good-bye." Callie confirmed.

"I did," Kerri said. "What's strange is that Lisa didn't answer me, but someone else did."

"Who?"

"I have no idea."

"What did they say?"

"Remember, I had said, 'Lisa, don't leave me', and the voice in my head said, I'm not going anywhere. Contact me anytime."

"Could you tell anything about the person—Young or old, male or female, friendly or unfriendly?" Callie asked.

"Hard to tell, but if I had to guess, I'd have to say it was an older man—middle aged, I think."

1

The Old World—present day

Eighteen years after Amos Blund and Terry Stephens built an underground retreat in Aspen Valley, to avoid the aftermath of global thermonuclear war, the United States was still recovering from the devastation to the infrastructure and the population. Nearly one hundred percent of all microchips were destroyed by EMPs during the two-week war. Millions of people had died from disease, starvation, violence and natural disasters.

In addition to building the Preserve and stocking it to survive thirty to fifty years, Amos and Terry built the Observer, to diagnose medical conditions non-intrusively, and discovered its more mysterious capability, the Gemini Gate, a door between parallel, twin worlds.

The Nuclear Regulatory Commission, under the leadership of Dr. Chandra Robertson, a young female nuclear engineer, built twenty full-size nuclear power plants in the years after the war, to restore power to the nation. Patterned after the Blund mini reactor, of which there were now thousands spread around the country, the power plants provided safe, reliable, low-cost energy to major population centers.

When Amos Blund died in the battle for Aspen Valley, a year after the war, his son, Michael, used the Gemini Gate to find and meet Amos's counterpart in the twin world, Amos 'Doc' Blund, to exchange information that would solve problems in both worlds.

President James Seymour, successor to President Gregory McCormick, later attacked the Preserve to steal the Observer in the old world, for military use, but Mike evacuated the Preserve and valley into the twin world moments before the military arrived, having been alerted by sensors mounted around Aspen Valley.

Mike, Chairman of the board since his father's death, eventually moved the residents back into the original Preserve in the old world, where they all felt more comfortable and used Artificial Intelligence to try to solve social problems in the valley.

2

The Old World—eighteen years earlier

The world war that started when Al-Qaeda exploded a nuclear bomb in Washington, D.C., lasted less than two weeks, but left eighty-five percent of the infrastructure in the northern hemisphere damaged, and communications and electronics fried by EMPs. A few months after the war, the federal government developed a vaccine and began vaccinating citizens against Smallpox K, a mutated form of smallpox that had escaped containment as a result of the war. Named for former Vice President Art Klemp, who had caught the virus and gone renegade during the pandemic, spreading the contagion, and threatening to kill the president, the disease spread from its points of release in Georgia and Maryland. Almost a year later, based on the research and developments of the brilliant doctor and scientist, Amos Blund, and continued by his counterpart, Doc Blund, in the twin world, the government finally had the tools to stop the virus and rebuild the infrastructure, starting with removing nuclear contamination from water, soil and air, curing radiation sickness, and building nuclear reactors to supply safe, reliable electrical power and restore communications.

The U.S. government in the old world organized what remained of the military and the Corp of Engineers, to begin rebuilding the infrastructure, starting in several key locations in the northeast, southeast, Midwest and Rocky Mountains—they waited on the western states because of the massive destruction caused by several direct nuclear hits on major population centers.

With communications restored to parts of the country, the

government broadcast to anyone who could hear, its plans to rebuild the infrastructure. The military and Corps began hiring local skilled workers to assist the massive effort to rebuild airports, government buildings, hospitals, water treatment and distribution systems and freeways. Hiring local resources, including unskilled workers in support roles, the government would be supporting the local economies in much the same way as they had with the Civilian Conservation Corps—a voluntary public work relief program that operated from 1933 to 1942.

In the second year after the war, they reached the Wasatch Front, entering from the East on Interstate 80. Because of the explosion at Hill Air Force Base, north of Salt Lake City and the resultant earthquake along the Wasatch Front, the first thing they had to do was repair the damaged section of freeway where it crossed the Wasatch Fault and entered the Salt Lake Valley.

As soon as trucks could pass on the freeway, a military convoy entered the valley and spread out to various locations. The military leaders met with state leaders in Salt Lake City to set priorities and coordinate logistics. At the international airport, they cleared and repaired the runways and removed damaged aircraft, to allow military transports to land *en masse* with building materials and relief supplies. Small nuclear reactors were installed at power substations around the valley and connected to existing or new power lines, using pre-microchip technology. Power was restored to water treatment and distribution facilities, which were also repaired or rebuilt, as needed, with pre-microchip technology. Hospitals were repaired or rebuilt and new medical procedures to treat cancer and radiation sickness patients became commonplace, with amazing positive results. New facilities were than set up to treat water, soil and air to eliminate radiation contamination. Since the people still didn't have electrical power to their homes or gas for their cars, they still had to spend most of their time and energy gathering the basic necessities for survival.

As the work in Salt Lake City progressed, the effort spread north and south to encompass the entire Wasatch Front, then continued in all directions from there. All of the work along the Wasatch Front was monitored by Michael Blund and Terry Stephens from the Preserve in Logan Canyon, using the Gemini Gate.

The Twin World

In the twin world, where war had been avoided, due to the efforts of President Gregory 'Buck' McCormick and his advisors, with the secret help of Amos 'Doc' Blund, global reconstruction wasn't required. In fact, they enjoyed the benefits of those same energy and medical advancements without suffering the devastating loss and damage experienced in Amos Blund's old world. The only people who knew how all of it was accomplished were McCormick, his security team and top advisors, one female supreme court justice, and Doc and Lillie Blund.

Doc and Lillie lived in Logan, Utah, on a five-acre estate, with a government-paid security guard, Tyler 'JP' Morgan, and his family. When not at their estate, Doc and Lillie could usually be found at their retreat in Logan Canyon, Aspen Valley, which was a near duplicate of the Preserve, in the same location in the old world—Amos Blund's world.

3

The Old World—Fort Campbell, Kentucky, eighteen years earlier

"You've got a big ego for someone so small," the soldier said, but Aiden Short didn't want to hear it. At five-foot three—five-foot four and a half in his combat boots, Short barely came to the other man's shoulders; but the man was right, Short did have an ego, and it got him into trouble once in a while. Like now. He was tough as nails, but against someone trained as well as he was, he was at a disadvantage, unless he could get the drop on him—get in the first punch.

With both arms resting at his sides, his fist caught the other soldier off-guard, hitting him under the chin. The blow drove the man's teeth through his tongue, nearly cutting it off, causing it to bleed profusely. The soldier attempted to swallow a mouthful of blood, but a gag reflex caused him to spit it out, all over Short, while Short got in another couple of blows to the man's unguarded midsection.

Three other soldiers, standing nearby, anticipated the attack because of Short's reputation for violence and dirty fighting, and intervened. Two of them dragged Short away from the other man, while the third helped the man to a chair and called for a medic.

Later that day, Short found himself standing at attention in front of his commander's battered desk, trying to ignore his commander's grating voice as he read, out loud, the regulations that Short had violated and the discipline he would receive as a result.

Short would tolerate the discipline—it was never too harsh—knowing that the other guy had it worse, lying in the post hospital, nursing a swollen, damaged tongue and sore jaw. It was always worth it. He would teach them respect, even if he had to hospitalize every soldier on the post, including his commanding officer.

Short amused himself as he cleaned latrines, thinking about the woman he had spoken to earlier that day by mind-speak. He could tell it was a young woman from her voice and her frantic pleading. She had seemed surprised that anyone besides her dying girlfriend could hear her; but he had been listening to people all over the country mind-speak to each other, ever since . . . well, as long as he could remember. It was his gift, and one that made him better than other men. He knew a time was coming when he would use his gift to control the destiny of the country, maybe the world. He hadn't figured out how, yet, but knew his time was coming. This was the first time he had used his gift to communicate with someone outside his circle of close associates—he couldn't say 'friends' because he never cultivated friendships—so he would remember her voice and call her again, if she didn't call him first.

☢

Months later, a mutated Smallpox virus spread along the east coast and Short was assigned to one of the military's elimination teams. He was always underestimated because of his short stature. He enjoyed the assignment because it gave him power—an excuse to belittle people, be mean to them if it pleased him, and shoot them if they didn't follow his instructions.

During a typical assignment, the squad would stop a group of citizens who were out on the street and question them. 'It looks like you have the virus. Why are you outside during curfew? Climb in the back of the van. If you resist, I'll have to shoot you.' One man sent a message by mind-speak, which Short obviously heard. "You wouldn't dare," the man had thought. Short, who had looked away at the wrong time and thought the man had spoken out loud, turned and shot him in the chest. The man died and Short was sent before his commanding officer.

"It looks like you have a history of violent confrontations, the officer said, looking in Short's service record."

"All of those cases were self-defense," Short complained.

"This one says the other guy didn't even swing a fist, yet you hit him hard enough to nearly cut off his tongue. How was that self-defense?"

"He was going to hit me, so I hit him first."

"He reported that all he did was make fun of your name. This one says that you hit a guy for asking you to leave his girlfriend alone. He said you were hitting on her—his words—and you became physically abusive to her."

"She came on to me, then acted offended when her boyfriend showed up."

"So, you tried to rip her dress off?"

"I stumbled into her and it tore."

"This latest one says an unarmed man resisted arrest so you shot him in the chest, in front of his family. Were those your instructions?"

"Not exactly."

"Not exactly?"

"Not exactly, sir."

"Short, we're in the middle of a crisis. Public relations is a delicate matter right now."

"I know . . . sir," Short interrupted.

"I know you do. You've probably heard that every day, and don't interrupt me again."

"Sorry, sir."

"Short, I'm sorry, but there's no place for your ego here. I'm discharging you. You can go pack your bags and we'll get you home to Montana. Dismissed."

"Sir . . ." Short tried to say more.

"I said 'dismissed' soldier. Unless you want a court-martial in addition to a discharge, get out of here."

Short saw the futility of arguing. He considered shooting the officer, but knew he couldn't get away with that, with guards just outside the door. He had finally lost a battle, and it wasn't even a physical one, but a battle of wills. He turned on his heels and left the office. Next stop—Montana.

☢

Short was tired of defending his name. He was going to change it. At the same time, he wanted a name that described who he thought he was—who he wanted to become. All the way to Montana, he thought about mind-speak and the young woman he had spoken to. It was as if they were the first two of their kind to appear, kind of like Adam and Eve. The more he thought about it, the easier it was to imagine himself the leader of a huge society of mind-speakers—a new race of people. He would be Adam—it wasn't much different from his real name, Aiden—and the young woman would be his queen, his Eve.

"I'll begin calling people to me using the ham radios and mind-speak, including Eve," He thought aloud.

☢

Technically, he was a member of a small militia in Western Montana that had organized long before the war started. They were a bunch of like-minded survivalists, who didn't want to be ruled by the federal government. So, at the beginning of the war, they had consolidated their resources in the underground bunker of one of their number and he had become their military commander. The militia realized quickly that they were short on certain supplies and asked for volunteers to join the U.S. Army to acquire what they lacked, which meant stealing ammunition and M.R.E.s. Aiden was one of the volunteers and managed to steal a quantity of both before being drummed out of the service for his violent behavior.

Upon his return to the militia, he convinced himself that he was a hero and should be treated and rewarded like one. He insisted on being called Adam, which everyone seemed to think was a stupid affectation. He ingratiated himself to their commander, in order to gain special privileges and assignments, his favorite one being the quartermaster, or the keeper of the armaments. He liked knowing how many rifles, handguns and bullets they had and who had what in their possession at any given time. It was a powerful position and he imagined that with his knowledge, he could take over control of the militia at any time.

Aiden convinced nine of the twelve people in the militia who had ham radios, to work with him to gather survivors of the war who wanted to reshape the world in their own image. He wrote a clever script for the radio operators, then asked them to begin calling all their contacts and inviting them to join his crusade.

The first part of his plan—to gather people to him—was slow, but was fairly straightforward. There were always people looking for someone with a cause, who they could link up with, it seemed, and gradually, over time, he gathered a lot of them to his militia in Montana.

When the commander and his lieutenant got into a serious fight over control of the militia, Adam saw his chance to gain more control. He sided with the lieutenant, agreeing to help him become the commander if he would name Short his new lieutenant.

Eventually, it came to a vote—no bloodshed—and Short's followers tipped the balance of power in favor of the lieutenant. The commander was banned and left his own bunker, never to return. Then, with his position solidified and his role in the battle acknowledged, Short convinced one of his followers to murder the new commander in his sleep. He was the one to raise a clamor of murder, his follower was banned and ejected from the bunker, and he was elected and installed as the new commander.

Short convinced himself that he could take over the government in much the same way; he just had to continue building his army of followers, and he was amazed, when he thought about how many they had talked to that still hadn't joined him. What he really wanted though, was to find Eve.

4

Presidential Palace, Brasilia, Brazil, present day

In a country where every young man was required to serve in the military, it was no surprise that young men in uniforms walked the streets of Brasilia. What was not normal was having the military occupy the presidential palace and conduct meetings of the House and Senate. General Ramos's staff had escorted the president's family from the palace and arranged for them to return to their family home in Curitiba, under house arrest. General Ramos stood at the podium in the Senate chambers and addressed the men and women assembled there.

"Where is the president?" the president of the Senate asked.

"He's is in detention awaiting trial," the general said.

"What are the charges against him?" the president of the Senate asked calmly, not becoming upset or belligerent in any way. It was a reflection of the attitude of the government leaders toward the military. "And what's the timetable?"

"He is charged with misbehavior toward female members of his administration, unbecoming of a national leader and the trust we place in him. The timetable has not been set, but the Senate and House will be involved in setting the timetable."

The Old World—Philadelphia, Pennsylvania

"What is it, Jim," President Greg McCormick asked his vice president, Jim Seymour.

"You've heard that the Brazilian president has been removed from the presidential palace and placed under arrest?" Jim asked.

"I have. What's the latest?"

"General Ramos has assumed power and is holding the president in detention awaiting trial."

"This is a major concern for us. Brazil is the *stable* government in South America. If they can't hold it together, it could destabilize the remainder of the continent, including Central America. What can we do?"

"We could send troops," Jim suggested half-heartedly.

"They don't need our soldiers. They have more than we do."

"Yes sir, they do. Maybe, if we had Doc's Gemini Gate, we could infiltrate their government, assess what's going on, and prepare a plan for helping."

"You know how unlikely it is for Doc to give us his gate, don't you?"

"Maybe you can order him to give it to us."

"Unlikely to make a difference. Doc won't voluntarily give us his technology."

"He gave us the mini nuclear reactor."

"Yes, he did, at great cost to me personally, and to our friendship."

"Is your friendship more important than peace in the western hemisphere?"

"Let me think about that, Jim."

5

Aspen Valley—January, Seventeen Years Earlier

"Hi, I'm Rick," the man sitting next to Kerri said, "and you must be Kerri."

"Guilty as charged," Kerri said, trying to be funny, since all she knew about Rick was that he was one of the widowed men from Garden City and had come to the valley as an invader, to help Jason Carlsen take over the Preserve. He had surrendered rather than being shot. "Are you from Garden City?" she asked, the only polite thing she could think of to say.

"Actually, I'm from Brigham City," he said. "I come from a family of nurserymen and had started a wholesale nursery business in Bigham City when all hell broke loose on the Wasatch Front. Even before the explosion at Hill Airforce Base, people were coming through Bigham City to escape the threat of war that was on the news. Military installations were being bombed across the country and we had three of them within about fifty miles of us."

"Why did you go to Garden City?" she asked.

"We had a cabin there,"

"You and your wife?"

"It belonged to her dad. It was the family's emergency gathering location. We took our three kids and expected to meet up with all their cousins. The kids thought of it as a vacation."

"How old are your kids?" she asked, not realizing that they had all died from the Smallpox plague.

"They were five, seven and ten. We married when I was eighteen."

When she considered his comment and the fact that the kids weren't with him, she realized that they must have died. "I'm sorry," she said, placing a hand over her mouth.

"That's alright," he said. "I'm beginning to reconcile myself to my fate."

"So, did they get to have that vacation with their cousins?" she asked, hoping she wasn't making another faux pas—that the kids' last days were fun.

"Actually, by the time we got to the cabin, several other groups had beat us there. They weren't family. People had broken in and were making themselves at home, eating the food we had stocked it with. We called the police, but they said breaking and entering was low on their priority list because there were thousands of extra people in town and crime had skyrocketed. Food was so scarce and B&E was so common that they didn't have time to follow up on all the cases."

Kerri opened her mouth to say something consoling, but nothing came out. She didn't know how to apologize for other people's insensitivity, bad manners, crimes, or whatever he judged it to be.

"The people left when we told them we were the owners. But they took everything they could carry out of the cabin, with them; food, blankets, toilet paper. They didn't leave us much."

"I'm sorry," Kerri said, but it sounded hollow to her ears. "Did your family arrive safely?" she asked.

"They never arrived at all. We heard on the news, before all the stations quit broadcasting, that there were natural and manmade roadblocks south of Brigham City and that the police were evacuating people in all directions. Who knows where they ended up?

"Then there was the explosion at Hill Airforce Base," he continued. "They said there were fires, but none of them reached us in Garden City. Even so, there were so many people around the lake that city services were inundated quickly and even water was rationed within days of our arrival. Businesses closed. We really missed the raspberry shakes that Garden City was famous for. I think that bothered the kids more than anything else.

"Several family groups camped in our yard. When the first cases of smallpox appeared, everything shut down, stores, schools, resorts, everything. When our five-year-old got sick—we guessed it was from playing with other children camped in the yard—a Doctor visited and called it a plague, not knowing specifically what it was, and told us to quarantine him. He was so sick and in pain, but we couldn't do anything to give him relief. It was hardest on Marie—my wife. She cried constantly.

"Two days later, the other two caught it, then Marie got sick and I had to take care of all of them by myself. I tried heating pads, cold packs, aspirin, ibuprofen. I couldn't get the doctor back. Someone said he was sick, too. I must have had a mild case; I had all the symptoms, but wasn't sick like the rest. When Sammy died, I felt like lying down next to him and dying. The other two children died within the week, then Marie died later that same day; I think she just gave up.

"When I heard the rumor that Jason Carlson had a retreat, with clean water and food, I followed him around for days, trying to learn more. Could I have saved my family if we'd acted sooner? Could I still save myself? I was all alone. I think I was becoming despondent. Half the time I wanted to die. I went with Jason to the valley out of despair, hoping to find hope. I had a gun, but it was obvious immediately that Jason had lied about his ownership of the valley. I never fired a shot. I surrendered and asked to be allowed to stay in the valley with the other survivors from Garden City. So, here I am."

"I'm so sorry for your trials and for the loss of your family," Kerri said, her eyes moist with sympathy. "Are you beginning to feel comfortable here?"

"Everyone here has been so kind," he said. Tears came to his eyes. He wiped them away with the back of his hand. She placed her hand on top of his, in sympathy and consolation; but he may have interpreted it as something more, since he started from that time forward, to seek her out and spend time with her.

"Who's your friend," Callie asked Rick at breakfast, motioning to the man sitting across the table from them. Kerri sat on one side of Rick and Callie sat on the other.

"His name is Taylor," Rick said. "Taylor, let me introduce you to Callie and Kerri."

"Hello ladies," Taylor said, his voice filled with melancholy.

"What's his problem?" Callie asked quietly.

"He's still mourning the loss of his family in Garden City," Rick said.

"That must have been terribly difficult for both of you to lose your entire family to the Smallpox pandemic," Callie said.

"We heard that only about thirty percent of those that caught it actually died from it, so it was rare for entire families to be wiped out," Rick said.

"I have an idea," Callie said. "Why don't the four of us go on a picnic?"

"I'll warn you now," Taylor said, "I'm not very good company."

"Come on," Callie said. "It's going to be a beautiful day and we should enjoy it."

"Besides," Rick said, "You don't want to leave me alone with these two beautiful young ladies."

"Beth told me she has a job for you two," Kerri said, "so why don't you see what that is and we'll make a lunch, then we can leave when you're ready." The agreement with the Garden City survivors was that they could stay in the valley if they agreed to help out. Since Beth was the de facto leader in the valley, in much the same way that Mike was the leader in the Preserve, she would be the person telling people what needed to be done.

Rick and Taylor found Beth coordinating housecleaning in the big cabin, directing adults and children to specific tasks, inspecting their work when they reported that they were finished, and directing some, particularly the children to "try again and get it right this time".

"Taylor" Beth said, "I understand that you worked for the power company."

"I did, Beth," he said, "I lived in Coalville, next to the power substation, monitored the station, and performed maintenance on all of the power company equipment across the Summit and Wasatch counties. That is, until the EMPs blew the transformers and sent sparks everywhere. My last task at the station was putting out brush fires, before they spread.

"Well, Doc asked if you would help with the communications in the valley. He knows that's not quite the same thing, but would appreciate a second opinion on things."

"I'd be happy to, but Callie and . . ."

"Not right now," Beth interrupted. "I know the girls planned to invite you for a hike and a picnic today. But I would appreciate you spending an hour clearing and lining the trail between the cabins before you go. Would that work for you? Even that doesn't need to be finished today."

"You bet," Rick said quickly.

"That would be fine," Taylor said at the same time, but with less enthusiasm.

An hour later, Callie and Kerri found them hauling logs and rocks to line a path between the cabins. They were covered with dust and dirt. There was still grass in the path, but they figured what didn't die from being trampled, they could clear later.

"Do you want to clean up a little before our picnic?" Kerri asked them.

"Probably a good idea," Rick said, brushing his hands together and brushing off his jeans, making a cloud of dust, like Pigpen in the Charlie Brown cartoon. They went to the cabin and washed up, then returned to the yard where the women waited patiently.

"Would you rather take a fifteen-minute walk or a two-hour hike before lunch?" Kerri asked.

"I'm up for either," Rick said.

"How about the short walk before lunch and see how we feel after lunch," Taylor asked. "I'm hungry."

"A short walk it is," Callie said. She took Taylor's offered hand and started walking up the path that led out of the valley. A few minutes later, Taylor dropped Callie's hand and placed his arm around her waist, while he told her about his duties for the power company. Eventually, Kerri and Rick, walking behind them, held hands and talked quietly about what the Outcasts had gone through to get to Utah and the valley.

☢

They crossed the highway and settled under the one tree in the field that offered any shade, which wasn't much in the middle of the day, in the middle of winter. None of them were cold as a result of the metabolism changes caused by the virus.

"What are you talking about, Kerri?" Callie asked.

"I'm telling Rick about our travels," Kerri asked. "Would you like me to speak louder so Taylor can hear?"

"Yes, please," Taylor said, as he laid out a blanket on the snow-covered ground and they all sat. Kerri continued. "We walked miles a day, from Georgia to the Mississippi, all the way to St. Louis, then to Wyoming, where we got caught in an early winter storm and stopped for the winter."

"Miles a day?" Taylor asked.

"A side-effect of the virus is increased stamina, so we seldom tired from the journey. We were more affected by the encounters with angry people, the accidental deaths, and dealing with Jason at Laketown."

"I've noticed the increased stamina and resistance to cold," Rick said, "but had no idea why I seemed to have more energy. I thought it might be from eating better food. Who built the cabins?"

"We all helped, with supplies provided by Amos," Kerri said.

"And Amos died?"

"Yes, in the battle for Aspen Valley."

"I thought I heard someone say Doc was Amos in a different world," Rick said.

"That's right. The twin world."

"I'm still having trouble with this twin world thing."

"If I hadn't been through the gate, and seen the other world, I'd still have trouble with it," Kerri said. "But it's there. I've been there. Taylor, Rick told us how he got here. What's your story?"

"It's not very interesting," he said.

"I'd really like to hear it," Callie said. "Please tell us."

"Alright, but if you yawn or close your eyes from boredom, I'll stop talking," he said.

"I'll try not to close my eyes or yawn," Callie said.

"Okay. We lived in Coalville, Utah, next door to the electrical substation. When an EMP blew out the transformers in the station, they exploded, sending sparks everywhere, setting off small grass fires as far away as two hundred yards from the station. I put out all the fires, but the phone rang continuously, people trying to find out what happened to their power. Then the power went out completely, a few minutes later: I used a two-way radio to call the office in Salt Lake City to find out from them what had happened.

"The entire coverage area, including all of Utah, and parts of the surrounding states and the northwest, had blacked out from the EMP. The rumor was that war could come to Utah at any time because of the nearness of military installations—Hill Airforce Base, Camp Williams and Fort Douglas—so I packed up the family, in our camper, for at least a week-long stay away from home, and prepared to leave. By the time the bomb hit Hill, half the town had evacuated for Evanston, Wyoming.

"The highway patrol had blocked all roads leading west, toward Ogden and Salt Lake and had converted all traffic lanes to eastbound traffic. In Evanston, we wasted a couple of hours looking for a place to camp. Finding nothing, we turned north and headed for Bear Lake, thinking there must be something there. If nothing else, we had friends who owned a cabin that we could mooch off of. We were shocked when we got to Bear Lake, finding, if anything, that there was less room for camping than in Evanston. I even considered going back to Evanston, but my wife . . ."

Taylor choked up and couldn't continue.

"It's okay, Taylor. Losing someone so close to you has got to be hard."

After a few moments, Taylor had himself under control and continued, "My wife suggested that since people were still headed east toward Evanston, conditions would soon be as bad there as at Bear Lake.

"I drove to our friends' cabin, north of Garden City, but couldn't get in their driveway because of all the cars. People we didn't know had camped on their front lawn, but that didn't account for all the cars. I went to the door anyway, only to confirm what appeared to be happening; they were overrun with friends, family, and strangers, but they suggested we park the camper across the bottom of the driveway. Our food ran out a week later. The cabin ran out of food a few days after that because they were sharing. As the transient population grew, everything started to shut down. There was no food to buy, and water became rationed. Even the sewer system backed up and people started dumping sewage in the lake.

"We heard a rumor that people were getting sick closer to town; then people began to die. Our son got sick, then my wife, who was trying to treat his fever and rashes." Taylor stopped talking and looked at Callie, his distress evident in his face.

"You don't need to continue," Callie said sympathetically.

"No," he said. "I'll be okay. Just give me a second." He sucked in a breath and let it out noisily, then continued.

"I had to take care of both of them. They got so weak they couldn't even go to the bathroom by themselves. When our son died, I think my wife just gave up. She died later the next day. I couldn't even bury them," he said, agonized. "The life went out of me, but I carried on, one day at a time. Then Jason showed up with his fantastic story of a retreat in the mountains where there was plenty of food, water and medicine. I didn't believe much of what he said; if it was true, why would he leave? It was unbelievable. I decided to follow him; even if none of it were true, since it would get me away from the pandemic and I would be taking action instead of sitting and doing nothing.

"Jason said to take a gun, but I didn't have one and wouldn't use it if I did. I couldn't shoot someone, even if I got shot at; so I was surprised at the ambush in the valley. I wasn't surprised that Jason wanted a gunfight; he was an angry and selfish man. The death of the invaders didn't trouble me. I reasoned that death might be better than the living hell we'd been living in." Taylor stopped talking and bowed his head. A tear dropped from his nose into his lap. Callie handed him a napkin to dry his eyes and blow his nose. Then he looked into Callie's face and saw the compassion there.

"Thank you, Callie," he said, "for letting me talk. It was good to get that out."

"You're welcome, Taylor," she said. "Thank you for feeling like you could bare your soul to us."

"Can I have some more salad?" he asked.

"Absolutely," she said, "Then maybe you'd like to hike up that hill over there," she said, pointing, "before we go back."

"So long as it's not so muddy that we spend the whole time sliding backwards," he said

---

"How was the picnic," Beth asked Kerri when they got back to the valley.

"It was a good change of pace," Kerri said. "Rick is definitely more at ease here than Taylor is."

"Oh? How's that?"

"Taylor really misses his wife and son. Rick misses his family, for sure, but he doesn't get weepy every time he talks about them."

"I see," Beth said. "What does Callie think about that?"

"She's right here. You can ask her yourself."

Callie entered the cabin, followed by Taylor and Rick, which made it awkward for Beth to ask, so she changed the subject. "I saw how much you two got done on lining the path between the cabins. A little more and I think we can call it good. What do you think?"

"I think," Rick said, looking at Taylor for a reaction, "that we could finish it in less than an hour. What do you think Taylor?"

"I agree. Would you like us to do it tonight? Now?" Taylor asked.

"Whenever you like." Beth said. "There's no hurry."

"I'd like to go to the gym," Rick said, "if I have time tonight."

"I'll join you," Kerri said, "and we can do the sauna and pool after that."

"Would you like to do that, Taylor?" Callie asked.

"Not tonight, thanks," Taylor said, "but you go ahead and enjoy yourself. I'll catch you another time."

"Callie," Beth said, before Callie could commit, one way or the other, "can I speak with you for a few minutes?"

"Sure Beth. Thanks, Taylor, for a lovely afternoon," she said to Taylor's back as he left the cabin. "What is it, Beth?"

"Do you think Taylor enjoyed the picnic?" Beth asked.

"I don't know," she said. "He's pretty quiet, says very little unless asked a direct question. Why?"

"He's my responsibility now. I want to know how he's adjusting. Does he seem to be adjusting?"

"He's still very much focused on his wife," Callie said. "Is that your only reason for asking?" She smiled mischievously at Beth.

"Oh, you know me too well, Callie," Beth said, with a sigh. "I also want to know how much you like him."

"I'd like to help him come out of his shell," Callie said, "but I'm not much of a conversationalist, myself."

"You might be exactly what he needs, Callie."

6

The Twin World—Aspen Valley, present day

Life in Aspen Valley settled into a routine. There were no dangers, from external sources or from within. Everyone got along fine—suffering only little squabbles and disagreements that are common to human nature--and there were no intrusions from outside the valley. Most of the residents of the valley were content with their lives, marrying, having children, building homes, raising crops and tending fruit trees. With no interaction with the outside world, there was little to look forward to and little variation in their routine. The Outcasts spent most of their time learning to live in their new environment, finding hobbies that revolved around what they found in the valley, including hiking, swimming, gardening and decorating their homes.

Interaction with the residents of the preserve was inconsistent. Mike supplied building materials and advice on construction of the Outcasts' first and second homes. Terry provided medical supplies and advice. Doc, who everyone had come to rely on as the source of all knowledge, advice, and access to the rest of the world, generally left all decision-making to Mike, the chairman of the board.

Mike, Terry and Doc continued experimenting with the Observer. Terry worked on understanding its medical applications, while Doc and Mike played with its AI capability. Each of Doc's AI experiments disrupted everyone's lives for a time, then things would settle down again until the next experiment.

Becca periodically spoke with one or more of the Outcasts, by radio, about meal preparation, recommending menus to vary the Outcasts' limited diet. She also made food ingredients available that the Outcasts couldn't obtain for themselves, ingredients that she sometimes had to rely on Doc to obtain from the twin world.

Katie and Rachel recommended activities for amusement, exercise or learning, often donating books from their vast school library, after the radiation contamination in the valley had been cleaned up.

Callie and Taylor had plenty of time to become good friends, then lovers, then man and wife. As did Rick and Kerri.

☢

"That man contacted me again," Kerri said to Callie as they watched the children play games in the yard. The snow that had covered the ground for over a year after the war, had finally melted after the effects of radiation had been controlled, and the weather went back to a more normal seasonal pattern.

"What did he say this time?" Callie asked.

"The same as before, he wants to know why I won't tell him where I am or what's going on."

"What did you tell him?"

"I stopped answering, hoping he'd give it up. Maybe he'd think I was dead and go bother someone else."

"Why don't you answer him?"

"Before Amos died, he told us that he wanted the existence of the valley to remain a secret, and I haven't heard Mike say anything different since he took over. I won't tell this guy where we are unless Mike approves."

"But if Mike doesn't know you're talking to the guy, he won't have an opinion. In effect, you're making the decision for him."

"And you haven't heard him?" Kerri asked Callie.

"Not that I'm aware of," Callie said, "I don't have your talent."

"I hear other voices, too, sometimes. There seem to be a lot of telepaths out there, trying to talk to each other, maybe because all other communications are down."

"Can you tell what they're saying?" Callie asked.

"They seem to be far away," Kerri said. "I tried to follow one conversation, a couple of year ago, but it sounded like they were just practicing and really had nothing important to say."

"Do you think your guy has something important to say?" Callie asked.

"First of all, he's not my guy" Kerri said, "Rick's my guy; and second, I'm not going to talk to him unless Mike says it's okay." Kerri and Rick had been happily married for about four years, the same as Callie and Taylor, having been married on the same day, by a minister that Mike had found in Garden City.

"Then you're going to talk to Mike about him?"

"I guess I better, so you'll get off my case."

"I'm sorry, Kerri, but if I were hearing voices, I'd want to know what they were talking about. Maybe they need help or have something to offer."

"Well, we can't help them, and we don't need anything from them, so I don't see the point."

7

The Twin World—The mouth of Logan Canyon, present day, June

David Murdock breathed a sigh of relief as the ribbon cutting ceremony ended and he hadn't been asked to make a speech. Technically, the upper Logan Canyon project was his, but Evans, his supervisor, and his superiors in the highway department were taking all the credit and the bows for its successful completion, on time and under budget, something rare for a highway project. He knew that the parking lot and all the folding chairs that had been set up in First Dam Park at the mouth of Logan Canyon had been filled by state, county and local politicians and reporters, which bothered him only because his team of engineers, who had helped him design the road and manage the project, had to sit on the grassy, sloping verge of the parking lot.

David loved Logan Canyon, his favorite place to hike, camp and fish. He had been lobbying for this project ever since he'd graduated from the University of Utah and gone to work for the highway department, ten years earlier. With the mushrooming population around Bear Lake, the highway from Logan to Garden City had become overstressed, unable to handle the traffic load, and that had been the case ten years earlier. The population growth in Utah had been high for decades, especially since the war, when people recognized the relative safety of living near the mountains, in the middle of the continent. The growth spread out from the Wasatch Front in all directions. Highway 89 had been a lower priority than the interstates and some other highways; but its time had finally come.

When the request for proposals had gone out from the state, several large design firms and construction contractors had submitted proposals. David's proposal was the only unsolicited one and it was rejected out-of-hand by Evans because, Evans said, it was a conflict of interest. David worked for the department that would manage the construction. David believed Evans felt threatened. David could easily be promoted above Evans, if his role in this project became known and the opportunity presented itself.

David had a good eye for design. He trusted his design team to help him put together the perfect proposal for the new road. Evans's rejection meant that they would not even be given the chance to prepare their proposal.

As it turned out, the newly elected governor was a family friend of Ty Davis, one of David's team members; and before David knew it, Ty had asked the governor whether Evans had the right to reject their proposal.

The governor spoke to the head of the state highway department, two levels above Evans, who passed the word down that David's proposal would be accepted. The state wanted the best design for the road and didn't want to restrict where it came from. Evans had reluctantly notified David of the department's decision, with a warning that none of the proposal preparation would be performed on department computers or during normal work hours. So, the entire proposal was drafted in the basement computer lab of Ty's parents' home, where Ty designed Virtual Reality computer games in his spare time. Ty, who had a lucrative side business in VR games, had agreed to delay the release of his latest invention while the design team worked on the road proposal in evening and weekend sessions.

The proposals were submitted and judged by an independent team of industry representatives and university professors appointed by the lieutenant governor. David's team design won, which surprised Evan's because of all the roadblocks he'd placed in David's path, and the project moved forward to the solicitation for road construction bids. David's team had no construction resources, so they didn't bid, but they were given responsibility to manage the project, which suited David just fine; after all, he was a professional project manager and this was his design.

The construction had been completed on time and under budget, which was rare for a highway project, and David credited his team for their close supervision of the contractors and his innovative ideas for cutting costs without compromising quality or integrity. His team members had spent so much time in the canyon, watching the contractors, that they knew where all the good fishing holes were and where the wildlife roamed.

Now that the speeches were finished and the ribbon across the highway was cut, the dignitaries that wanted to be seen as supporting a successful project, piled into their cars and headed up the canyon to the starting point of the project, near Cottonwood Canyon, the upper twenty-one miles of highway 89 ending at the Bear Lake Highway in Garden City.

David had thought that with this project completed, Evans would find someone else to pick on, but it was not to be. Evans had already refocused on another of David's projects and wanted to micro-manage it like he had tried with the Upper Logan Canyon project.

David clicked the remote to unlock his red Camaro convertible, lowered the top and fired up his new ride. The car had been his gift to himself for a successful project, paid for from his bonus, and he loved it. He loved the smooth ride and the horsepower under the hood. He'd only had it a week and he'd already noticed the looks he got from women, and the notes left under the wiper blades with phone numbers and the message, 'Call me'. The three team members who had helped manage the project walked over and David said, "Climb in!"

Ty opened the passenger side front door, set himself carefully in the seat and closed the door softly, showing the proper respect for David's baby. Tanner and Cody climbed in the back and set the plants, that had been setting on the seat, on their laps. Checking that they all had their seat belts buckled, David revved the engine and within minutes, was cruising just below the speed limit up his favorite canyon, near the tail end of the line of cars and trucks. He loved the fresh smell, from a recent rain, on the plants and trees. The sun broke from behind a cloud and the sunlight glistened off the wet, vivid green leaves. He lowered his sun glasses from the top of his head to the bridge of his nose. He listened to the swishing of the tires on the wet asphalt and noticed the pools of rainwater in the ditches on the sides of the roadway. *Ah,* he thought . . . and smiled. *This is my world. This is where I belong.* He felt like he had entered a new and pristine world meant only for him.

He noticed how the sun, warming the asphalt, caused steam to rise from the roadway, creating a mirage of shimmering light ahead. One of the absurdities of nature, that mirage, giving the impression of something being there that was not, like a lake in the desert.

He chuckled at the thought and shook his head. The absurdity in his life was that he was taking a carload of potted plants, jewelry and other presents to propose to a woman he wasn't sure he loved. He wasn't sure he was capable of loving another woman, not since Heather's automobile accident and death twenty months earlier. It was so difficult for him to open up to people anyway. He had lost a big part of himself when Heather died after the accident. The two weeks that she lay in the hospital in a coma, hooked up to all the machines, had seemed like an eternity. He had spent every spare moment in her hospital room, holding her hand, talking to her, and listening for any response; but there was none, and she had passed on, likely not knowing he had been there.

The guy who had run into her car had been convicted of a DUI and spent six months in jail. A week after his release, he was arrested again—another DUI. It had taken David a long time to forgive the guy, but he didn't know if he had anything left to give to Stefani. Perhaps he was afraid of losing her, too.

Upper Logan Canyon

As the motorcade reached Cottonwood Canyon, the starting point for the project, some cars stopped, their occupants getting out to look around; but most of the cars turned around and headed back to Logan, without stopping. They had shown their support and the local media had been on hand to take video, so they would be remembered at election time. David stopped and let his team members out so they could catch a ride back, then he continued up the canyon, admiring their work. From here on, he was on a divided highway which hugged the contours of the canyon, crossing the river when there was insufficient space on one side or the other; but always blending in with the landscape.

His Camaro swept around a banked curve, one that David, himself, had designed. "We did this right," he thought. Then, 'Stefani should be pleased with the potted plants.' She was studying botany at Utah State University and was always talking about this or that plant. She thought David wasn't interested and accused him of not paying attention when she talked about her plants. But he had spent weeks looking for just the right ones. When he had asked her, "Why botany? You can't make a living with a botany degree," she had disagreed, becoming almost hysterical, and insisted that there was a demand for botanists.

As the Camaro swept across a bridge over the river, he thought about the care his team had taken to ensure that the new road blended in with the landscape. Even the bridges were partially hidden by the trees and brush, and decorated to look like the forest around them. Anyway, Stefani figured she'd get married and settle down with children and home-making before too many more years. She already had the family cabin in Garden City, which she'd inherited from her grandparents upon their deaths in a plane crash. So, it wasn't like she had to make a lot of money to live. She had told David on several occasions that they could live there once they married, but it was always, 'her home' they would live in, which grated on his nerves.

He guessed that it was her self-confidence and sense of direction that attracted him to her. 'Well, that's great for her to know what she wants. But what am I doing with a carload of plants, the names of which I can't even pronounce; about to make a commitment I'm not sure of?'

David snapped out of his musings suddenly, as he realized that the mirage ahead of him was not acting normally. The roadway had just curved to the left and was about to make a long, gentle sweep to the right before climbing to the overlook. The sun was now slightly off to the left, so the mirage should have disappeared, but it didn't. David was about to pass off this phenomenon as a result of the bank of the road surface, but his eyes were playing other tricks on him. He knew a mirage should move forward along the roadway, keeping about the same distance from the car at all times, due to the angle of the sun. But he could swear the mirage was closer than a few moments ago.

He thought about that place south of Rapid City, South Dakota, where the trees didn't behave normally, bending in toward each other due to some strange energy field phenomenon, so they said. It taxed the imagination. This mirage was like that, catching his attention because it wasn't behaving normally. Maybe there was a similar energy field in the canyon, but he'd never encountered anything like this, in all the time he'd spent here.

As his engineer's mind recalled, reviewed, evaluated and rejected ideas, he wanted to pass this off as an optical illusion, but his mind and his attention were totally captured. Even so, he was about to cast aside his mental exercise and accept the fact that nature is full of surprises, when yet another oddity shook him. He was now close enough to notice that the mirage was not lying flat on the roadway, but appeared to be standing on edge, intersecting the pavement. It appeared as an oval shaped plate of glass or polished steel might, if erected on the road. He guessed steel, since it reflected blues, greys and browns from the hillside instead of the natural greens.

With his attention totally focused on the odd shape and color of the object, it took a few more moments for his mind to grasp the fact that he was on a collision course at high speed with an object, the consistency of which he had no idea, which by then had grown to completely block the roadway. If he didn't stop the car, he was going to hit it and do who-knew-what kind of damage to the car, and to himself, and there was now no way around the object. David's body tensed and he slammed on the brakes, throwing the car into a drunken skid on the slick roadway. David instinctively turned the wheel into the skid to keep the car from leaving the roadway or turning sideways and rolling. His mind raced as his eyes searched for an escape around the grotesque object which now, against all logic, had grown so large as to almost rest against the embankment on the left side of the road and extended beyond the edge of the roadway on the right.

With no time left, and certain death imminent, his heart raced. He braced himself for impact. Then, on an impulse, he threw himself to his right, across the console, to avoid any shattering glass or being stuck behind the wheel on impact. He closed his eyes and threw his right arm in front of his face.

The inevitable collision didn't happen. He still had one hand on the wheel and his foot on the brake, so he could tell the car was slowing quickly. The roadway was suddenly rougher, but there was no impact, no shattering glass, no screeching metal.

The car came to a stop with a bump. David lay still with his head resting in the crook between the passenger seat and thc seat back. He dropped his arm and tried to collect himself. He opened his eyes to see the dashboard and, above it, a gray sky; not the grey of swollen rain clouds, but high thin clouds that totally covered the sky.

He had always heard that right before you die, your entire life passes before your eyes. In a way, he was disappointed. He had always wanted to see his early life and figured that his death was the only way it was going to happen. Then he chastised himself for his levity in this dire situation. He had obviously gotten around the object, or he would be a pile of twisted metal and flesh now. All he felt was a little stiff from tension.

Maybe he had imagined the whole thing. Maybe he was going to sit up and see that there was no object in the road. Maybe he had panicked because he really wasn't ready to commit to marriage with Stefani. Wasn't that going to bc embarrassing?

As he tensed to sit up, sudden terror ripped through him and he lay back down. His mind filled with doubts again as he realized that there was actually a different feeling about the air around him. He chuckled humorlessly and wondered if he had died and gone to some other existence. How else could he explain a collision that should have mutilated his car and himself, but didn't, and a gray sky overhead? Well, if he had died, what they said about not being able to "take it with you" wasn't true. Here he was, lying in his Camaro. He could tell by the feel and smell of it. It was the air around him that felt different. He didn't think he was in his favorite canyon anymore. But that was ridiculous. He must have rolled off onto the soft shoulder before impact and either stopped short or gotten around it somehow.

The Old World

He collected his wits about him and pushed himself upright, looking out through the windshield. What confronted him was so unreal as to make his mind whirl. As he looked quickly around at the landscape in front and to either side of him, his heart raced, sending pains outward through his chest. His temples pulsed, his neck sent sharp, jabbing pain down his back and into the back of his head. His eyesight narrowed until all he could see was a sliver of what was in front of him. He closed his eyes, put his head in his hands, and leaned against the steering wheel until his head stopped spinning. He placed a hand to his pounding heart, fearing a stroke or heart attack. What he was seeing *was not possible!*

The scene before him was burned onto the back of his eyelids. His Camaro had, indeed, rolled to a stop in the ditch on the left side of the road. But all that remained of his beautiful forest were leafless, charred and blackened skeletons of trees, many of which were laid over on their sides. There was little other groundcover, mostly gray, lifeless dirt. The road was an old, pot-holed, two-lane, with a faded yellow line running down the middle. There were no shoulders, only the ditches normally found on old country roads.

A cold breeze brushed against his face. Not the cool breeze after a rain storm, but dry, winter cold. Maybe I turned onto a side road, David thought hopefully and looked around to see if, somehow, his canyon was behind him. New pains shot down his back and through his skull. He stopped and closed his eyes again, to regain his equilibrium. But when he opened them again, the landscape had not suddenly turned green again. And when he carefully turned his body around to look behind him, all he saw was a continuation of the old, broken road. "Noooooo," he moaned, and laid his head in his hands. "*This can't be!*" Then he got angry.

Was someone playing a trick on him? Had they somehow disguised this portion of the canyon to appear like something it was not? Who could do that? A magician? Why? Were they in league with Evans, trying to make him lose his mind? No, none of that was possible, but neither was what he was seeing, possible. He laid his head back on the headrest and closed his eyes, hoping that in a few minutes, everything would return to normal.

Sometime later, David stirred, pulled himself together, and thought about what he should do. It looked like he couldn't go back, but he thought he would try anyway. Maybe there was some kind of weird phenomenon in this particular location, like the site in South Dakota, and he just had to drive out of it. The car was still running, but he needed to know if he'd caused any damage to it that made it undrivable, so he opened the door carefully and stepped out onto the soft shoulder, which was muddy. He did a walk-around, looking under the car from both sides. Then, seeing no damage, he climbed back in, careful to knock most of the mud off his shoes before putting his feet on the floor mat. He backed the car carefully onto the roadway, did a three-point turn, then drove back down the canyon for a couple of miles, stopping when he got to the turn-off for Tony Grove and the Lewis M. Turner campground. He gave up trying to figure out what had happened and turned around again. His best chance to find civilization and get answers was at Garden City, because it was closer than Logan, or any of the towns between here and there.

He had gone a couple of miles back toward Garden City when the Low Fuel light lit up on the dashboard. He remembered that he was going to fill up before he left Logan, but had forgotten to do so in the rush of activity earlier. He thought he had enough gas in the tank—about two gallons—to easily get him to Garden City; but, based on how his day had gone so far, he feared that some catastrophe would stop him from getting to Garden City.

He looked around again at the landscape. Most of the trees were bare of foliage and appeared to have suffered fire damage sometime in the past. There was new growth on the ground — bushes mostly—but it looked stunted. All except the valley to his right, which was greener than the trees on the hillsides. There were new leaves on some of the branches; but they still looked a little anemic compared to what they should look like. He noticed two cabins in the valley, where, he was sure, there had never been buildings in the past. Looking more closely, he could see a garden and fruit trees next to the cabins. Maybe he was mistaken about there never having been buildings here before. Maybe he just hadn't noticed them when the valley looked healthier.

He stopped the car and looked around, praying for a miracle, but expecting none. He was ten miles from Garden City, with nothing but campgrounds for miles in the other direction. When he thought about calling AAA for a tow, he pulled his phone out of his shirt pocket, looked up the phone number in his contacts list and dialed. He immediately got a message stating that he did not have service. That surprised him, since he had been using his phone in the canyon for over two years during road construction.

He got the same error when he tried to call the office, then Stefani at the cabin.

He debated with himself and finally decided to go as far as Stefani's cabin. He could use her car to get gas if she didn't have a can of gas at the cabin. He drove as fast as he dared on the old roadbed, to the Bear Lake overlook, then down the other side toward Garden City, taking the side road on the right. Her car wasn't in the driveway of the cabin and no one answered his knock. He debated waiting for her but had no idea where she'd gone or when she'd be back; it could be days.

He got out and looked around, taking a few moments to look out over Bear Lake. He was positive that the field below him, on the approach to Garden City, had always been a field of raspberry bushes, but what was growing there now didn't look like raspberries—the plants were too low to the ground. He was too far away to see any more than that. Confused, he thought about the cabins he had seen back a few miles, and decided he should go there. He hadn't seen any cars or trucks there, either, but maybe the owner would be there when he got back.

The Old World—Aspen Valley

There was a trail leading into the small valley, he remembered, and pulled the car off the highway onto the trail when he saw it. It was deeply rutted, as though from heavy runoff and little use, so he stopped partway into the valley, watched for activity, and tried his phone again. Same result. This was frustrating. Not knowing what he would find, friendly farmers or gun-toting partiers, he decided he had to approach the cabins. He got out of his car, once again amazed at the poor condition of the path and the trees, and began his approach down the muddy hillside.

One of the sensors on the wall beeped, letting Mike know that something had entered the valley. He casually looked around toward the wall of monitors, expecting to see a deer or large bird, the usual suspects, but wasn't surprised to see a splash of red across the valley on the approach road. He had invited Mr. David Murdock into the old world by sending the gate to the twin world, to the highway just West of the turnoff. He suspected that David was uncomfortable with the way he had arrived, but there was no help for it; they couldn't announce their presence to the twin world. The Observer had been following David for weeks, using the Gemini Gate, and this was the first chance Mike had to bring him across to the old world.

Mike called Terry on the radio and Doc on the phone, asking them to come to the lab. Terry, who had been over in the large cabin, meeting with Bryce and Justin to discuss a bacterial growth on a peach tree, excused himself and said he would check his gardening books and get back to them. Doc, who was taking an afternoon nap with Lillie, woke groggily and promised to be there within a few minutes, after he was awake.

"What have you got," Terry asked when he entered the lab a few minutes later.

"Just a minute," Mike said. "I can see Doc. He's only a minute away."

When the three men were together, Mike told them what the Observer had shown him and what he had done about it. They could see the red Camaro on the trail and asked Mike what he planned to do.

"I'm going to let him come to us," Mike said, "rather than approach him. I still feel badly about the last three people we invited here, who failed to assimilate."

Terry laughed, then coughed into the sleeve of his lab coat. "That's a sterile way to say they committed suicide."

"Well, I don't think it's our fault that they didn't like it here," Mike said in his defense. "Jesse Newman did fine. I think the difference was trying to introduce them to the technology too quickly. They weren't ready for it emotionally or intellectually."

Mike watched as David slipped between the trees, figuratively and literally, heading straight for the cabins, rather than taking the easier path around the valley to the clearing. He held onto limbs or tree trunks to maintain his balance on the muddy slope. Actually, Mike realized, the roadway was so muddy that it probably wasn't any easier to navigate than what David was doing.

"Why's he doing that?" Mike asked anyway.

"Maybe he's frightened," Terry suggested. "if he's familiar with the canyon, which we believe he is, it must be a shock to him to be here. He's probably scouting out the area before stepping into the open and letting us see him."

As David approached the cabins, he stopped, looking around carefully, not stepping out of the tree line.

⊛

Mike picked up a radio from the worktable in the lab and called Beth, who answered right away.

"This is Beth," she said. "Am I speaking with Mike?"

"It's me, Beth," Mike said. "You have a visitor, stalking through the trees toward the cabins. When you see him, don't act surprised. In fact, I would appreciate you going out and meeting him if you have time. We invited him here, but he doesn't know where 'here' is."

"Like the others?" Beth asked.

"Similar," Mike said. "We think we've vetted this one better than the previous ones, so if you have room, would you make him feel at home?"

"Happy to do that, Mike," Beth laughed, probably at his explanation that he had vetted David. "We'll put him in Bryce's cabin."

"Great. Thanks, Beth."

Beth stepped out of her cabin and turned toward the trees, coming almost nose to nose with David, who was on the porch by then.

"Hi," she said. "Can I help you?"

"Where am I?" David asked.

"Logan Canyon."

"It doesn't look like the Logan Canyon that I know."

"Are you hungry? We're about to sit down to dinner. Would you join us?"

"I'd rather just be on my way," he said, "could I use your phone, or maybe get a lift back to Logan?"

"Sorry . . . I'm Beth," Beth said. "What's your name?"

"David," he said and waited for her to answer his question.

"Sorry, David. No phone and no transportation. Now, how about that meal?"

"I guess that works," he said, frustration showing in his demeanor. "Maybe you can tell me where I am in the meantime."

Beth turned back toward the cabin and walked away, looking back only once to confirm that David followed.

They stepped into the cabin. The main room took up a major portion of the cabin, with a high ceiling—two full stories. There was a fireplace on the right wall, with a swing in front of it, hanging from the ceiling. The swing was full of noisy children, at least five of them, he wasn't positive because of all the wiggling. On the left stood a long table, with benches on either side, set for at least twenty people. As he watched, a young woman entered through a door in the back wall and placed another plate, cup and silverware, along with a folding chair, at the near end of the table. Based on the rustic look of the cabin and the barefoot children, David decided that he had stumbled upon a group of hillbillies, or maybe polygamists. He would be careful what he said, so that he wouldn't offend anyone, just in case the men carried guns and had attitudes.

A bell rang and people appeared from several directions, filling the benches. What appeared to be a family of three, a man, woman, and beautiful young woman, probably in her late teens, entered the front door and moved to the far end of the table on one side. Several of the men approached David and introduced themselves, but he promptly forgot their names. When everyone was seated, they all bowed their heads and the father of the young woman said a short, but sincere prayer, giving thanks for the food and asking for protection for the family. When he was finished, David waited to see what would happen, certain that everyone would dive in and inhale the food that was on the table. He was surprised at the calm and organized manners of the group, taking small portions and passing the food around the table, all in the same direction, as though this were a common, practiced behavior. All of the activity was accompanied by polite talk around the table.

The woman, Beth, sat to his right and encouraged him to help himself as she passed dishes full of fresh fruits and cooked vegetables to him. She explained that this group consisted of several families and individuals that had come together over a period of years, all refugees from the war.

"What war?" David asked, looking at Beth sharply. There was a clue in what she said, to where he was and what had happened outside. Beth looked down at her plate and stopped talking, and nothing David could say could get her talking again.

Finally, David worked up the nerve to ask about the young woman. She was the only woman her age in the room. "May I ask her name?" he asked.

"Lisa Beth," Beth said. "Would you like to meet her?"

"Is that her dad who said the blessing on the food?"

"It is, and her mother is the one sitting on the other side of her. They've been here the longest, along with me and a couple of the others."

Concerned that he had acted inappropriately, or that his inquiry might be unwelcome, he decided to stop asking questions. It was none of his business. They would tell him what he needed to know.

When dinner was complete, everyone picked up their dirty dishes and leftovers and carried everything to the kitchen, which was through the doorway at the back of the room; then one person wiped down the table while two of the children straightened up the room. The others found other things to do. Beth took David by the arm and led him to the family of three to introduce them.

"David, this is Bryce, Sheryl and their daughter, Lisa Beth. This is David. He arrived a little while ago from Logan," she said.

"How long are you staying?" Bryce asked.

"I don't know," David said. "I'm not even sure where I am."

"You're in Logan Canyon," Bryce said, then looked at Beth with a quizzical look on his face. When no explanation was forthcoming, Bryce looked back at David. "Would you like to look around? Lisa Beth, would you give David a tour?"

"Sure," Lisa Beth said, then touched David's arm to get his attention. She offered a hand, which he took. Then she led him out the front door into the valley.

"This is our vegetable garden and fruit trees," she said as they walked, pointing out some of the things they had growing. "This is where I live," she added, as they approached a smaller cabin. "We like to eat together when possible, for the social interaction."

"Is Beth a leader of some kind?" he asked.

"Beth is a doctor, who led a small group from Georgia to Utah after the war, years ago, to escape the military."

"What war?" he asked.

She studied him without answering. When the silence became awkward, he asked a different question. Maybe she didn't know about the war. Or, maybe, as he suspected, there had been no war.

"What did they do to attract the attention of the military?" he asked, thinking that Lisa Beth might admit that they were polygamists.

"The military lost interest in them years ago," she said. She seemed reluctant to explain further, so he decided to drop that subject, too.

"What brought you to Aspen Valley?" she finally asked.

"You call this Aspen Valley?" he asked. "It has no name on the maps that I've seen. I knew it was here because I'm familiar with the canyon, but I didn't know anyone lived here." He looked around, once again struck by how much he liked this canyon. This valley—Aspen Valley—was now the prettiest part of the canyon. "It's pretty, like you."

She blushed, and he thought he might have gone too far.

"Thank you," she said. "I think I'm just average."

"I think you're beautiful," he said, now fully committed.

☢

"Hey, what are you doing with my girl?" a voice called from behind them. "Leave her alone. Quit holding her hand."

David dropped Lisa Beth's hand and turned to see whose ire was directed at him. There were two young men—they looked younger than Lisa Beth—quickly catching up to them.

"Leave us alone, Matthew Jr.," Lisa Beth said. "I'm not your girl."

"The name's Matt, and you've been my girl since we were born, months apart. My mom said so."

"Well, your mom's wrong, and you can tell her *I* said so." She retook David's hand and held it in both of hers, in plain sight of the boys.

Matthew Jr. and his friend walked right up to David and tried to stare him down. It amused him, since both boys were probably ten years younger and head and shoulders shorter. He spread his feet and got a solid stance, just in case they tried something, but they must have thought better of it. They backed down and took a step back.

"You just remember," Matt said, "that she's been claimed by me, and don't you butt in where you're not welcome." Then they walked back toward the big cabin, the way they had come.

"Pleasant young man," David said and chuckled.

Lisa Beth rolled her eyes, then raised David's hand between their faces. "He has no say about what I do and who I do it with."

When they arrived at her cabin, she took him inside. He could see that it was set up more like a house, with a sitting room in the entry and a hallway into the back of the cabin, presumably to other rooms, like bedrooms. Her parents were sitting on a couch.

"Matt Jr. was bothering me again," she said. "He insulted David."

"I'll speak to his mother," her mother said. "Don't worry about him."

"If he bothers you again, come and get me," her father said, "and I'll deal with him."

"Come and tell us about yourself," Sheryl said to David. Lisa Beth led him to another couch, turned ninety degrees to the first, and they sat side-by-side.

⊕

"Sheryl, is David here?" Beth asked at the open front door of the cabin, late in the day.

"Come in Beth. He is. David, Beth wants to speak with you."

David stood from the table, where he and Lisa Beth sat side-by-side, eating a snack of apple slices, talking quietly. He met Beth partway.

"What is it?" David asked.

"We need to find you a place to sleep," Beth said.

David realized that it was dark outside and he had failed to figure out what he was going to do. He hadn't intended to spend the night. He needed to get going, but he had no gas and no way to communicate with anyone he knew who could help.

"I'm sorry to be a burden, Beth. I can leave." He said apologetically, still not knowing what he could do. He would just have to sleep in his car. He stood and turned toward the door.

"You'll do no such thing," Beth said, then turned to Sheryl. "Sheryl, can you make room for David tonight, then we'll find something more permanent tomorrow?"

"More permanent?" David asked.

"Tomorrow, I'll introduce you to Michael and Doc," Beth said, "who can explain a few things to you. You may decide you want to stay awhile."

Lisa Beth led David toward the back of the cabin, gathering some bedding from a closet on the way.

"This is my room," she said, as she showed David to a bedroom.

"I'm going to move in with my siblings while you're here."

"I can't take your bedroom," David said.

"It's alright. Just help me change the sheets." He did, then she found him a pair of pajamas that she said were her dad's, and a new toothbrush. She showed him where the bathroom was located, between his bedroom and hers. Before she left him in his room, she kissed him on the cheek and wished him pleasant dreams.

In bed, all David could think about was walking through the trees, holding Lisa Beth's hand, and her chaste good-night kiss. There seemed to be no guile in her; she was sweet and innocent and he was instantly in love with her.

He tossed and turned, thinking about Lisa Beth, sleeping just two doors away. He wondered what she would think if he went to her room . . . just to talk . . . and decided it was a bad idea, even if he really wanted to. He thought about Stefani, wondering what she was doing and if she was missing him. What would she think of all this when he told her? When he met this doctor tomorrow, he would find out what was going on and how to get back.

After what seemed like hours, and he thought it must be getting close to dawn, there was a light knocking on his bedroom door and it opened just far enough for David to see a pretty face, with light blue eyes, long lashes, and a freckled nose in the crack.

"Can I come in?" Lisa Beth asked quietly.

"Please, come in," he said, and sat up in bed.

She opened the door, entered, and closed it behind her. She was wearing a long, modest white nightgown, that rustled against her ankles as she walked softly over and sat cross-legged on his bed.

"I couldn't sleep," she said. "I thought I would check on you, thinking you would be asleep, but hoping you would still be awake. I just wanted you to know that I enjoyed our time together today and hoped you did, too."

"I did," he said, but couldn't continue, because she kept talking.

"There aren't any young men here my age. Matt is the closest, a few months younger than me. We used to play together when there were just the two of us—the first two of the next generation—but he hasn't grown up. He's still a little boy with little boy interests. You're older, nice to talk to, and fun to be with," she said boldly.

He had also enjoyed their time together and wondered why she had come to his room in the night. Did she want more from him than he was prepared to give?

Suddenly, she twisted around and laid her head down on his pillow, bumping him with her hip. He moved over a little to give her room to lay by him. She lay on top of the covers, with her knees up, and continued to talk, as if she hadn't had an opportunity all day. She spoke of simple things, of living in the cabin, of a simple life, of taking care of children, of cleaning the cabin, of gardening, of her hope to one day see more of the world than this valley, although she said she was perfectly happy staying in the valley. She talked for a long time, totally at ease with the situation, until David's eyes closed momentarily.

"I should let you sleep," she said, as she jumped up and hurried to the door. She peeked out to see that the hall was clear, then blew him a kiss and left, closing the door softly behind her.

⊛

Doc happened to be at the cabin and saw Kerri and Rick sitting on the swing, close together, holding hands.

"Hi kids," he said, making Kerri smile. "How are you getting along?"

"Everyone thought that Rick, having been married before,

would be a problem for me," she said, with a wink at Rick, "but we've adjusted just fine. I don't try to compete with Rick's memory of his first wife and he doesn't compare me to her, at least not where I can hear."

"I don't compare you," Rick said. "I know which side of the bread is buttered."

"What does that mean?" Kerri asked, more curious than questioning.

"I really don't know," Rick said and they both laughed. "Maybe it was a dumb thing to say, but it seemed appropriate when I thought of it."

Kerri leaned over and kissed him, then ran her hand through his hair, "I love you," she said.

"Looks like you're getting along just fine," Doc said and turned to leave.

"Doc," Kerri said, stopping him, "can I ask you a question?"

"Of course, Kerri."

"You knew that Lisa and I were able to communicate telepathically on occasion, right?" she asked.

"I've heard that. So it's true?" he asked.

"Yes, it's true, and now I'm hearing someone else's voice in my head. Actually, it started when we were in Wyoming, on our way here, and Lisa was so sick. She sent a message to me, telepathically, and when I answered, someone else responded to me. That other person has tried to contact me several times over the years since. At first, I spoke to him, but I haven't since we arrived in the valley. He called again a few days ago. Do you think I should talk to him? The last thing he said to me was 'Where are you? I'll come to you.' "

She had Doc's full attention and he was concentrating on what she said, likely trying to ascertain what the man's interest in Kerri could be.

"What do you know about him?" he asked. "It was a man, right?"

"It is a man, and I know nothing about him. He sounds about your age, but that's all I could say from his voice."

"And now he wants to come to you?" Doc asked. "Did he say why?"

"No, nothing. I know Amos wanted to keep the location of the preserve a secret—I don't know why—but I thought I better ask you or Mike before I answered him again."

"I appreciate that, Kerri. Let me think about this. Maybe we could contact him together and try to get some information out of him. I'll get back to you."

David couldn't remember laying down or closing his eyes—anything really—until Bryce stuck his head in and told him that breakfast was ready. Breakfast was simple; creamed wheat cereal, with wheat toast and orange juice. When breakfast was finished, and he had brushed his teeth and dressed in yesterday's clothes, Lisa Beth asked if he would like to help in the garden.

"Doing what?" he asked. "I don't know much about gardening."

"I'll show you," she said, took his hand, and led him out of the cabin and into the orchard. He could tell when they reached the orchard because of the fruit trees, covered with small fruit. The grass was shorter, and they had obviously dug up the ground between the trees at some point.

"It looks like a bumper crop," David said. "It looks like the fruit is crowded for space."

"Actually, there's too much fruit on the trees," Lisa Beth said. "We need to thin the fruit, so that what we leave will have room to grow. The apricots are farthest along, so that's the first tree we'll thin. How big do you like your apricots?"

David held up one hand, with his fingers curved to show a ball about three inches in diameter. "About this big," he said.

"Well," Lisa Beth said, "we've never grown them that big, but the idea behind thinning is that whatever size you want at the end of the season, you don't want to have another fruit in the way of it getting that big." She studied one branch, selecting which fruit to leave on it, then plucked the rest of the fruit off, by twisting the fruit, and letting it drop to the ground. "Ideally, we wouldn't drop the fruit on the ground, since it can be the cause of disease later on; but we can pick them up later, too."

"Do you have something to put them in now, so we don't have to pick them up later?" David asked. "No reason to do this twice."

"I like how you think" she said, smiling sweetly. She retrieved a bucket from the edge of the orchard and they picked up the dropped fruit that they could find. "Now you try this one," she said. "Which fruit would you save?"

David eyed the branch and pointed to the ones he thought were the right distance apart.

"Very good. In this case, these two are so close together, that it doesn't matter which one you pick. I like to think that the one on the bottom of the branch would be best to save, because the weight of the fruit won't act against it, causing it to break off later if it gets bumped. You decide." When David just stood there, she added, "Go ahead." He did.

"That's good," she said when he had finished that branch. "Let's finish this tree together, then I'll show you the peach trees."

"These two appear to be growing together," he said after a while. "Should I try to separate them and leave just one of them?"

She looked to see what he was talking about, standing so close that he could smell her soap—a clean, fresh smell. When she turned to answer him, they were nose to nose. She backed away a step. "I would probably choose a different one to save," she said, her voice a little husky. "those two will still look like that when they're harvested. The fruit will be fine, but won't be as big or good looking."

After the apricot tree, they thinned two peach and one nectarine tree, then went on to thin the pear and plum trees, working together on most of the trees. At one point, Lisa Beth got a ladder so David, who had offered, could get the fruit in the tops of the trees. Lisa Beth told him that all of the trees were semi-dwarf, so they wouldn't grow over about twenty feet tall, but her dad, Bryce, had pruned them down to about eight feet. "Easier to reach the fruit," Lisa Beth had said. It was tedious work, but he hardly noticed. Working with and thinking about Lisa Beth distracted him. He watched her as she worked alongside him, admiring her poise and beauty. She periodically checked on his work, touching his arm or cheek when she spoke to him. He enjoyed her company and the attention.

Beth showed up when the sun was high in the sky and brought them each a sandwich and drink. David hadn't realized how hungry he had become, but relished the chance to sit in the shade of one of the trees, with Lisa Beth sitting close enough to touch thighs, and talk. Beth returned late in the afternoon and told David that Mike wanted to talk to him, but that tomorrow was soon enough—no hurry. "You'll like him," Beth said. "You'll like his whole family."

Beth met them near the orchard and walked back to the cabins with them at the end of the day. "We've been trying to figure out an automatic watering system for the orchard," she said. "We have access to sprinkler parts and supplies, so we thought that with your engineering experience, you might be able to help us." She took him to a shed that contained sprinkler parts, showed him the water source and asked what he thought.

"This is all the parts you have?" David asked. "I'll take inventory and think about the best way to do it." He hadn't figured it out before dinner time, then it was game night and everyone joined in with red rover, kick-the-can and other physical activities. He watched Lisa Beth as they played, catching her eye once in a while. When he did, he would wink and she would lower her gaze timidly, and sometimes blush.

After dark, when the games were finished and everyone was worn out, he walked Lisa Beth to the cabin and to her room. They sat on her bed and talked about the games, which he'd never seen before and performed poorly at. She complimented him on being a good sport about it. Finally, her mother, Sheryl, came to check on them, ushering her brother and sister into the room to go to bed, encouraged Lisa Beth to get some sleep, and asked David what he was going to do the next day.

"I didn't get back to the orchard to plan a sprinkling system," David said. "Please tell Beth that I'll look at it again in the morning."

"That's fine, David," Sheryl said. "I'll tell her."

Once again, David couldn't sleep, and once again, Lisa Beth came to his room in the night. She laid her head on his pillow, which was really her pillow, like she had the night before.

"I'm cold," she said, and wrapped his blanket around her, "from playing games outside. And I'm excited about the sprinkling system. I can't wait to see how you build a sprinkling system. Can I help?"

"I'd love to have your help. It will go much faster."

"You look tired," she said after a while. He realized that his eyelids were drooping. Yes, he was tired from a long day of doing things he was not used to. She got off the bed and went to the door.

"All clear," she said after sticking her head out into the hallway. Then she left the room.

He lay on his bed for a long time after that, thinking about her. He liked how she had enough self-confidence to do what she wanted. He also liked her innocence and unassuming behavior. His initial reaction to her, that he could love her, was reinforced by her actions toward him.

⊛

He fell asleep thinking about her, and didn't wake until she returned, dressed for the day, and told him breakfast would be ready in ten minutes.

After breakfast, she went with him and watched, while he took inventory of the PVC pipe and fittings in the shed, then continued to sit and watch as he stepped off the distances between trees and drew a diagram of the orchard. He superimposed a network of piping from the pump to each tree, calculating the amount of pipe needed to complete the job. It took him a couple of hours to complete the layout, commenting that it was a good thing this was a simple irrigation system. He'd never designed one before.

When he told Lisa Beth that he needed a break, she reminded him that they still had a couple of fruit trees to thin. And the garden needed to be weeded.

"Does anyone else help with these chores?" he asked.

"The children help when they're forced," she said, "but they're not really interested in helping and they don't do a good job. I have to go behind them and redo much of their work. When the adults help, which isn't often, they do fine, but quit before we're done, having some excuse about other priorities. Do you mind if just the two of us finish the thinning?"

"I don't mind at all," he said, taking her hand in his. He moved closer to her to see if she would back away from him or hold her ground. He wanted to kiss her, but he wanted her to want it, too. When she didn't back up, but didn't approach him either, he realized she wasn't ready and turned back to his task. It took the rest of the day to assemble all the pipe, gluing each joint, then another day waiting for the glue to dry before they could test the lines.

"It's not perfect," David said, when they finally had the water running and there was water delivered to each tree.

"I think it's fantastic," Lisa Beth said. "If you need to make changes, we can do that later."

"It's wonderful," Beth said, when David had the timer on the line and it turned on at exactly the time he wanted. "Can you set up a similar system for the garden?"

"If there's enough pipe and fittings left," he said. When he had built a header that distributed water evenly to each row of vegetable plants, he was just about out of pipe, so he was pleased; and it had only taken him an extra day to complete it.

❀

The next morning, Doc went to the cabin and asked for Kerri.

"Do you know how to contact this mysterious voice?" Doc asked, when she came into the main room.

"Do you want me to try it now?" she asked. He nodded.

"Hello," she sent, in the voice she always used to contact Lisa, "Are you there?"

"I'm here," came the stranger's older, male voice, immediately. "Oh, it's you. How's your friend? Did she recover and come back to you?" Kerri knew immediately that he was referring to Lisa and the incident in Wyoming.

"She did," she sent.

"I'm glad," he said. "Where are you?"

This is where she needed Doc. She hurriedly wrote down his question and showed it to Doc.

"Tell him you're in Utah, but don't be more specific. Ask where he is and his name," Doc said.

"We're in Utah," she shared. "Where are you and what's your name?"

"Montana, and you can call me Adam."

"That's obviously not your name, so why Adam?" She shared.

"I'm the first," he said, not trying to deny that it wasn't his real name.

"The first what?" she asked, as she quickly wrote her questions and his answers for Doc.

"The first of a new species, born out of the ashes of a dying world," He said. "What's your name?" he asked.

"I'd rather not say at this time," she shared.

"Ahh, you're bashful," he concluded, "because we don't know each other well? We'll correct that situation. Since you were the first woman I communicated with after the change, I'll call you Eve. I believe Eve would have been bashful at first, too, being naked and all. We need to get together."

Even though Kerri knew Doc couldn't hear their conversation, and she could tell him whatever she wanted, she was embarrassed by Adam's comments and couldn't look Doc in the eye. Finally, she looked at Doc to see if he had any suggestions, but he shook his head. "I need to think about this some more," he said.

"I have to go," Kerri shared, but Adam spoke hurriedly.

"Tell me where to find you and I'll come to you. There are others like us and I'll gather them on the way to Utah," he said.

"I have to go," Kerri shared again, and cut his voice off, but not before she heard other voices demanding her attention.

"That was weird," she said to Doc and realized that using her voice felt weird for a second.

"Tell me about it," he said.

She repeated the conversation for him, leaving out the embarrassing part, but including the other voices at the end.

"Now give me your impressions," he said.

"I felt like I was talking to a machine," she said. "Well, that's not exactly right, it was like he was listening to me, then he was listening to himself, admiring his own words, as if it was the most important thing that could be said. What do you think?"

"I've run into people like that before. It's called a narcissistic personality disorder, but I call it a 'god complex'. He wants to be the first of a new species and wants you to be his consort. Does that sound fun to you?"

"Heaven forbid," she said. "He scares me."

"I have several questions, which he probably won't want to answer; One—how did he know it was you so quickly? Does he have a voice recognition machine? Two—what other technology does he have? Can he track you to the valley just by talking to you once in a while? Three—is he a prepper, living in a shelter, and how well has he survived? Four—what's his motive for trying to find you? Is it benign, or is it evil, like taking over the world?"

"You're assuming he has bad intentions, aren't you?" she asked.

"You heard him. What do you think?"

"He scares me. I'd just as soon not talk to him again."

"Okay. For now, ignore him, if you can. If he becomes too persistent, as I imagine he will, let's talk about it again."

"What are you going to do?" she asked.

"I'm not sure. But one thing I know. We don't need him or

want him here."

⊛

David was ready for a break. He asked Lisa Beth what she recommended they do for diversion and she suggested a hike and picnic. There was a large field across the highway from the valley, where she thought they could go to get away from the confusion made by the children. He hadn't noticed any confusion; but thought maybe the children stayed out of sight so they didn't have to help. He agreed to the picnic, thinking maybe she just wanted to be alone with him. He certainly wanted to be alone with her.

She made the food and placed it in an old-fashioned picnic basket, including a red and white checkered table cloth, which he carried as they walked up the trail away from the clearing. On the way, they passed his car on the trail. She walked around the car and he followed,

"It's beautiful," she said. "Can we go for a ride."

"I'd love to," he said. "I love this car, but it's almost out of fuel." If I had fuel, he thought, I wouldn't be here. And, he realized, he wouldn't have met Lisa Beth. Did it matter, he wondered, if he had never met her? He was torn, but he supposed that as soon as he could escape this place, he would go to Stefani and propose marriage.

As soon as he thought about Stefani and marriage, his anxiety spiked. He didn't know if it was marriage that scared him or marrying Stefani. It was so refreshing to be with Lisa Beth. Even though she did most of the talking and he did the listening, he enjoyed being with her. He couldn't imagine tiring of her.

They found a shady spot in the shadow of one of the few trees in the field, a large cottonwood, and he laid out the tablecloth in the driest spot. They sat and she sorted out the food, setting dishes on the cloth and laying food on plates.

Suddenly, two young men came whooping and hollering across the field toward them; Matt Jr. and his younger brother, Dean, who had been with him when David had arrived.

"What now?" Lisa Beth asked, obviously frustrated at the disturbance. But when the boys arrived, she asked politely, "What can we do for you, Matt Jr.?"

"We weren't busy, so we came to join the picnic," Matt said and plopped himself down next to Lisa Beth, then reached into the basket to see what she had brought.

"I don't think you were invited," David said, struggling to keep his composure.

"Doesn't matter," Matt said. "We invited ourselves. Now we're here."

"Matt," Lisa Beth said patiently, "aren't they eating lunch back at the cabin?"

"Yes, they are, but your food is better."

"It's the same food," Lisa Beth said.

"Maybe," Matt said, "But you made this food, so it will taste batter."

"Thanks for the compliment," she said, "but there's only enough for two of us."

"Okay," he said. "You and me only makes two. Dean can go back and eat with the others."

"I meant," she said, still not losing patience with him, "I meant the food is for David and me."

"Who? That guy?" he asked, pointing a thumb over his shoulder at David. "He don't count for nothin'. I'll eat his share."

David had had enough. "Matt Jr." he said, anger in his voice.

"Do you hear anything?" Matt interrupted, likely knowing he was angering David, but obviously not caring.

"That's enough, Matt." David said. "Now go away and leave us alone." David tried to look menacing, although he really had no intention of doing anything to Matt. He just wanted to encourage Matt to leave and take his brother with him.

Matt spoke to Lisa Beth, ignoring David. "You really shouldn't be alone with him, look how mean he is."

"Matt," she said, frustrated now. "Please leave. You need to respect my privacy."

"Someone needs to protect you from him. He's not even one of us."

"That's enough, Matt," she said. "Now you've overstepped thc bounds of decency. Please leave."

"Don't make me," Matt pleaded, his voice rising in pitch so he sounded like a little boy. "Make him go away. He's not one of us."

David wanted to intervene, but when he started to rise, Lisa Beth motioned for him to remain seated. "Matt," she said, looking like she might explode, "please leave."

"I will if you kiss me," he said.

"I will not kiss you," she said and pointed a finger in the direction of the cabins. "Now go."

"Come on, Lisa Beth, just one little kiss."

"No! . . . one kiss, and then you'll leave us alone?" she asked. David wanted to object, but she waved him away.

"I won't bother you any more today," Matt said.

"A whole week," she said, sounding serious. "You'll leave us alone for a whole week," then added quietly, "maybe you'll grow up and act your age by then."

Matt moved closer and reached out his arms.

"Okay," she said, "one little kiss, then you'll go away." She pursed her lips and closed her eyes.

Matt moved over close to her, grabbed her around the shoulders, bent her over backward and gave her a long, sloppy kiss. She pushed against his chest, trying to break free. He finally let go and sat up straight. She fell backwards, landing on her back on the ground next to the tablecloth. Her eyes began to water and she thought she would cry, but she fought it back until she realized that crying might make Matt realize his actions had hurt her. So, she stayed on her back and began to cry. David came up on his knees, prepared to go to her, but she stopped him with a look. "Matt, you hurt me," she said.

Matt looked sad. "I'm sorry," he said and reached a hand out to her. She took his hand and he started to pull her up to a sitting position; but then he looked at David, on his knees and leaning forward, and let go, dropping Lisa Beth again.

"Oww," she said. "Why did you let go of my hand, Matt? That hurt."

Matt pointed at David. "He was going to hit me," he said.

"No, he wasn't, Matt. He's just worried about me, like you are. Are you sorry that you hurt me, Matt?"

"Of course, I am," Matt said. "I really care about you, and now I know you care about me. That's why you let me kiss you. Lisa Beth kissed me. She loves me. Lisa Beth loves me."

Lisa Beth came up sputtering. "That was too much," she said. "Never again, Matt. You took advantage, and you won't do it again."

Matt stood and started dancing up and down in place, kicking up dust and mud, all over David and Lisa Beth. As he ran off, with Dean following, he continued to chant his latest success, "Lisa Beth loves me."

"Did you have to do that?" David asked. "I mean, I know the type. They never give up, and each success prompts them to do more, to extend their boundaries."

"That certainly describes Matt," she said, "but I didn't know what else to do."

"Give me permission and I'll stop him from bothering you."

"Let me try it my way first."

"Alright, but I hate to see him taking advantage of you."

"Let's forget him and enjoy our picnic," she said.

"I'll try. Are you okay? Did he hurt you?" David moved around to sit closer to her, touching her hand, then her neck. He pulled a twig out of her hair, then brushed dirt off her back, which left a large wet spot on her top.

"I'm fine. Thank you," she said, pulling a comb out of her back pocket and running it through her hair. "See, good as new."

When they'd finished eating, she laid her head on his lap and looked up at the clear blue sky. "The air is really clear today, since the fallout is gone."

He was ready to try to give her a kiss, but her comment alarmed him. "Fallout? What do you mean?" he asked, looking around.

"The fallout from the explosion," she said as if he should know, then realized that maybe he hadn't been told yet. "They've cleaned it all up."

"What are you talking about?" he asked.

"You don't know." She said, realizing that she had spoken without permission. "I'm sorry. Never mind. Mike will tell you what you need to know when you need to know it." But she could tell from his reaction that he wouldn't be satisfied with that. The last visitor had killed himself over it, at least that's what she'd been told. She really didn't want David to kill himself. She really liked him. She didn't realize she was crying until a tear dripped off her cheek and landed on her hand.

"Tell me about the explosion and fallout," David said.

"I think it's time to go back," Lisa Beth said, standing, embarrassed by the tears.

David took her arm, stopping her, but she shrugged him off and walked away. He picked up the basket, folded the tablecloth, and finally caught up with her. He didn't ask again.

As they passed David's car on the way back, David looked it over, walking all the way around it, inspecting it as he usually did, frowning and nodding his head at one point.

"Is everything okay?" she asked.

"I'm not surprised," he said and pointed to the passenger side of the car, drawing her attention. There was a scratch in the paint, the full length of the car, made by something sharp, like a rock, or stick. "This wasn't here when we passed by earlier. Matt must have done it. I'll make him pay for it."

"What do you mean? He has no money."

"Then I'll take it out of his hide."

"Eve, Eve," a voice called as Kerri lay sleeping in the early morning. She thought it was Rick, but no, he was lying quietly beside her in the bed; then she realized the voice was in her head, Adam! She tried to ignore him, but his voice got louder and more insistent, until it seemed like he was screaming in her ears. She suspected that it was partly due to the quiet of the morning and her focus on the voice, but he may have some kind of amplifier.

"What do you want at this ungodly hour?" She asked.

"Ah, there you are. Sorry for the wakeup call. I just wanted you to know that I'm on my way to Utah. You can give me more directions when I get closer. I just passed Helena, Montana on Interstate 15, with my little band of followers. I can't wait to join with you." Just as quickly, the voice was gone.

Kerri's whole body shook. She was being stalked by a maniac.

The shaking woke Rick. "What's wrong, love?" he asked. "You're shaking like a leaf."

"It's Adam. He's on his way. It's creepy."

"Is Doc able to help?" Rick asked. He knew Doc was who she had gone to for help with this problem.

"I don't know what he can do, but I'll tell him about it the next time I see him."

⊛

"He said he's on I15 in Montana and has followers?" Doc asked when Kerri found him later that week.

"That's what he said," Kerri said. "What's creepy about it is that he seems to be able to project his voice, raise and lower his volume. Also, I can hear other voices, like they're in the background; but they're not in the background. It's like when you're listening to a radio station at night, and you can hear other stations on adjacent frequencies or the same frequency, farther away. What do you think it means?"

"I don't know," Doc said, "but I have an idea what to do about it."

⊛

"Jen," Doc said, speaking with former President Greg McCormick's former secretary on her mobile phone.

"Is that you, Doc?" she asked. "How are you doing? Are you still in Utah? We haven't heard from you in ages. How's the family?" Jen had been present when Doc had married Lillie in the valley several years before, so she knew about Doc's technology and the twin worlds. She had moved back to South Carolina when Greg left office at the end of his second term as president, but she had his contact information, which she gave to Doc.

"Take care, Doc. It was good to talk to you. Love ya," she said and hung up.

Doc called Greg and found him in his home office.

"What's up Greg?" he asked.

"Doc," Greg's voice boomed over the line. "Good to hear your voice. Sorry I don't have a cabinet position to offer you. So, what kind of crisis have you managed to get yourself into that I need to bail you out of?" They both laughed, knowing that it was always the other way around. Doc was always helping to bail the country out of sone kind of crisis while Greg was president.

"Actually, Greg, there is something you may be able to help me with. There's a group of people on Interstate 15 in Montana, headed for Utah. Their leader is a guy who calls himself Adam and he is fixated on one of my people. We're afraid he plans to make trouble for us when he gets here. Can you get the military to pass a satellite that way and tell me what to expect? I mean, is he on foot, does he have weapons or other technology that I should be aware of, that sort of thing."

"You think this is serious?" Greg asked. "Should I ask the president to send the military over there and disperse them?"

"Let's see what I'm up against first," Doc said, "and if you can't arrange to send a satellite, just let me know, so I can come up with Plan B."

"I'm sure you realize that I don't run the country now, but I still have friends in government who might be willing to help," Jim Seymour, who had been Greg's SecDef during his first term, and his vice president during his second term, had succeeded Greg as president, riding the high tide that Greg and Doc had created by wiping out most of the terrorists and restoring power to the country. Greg had little doubt that Jim would be happy to honor Doc's request.

"I'll talk to Jim and one of us will get back to you."

⊛

"Doc, Jim Seymour here," President James Seymour said, when he called Doc a couple of hours later. "I was able to get one satellite repositioned for one flyover. I waited to call you until it had actually flown over, so I could tell you what we found. The group you asked about is pretty obvious, just south of Helena, Montana. It reminded me of the 60s song *Convoy*—a big Hummer out front, with every lane filled with cars and trucks, several deep. There must be forty or fifty of them. What did you say this guy is doing?"

"So far he's being polite, but he seems fixated on one of our women, calling her his Eve, and letting her know he's coming for her."

"A stalker, huh?" Jim asked.

"That's what it looks like to me, but that's what I was hoping to confirm with the satellite. Did you see anything different?"

"Nah. No armored vehicles, no visible guns or other hardware. They look like what I said . . . a convoy."

"Did you get a look at the leader? Have you seen him before?"

"I saw him from an angle through his window. I sent his mug over to the FBI to see if they can ID him. I'll send you a copy."

"Thanks, Jim. I owe you," Doc said.

⊛

David and Lisa Beth finished thinning fruit on the last tree, just before dinner time. Lisa Beth's dad, Bryce, helped them and commented about how satisfied he was with their work. When David was able to get Bryce alone, he asked if Matt, Jr, had some claim on Lisa Beth. Bryce acted surprised at first, then smiled and said that Lisa Beth had been Matt's and Dean's babysitter years earlier and that Matt had often told her parents that he was in love with, and was going to marry Lisa Beth someday.

"Babysitter?" David asked. "I thought they were the same age."

"Lisa Beth is a few months older than Matt, but she was always much more mature and responsible. Despite their ages, Lisa Beth was often left in charge of the boys. Everyone knew she could be trusted to take good care of them and ask for help when she needed it. Why are you asking?"

"It seems he still has a crush on her," David said.

"Well, they're both older now," Bryce said. "I guess it wouldn't be so farfetched for them to marry." He studied David for a few moments, a puzzled look on his face, that changed to recognition a few moments later. "Oh, I get it," Bryce said. He must have realized that David was asking because he also liked Lisa Beth: but he didn't say more.

David wondered if he should drop the subject, but he was really curious about their customs. "Do you have rules here about courting and marriage?" he asked Bryce, drawing his attention again.

"Like what?" Bryce asked.

"Like arranged marriages. Has Lisa Beth been promised to Matt Jr.?" If Matt had a claim on her, he needed to know, so he didn't make a fool of himself by chasing after her. Should he just back away and let them do their thing?

"No David," Bryce said, with a laugh. "Nothing like that. She can date whomever she wants, and marry whomever she chooses."

That night, while he was getting ready for bed, Lisa Beth entered his room, sat on his bed, and watched him. He was bare-chested, putting on his pajama top, and her stare unnerved him for some reason.

"Hi, Lisa Beth," he said. "What's up?"

"Are you mad at me?" she asked after staring at him for a few more moments.

"Absolutely not," he said. "What would give you an idea like that?"

"The way you acted toward Matt earlier today, as though you were angry."

"If I was angry, it was at him, not you. I couldn't be angry with you."

"Not even when I let him kiss me?"

"That surprised me, is all. I don't know what social customs you have here, but where I come from, when a guy and a girl are together and want to be alone—we call that 'being on a date'—it isn't proper for another guy to barge in and kiss the girl. I'm not angry, just confused."

"Is that why you asked my dad about arranged marriages?" she asked, "because you wondered if Matt had a right to kiss me?"

"Something like that, yeah." He lowered his eyes from her face, embarrassed at having to talk about this with her.

"So, was our picnic a date?" she asked, staring at him boldly.

"Well, we didn't invite Matt and Dean to join us. They invited themselves, so I thought of it as a date until they complicated everything."

"So," she asked, "you wanted to be alone with me on our picnic?"

"Exactly," he said, "to get to know you better."

"So, do you know me better because we went on this date?"

"I'm not sure," he said. "I don't understand why you let him kiss you."

"So you *are* mad at me," she concluded from his response.

"No," he said, trying to think of another way to explain himself. "Maybe the best way to tell you what I think of you, is to show you. Do you trust me?"

"I hardly know you, but you seem trustworthy. At least you've given me no reason not to trust you." She said.

"Then stand up and come here," he said. When she stood, he saw that her top two buttons were unbuttoned, exposing a lot more of her than he expected. She didn't hurry to cover herself and didn't seem bothered by being partially exposed. Maybe she'd been in a hurry and didn't realized that she'd missed a couple. He looked away quickly.

"Umm . . ." he said awkwardly, pointing in her general direction, "Your top."

She looked down to see her top unbuttoned. She quickly turned her back to him and finished dressing. "I'm sorry," she said. "I embarrassed you, didn't I?"

"I didn't think it was on purpose," he said, "but I didn't want you to be angry when you noticed later and I hadn't said anything."

"Thank you for your concern," she said, her cheeks taking on a pink glow.

"Okay," he said. He stepped up to her, put his arms around her, and kissed her; not like Matt's immature, slobbery kiss, but a hard, passionate kiss, like he meant it. Then he stepped back and studied her face. Sometime during the kiss, she had closed her eyes. She opened them now and studied him with wide eyes.

"Where you come from," she said, "when two people kiss, does that mean they like each other?"

"Generally, that's what it means. And when they really like each other, they kiss a lot, and hug and spend lots of time together. Is that what it means here?"

"The same thing here," she said, "but Matt's kiss doesn't count. He's just a little boy."

"I'm glad that's how you feel," he said. "What should we do tomorrow?"

"I need to weed the garden," she said, "and we could plant more carrots. Have you seen the gardens inside in the Preserve? They're amazing. I want to learn to grow crops like that."

"They have a hydroponic garden indoors?" he asked.

"They do, and it's wonderful."

"Who do we ask?"

"Let's ask Beth," she said and turned toward the door.

He put out a hand to stop her, wrapping it around her upper arm. "We can wait until morning to ask," he said.

"Okay," she said. She turned and laid on his bed, with her head on his pillow, then looked at him. "Are you coming?"

"What do you mean?" He asked.

"Are you coming to bed?"

"In the same bed with you?" he asked.

"Where you come from, when two people like each other a lot, do they sleep together?"

"That seems to happen a lot," he said. "What are you thinking?"

"I'm thinking that we should sleep together. Do you want to?"

"Yes, I do, but I don't think your parents would approve. What do you think?"

"I think you're right. How about just laying by me for a few minutes?" He turned out the light and climbed on the bed, laying out next to her, his head on the pillow next to her head. She stayed and talked, her forehead touching his, until he started to dose. Then she kissed his lips, which were an inch from hers, and stood up.

"Did I fall asleep again?" he asked, opening his eyes.

"You've had a long day," she said. "I should leave and let you sleep."

"I'd rather you stay," he said. "You're so comfortable to lay next to."

"I like lying next to you as well."

"Can we think of a good excuse?"

"You mean, in case somebody—like my mom—notices and doesn't approve?"

"Yeah. Could we say we just fell asleep, talking?"

"We could try it and see how much trouble we get in."

"You're the one who would get in trouble, so it needs to be your idea."

"Okay," she said, snuggling against him. "Good night."

He tucked her in tighter against his side, then turned and gave her a kiss on the lips. "Good night."

They closed their eyes and were soon asleep.

The next morning, when he climbed out of bed, he could tell Lisa Beth was still in their shared bathroom. He hadn't heard her get up, so he didn't know if she had stayed the whole night or had gone to her own room at some point. He waited until he was sure she was finished in the bathroom, then quickly bathed, shaved and dressed for the day. When he arrived in the dining room, Sheryl had just placed breakfast on the table—oatmeal and wheat pancakes with peach preserves--and they had a visitor, Beth. David listened as Sheryl and Beth made small talk, then Beth got to the point of her visit.

"The garden flooded and some of the plants have washed out. David, will you check your lines and see what might have happened?"

"Sure thing, Beth," he said, wondering if she was blaming him for doing a poor job on the irrigation lines. He knew that when he'd tested the lines, everything had worked as it should and there were no leaks. "I can't imagine what could have happened, but I'll check it and make any needed repairs, to the lines and the plants."

"And I'll help." Lisa Beth said. He thought her look of concern might be accusatory, but hoped it was supportive of him and his workmanship.

They finished breakfast, then went to the garden. The first thing he noticed was that it wasn't the whole garden, just a couple of rows that had washed out, but half the garden was dry while the other half was saturated. That looked like a broken line to him. On close inspection, he could see that the header line had been shattered at one spot, by a heavy blow, and the water had run from that point down the next two rows, washing the soil away, along with many of the plants.

"What could have done that," Lisa Beth asked.

"A heavy blow," David said.

"Like from a shoe?" she asked.

"I don't think so. That could have been accidental, but wouldn't have caused this much damage."

"Intentional?" she asked. "How?"

"This was done with a hammer or hatchet, maybe a sharp rock. I doubt it was an accident. It looks like it was done to undo our work, intentionally." He was almost positive that Matt Jr. did it to get back at him for taking an interest in Lisa Beth.

"But who would do that?"

"You know your people better than I do. Who do you think would do it?"

"Matt Jr. or Dean are most likely, or maybe one of the younger children, not knowing better."

"We'll repair the line and clean up the damage, but is there anything else we should do about it?"

"Maybe you should tell Beth," Lisa Beth said. "She'll probably ask anyway."

"Then you tell her, if you want to. She thinks it was something I did wrong, and I don't want to accuse anyone unfairly."

Lisa Beth had to think about that. She appreciated his kindness, not wanting to get anyone else in trouble, but if this was sabotage, it needed to be stopped. She also didn't want David to be blamed, when she knew he had done such a beautiful job on the irrigation system. She remembered that her dad had said to tell him if Matt caused any trouble, but was hesitant to accuse Matt without proof.

It took most of the day to clean up the garden and repair the line, and the line would have to set for another day to let the glue dry. David thought they could replant the plants that got washed out, with few plants dying as a result. Then they watered the garden by hand.

Beth came looking for them late in the afternoon, after they had missed lunch to finish the job.

"Well, what happened?" Beth asked, not unkindly.

David stood with his hands to his sides, not offering anything. Finally, seeing that David wasn't going to say anything, Lisa Beth spoke up.

"It looks like the line was sabotaged by someone, intentionally," she said.

Beth looked from Lisa Beth to David and back again, waiting for more. When neither one spoke, Beth asked, "That's quite an accusation. Who would do something like that?"

Still, David wouldn't speak, but stood tight-lipped and silent. Lisa Beth looked at him, then down at the ground, then back at Beth, before answering.

"I think it was Matt Jr. or Dean," she finally said.

Beth looked shocked. "Why would either of them do something that hurt the whole community, including themselves?"

Lisa Beth hesitated, looking at David again. "Maybe they don't understand how important the irrigation system is. I'm probably wrong, Beth. I don't know why anyone would do it."

"Then why would you suggest such a thing?"

"Well . . . they interrupted our picnic yesterday . . . and Matt acted poorly. I think he's jealous of me spending time with David."

"That's ridiculous—" she said, then stopped and studied Lisa Beth more closely She wasn't the little, freckle-faced, coltish, girl she used to be. She was grown up and beautiful. Beth could easily imagine Matt Jr. being attracted to her, even jealous of her attention to this mysterious, older, single male. "Maybe I'll have a talk with his mother," she said instead. "Now you two run along and get your supper, before it gets cold."

"Beth," Lisa Beth said as Beth turned to go.

"Yes, dear?" Beth asked.

"Do you think David could see the hydroponic gardens?"

"I'm sure he can, but let me ask, and I'll get back to you."

⊛

It didn't take long. They were still sitting at the table, finishing their meal, when Beth sent word to meet her in a half hour at the door to the Preserve.

"You'll love the gardens," Lisa Beth said as David followed her across the orchard, toward a rock wall—a cliff—on the far side of the clearing. As they approached the wall, Beth stood at the cliff, in front of an open doorway in the rock face.

David looked at the doorway, then did a double-take, realizing that the door looked just like the rock around it, but had to have been man-made.

"Ingenious," he said. "What's it made of, graphite composite?"

"Actually, it is," Beth said. "You know about graphite composite?"

"I do," he said. "I interviewed with a company that uses composites to make thing like golf clubs, before I graduated from school."

A man, about ten years older than David, appeared in the doorway "Hi Beth, Lisa Beth," he said.

"Hi Jesse," Beth said. "David would like to see the gardens. He's been helping us with our garden and when we mentioned you had one down here, he said he'd love to see it. Can you give him a tour?"

"You bet," Jesse said. "Are you coming along, Lisa Beth?"

"If I may," she said.

"Absolutely."

They descended a staircase, walked down a long hallway and through a set of double doors into what appeared to be an airlock. David opened his mouth to ask, but his guide must have anticipated his question.

"Yes, it's an airlock, and yes, we're in an underground bomb shelter, what we call the Preserve. Just a minute and I'll answer the rest of your questions."

David studied Jesse, and everything they passed along the way, amazed by what he saw. He could tell the tunnel they walked though was made from corrugated steel pipe, the floor concrete. The airlock was impressive, with hazmat suits hanging in closets and a cleansing shower in the corner, like he'd seen on construction sites. They entered a large sitting room, with furniture arranged like a living room, and an entertainment center at the far end, about forty feet away. There were two other entrances to this room, one on the far wall and one, half-way down in a side wall. Jesse noticed where David was looking, led them to a couch and they all sat. "This is the community center," Jesse said, "and I'm Jesse. I'm a visitor here, like you. I've been here for about seventeen years. You want to know where we are, right?" Jesse asked.

"That's a difficult question."

"Why?" David asked. "Why is it difficult?"

"Let's begin with something simpler. Do you like it here?" Jesse asked.

"Haven't you figured out where you are after seventeen years?" David asked, "and why do you still call yourself a visitor?"

"I'm a visitor in the same sense that you are. We were invited here the same way."

David wondered why Jesse didn't say he was kidnapped. Why did he say 'invited'? Instead, he asked, "It seems a little primitive."

"I like to use the word, 'simpler'. Life is simpler here; narrowed down to what it takes to survive and not cluttered with all the social media and political turmoil. Do you like Lisa Beth?"

David looked at Lisa Beth, sitting next to him, and considered how to answer. Of course, he liked her, a lot. But with her sitting right there, what else could he say. "Of course, I do. What's not to like? Why? What's going on here?"

"Have you met Matt Jr.?"

"Yes. He made his presence known. Why do you keep asking me questions, without answering mine?"

"Would you like to stay here?" Jesse asked.

"You mean like you, for seventeen years?"

"Or longer?" Jesse asked.

"You know, I had a life before I ended up here, wherever 'here' is; and although I've had fun the last couple of days, it's been more like a summer campout than a real life, which I can still have if I can get some help getting back to it."

David noticed Lisa Beth frown at that response.

"Were you happy in your old life?" Jesse asked.

"Yes," David said hesitantly, after a slight pause, during which he thought briefly about his boss, whom he detested, his girlfriend, to whom he had been ready to commit for life, but in whom he had little interest beyond how well she kissed, and his job, which he enjoyed, but didn't receive the recognition that he thought he deserved.

"Were you *really* happy?" Jesse asked again. "How about your job? You don't seem to be appreciated for all of your accomplishments. They didn't even mention you at the ribbon-cutting ceremony, did they?"

"Well, no," David said, "but they used my team's design, and who cares if I didn't get the pat on the back for a job done exceptionally well?" Then he wondered how Jesse knew so much. "How do you know about the ribbon-cutting ceremony? For that matter, how do you know anything about me?"

"I think you're answering your own question." Jesse said. "What about your boss, Evans. He's not very nice to you, is he?"

"I could get a job anywhere, with my portfolio. I don't need him."

"But he blackballed you from getting any other job in the department, didn't he?"

"How do you know about that?"

"Not too much of a secret if it's discussed in department leadership meetings, is it? What did he call you? A pompous self-aggrandizing know-it-all, it didn't help for him to put that in your performance review, did it?"

"So Evans is a jerk. What of it? None of those things are true, and anyone who knows me, knows it."

"How's Stefani?" Jesse asked. "Were you going to see her when you got sidetracked?"

"When I got kidnapped, you mean? Yes, I was on my way to see her, to propose to her."

A quick look at Lisa Beth confirmed that she didn't like that answer either.

"When you don't love her?" Jesse asked.

"How do you know I don't love her. And what business is it of yours anyway?"

"Everything about you is my business, now."

"Why?"

"Because you're here and Mike asked me to take care of you,"

"And your idea of taking care of me is to badger and belittle me and make me feel like my life is worthless? Is that it?"

"Your life's not worthless, just . . . misdirected." Jesse said.

"Oh yeah?" David said, defensively. "What would you have me do differently?"

"Stay among people who really care about each other and who need you."

"I saw how much Matt Jr. cares about people."

"One bad apple doesn't spoil the whole barrel," Jesse said. "Besides, Matt Jr. just needs to get to know you the way some of us do."

David had to think about that statement for a few moments. What did Jesse mean? *How* did they know him and how *well* did they know him? And, more curiously, who were 'they'?

"I see you have some questions," Jesse said. "Will you go for a walk with me?"

"Do I have a choice?"

"You always have a choice. You just can't always predict or control the consequences, right? Like when you choose to contradict your boss."

"Okay, I'll bite. Where are we going?"

"On a little tour of the Preserve. I thought you might like to see how we live. This is the community center. There are twenty of us living here, plus another twenty-two living in the valley, above-ground, most of whom you've met already. People sometimes move back and forth, but that's the way things are set up at present. This tunnel leads to the bedrooms, we have one vacant room in this first hallway, so I'll show you what they look like; they're all about the same."

"Very impressive," David said, when he saw the room. "Modern and clean."

"On the left we have the library, school and exercise rooms. Would you like to see them?"

"Why not?" He was not expecting to be impressed, but was. "That's quite a library," he said. "and the exercise equipment looks new."

"Well used and well cared for," Jesse said.

"Back the other way are the hospital, nursery, office, lab, store rooms, and gardens."

"Lab? I'm almost afraid to ask what you do in the lab?"

"Besides being a doctor, Doc and his partner, Terry, are scientists and inventors."

"What do they invent?"

"Mostly, medical hardware, like artificial limbs, but they've invented some other things that are quite curious."

Just then, someone said, "Jesse" and he plucked the radio off his belt.

"What do you need, Beth," he said into the radio.

"If you're through with David, I would like to talk to him before bed about something."

"Actually, we're at a good place to stop. We haven't been to the gardens, but we can leave that for another day. I'll show him back to the door."

"Why don't you continue. What I need him for can wait."

"Fine. I'll let you know when we're done," Jesse said, "If we don't finish today, we can continue another day."

"Are you going to answer my questions?" David asked.

"We have plenty of time," Jesse said. "Let's show you the rest of the preserve first."

David wasn't satisfied with that response, but decided to wait a little longer for his answers. Jesse seemed to want to answer his questions, if he ever got around to it. They had been so nice to him, maybe he could be patient. Besides, he was curious to know what Beth thought he could do to help. It looked to him like they had everything they needed, even if they seemed a little backward. Lisa Beth took his arm in both her hands and held tightly to him, as if she were afraid he might leave her.

"Is anyone else here?" David asked, noticing how quiet it was.

"Actually, twenty people live here, but they're all occupied in other parts of the Preserve. We may see some of them in the gardens." Jesse led the way into the side tunnel and through a series of bends until they reached a door with a large 'G' in the center. He opened the door and they entered a large, humid room, with planting beds down both sides and in the center of the room. Green plants grew everywhere, under grow lamps, and several people milled about, talking and carrying plants or containers that looked like water or fertilizer. They walked down one of the two aisles between plants, many of which David recognized from his dad's garden back home, but his dad's plants looked anemic compared to these.

A door in the side wall opened and a thirty-something man entered. "Hi Chris," Jesse said. "I'm showing off your garden to our visitor. This is David."

"Hi Lisa Beth," Chris said. "Welcome, David. Do you like gardening?"

"He just designed and built an irrigation system for our garden and orchard," Lisa Beth said proudly.

"I recognize a lot of your plants from my dad's garden in Smithfield, but your plants look healthier than his ever did."

"I know where Smithfield is," Chris said, politely. "I dated a girl from there for a while, before all the trouble."

"What trouble?" David asked.

Instead of answering, Chris looked at Jesse with a questioning look.

"I'm waiting for Mike to say he's ready to talk," Jesse said.

David wondered why they wouldn't explain their cryptic comments, but stored it away along with Lisa Beth's comments about fallout and explosions and Matt, Jr's. comment about him not being one of them. Somebody needed to start explaining things soon or he was going to lose his temper.

"Has David met the rest of the residents?" Chris asked.

"I presume he's met the Outcasts," Jesse said.

"He's seen everyone," Lisa Beth said quickly, "but hasn't been introduced to them all. We figured he would get to know everyone as he interacted with them."

"Outcasts?" David asked Lisa Beth quietly.

"I'll explain later," she said, so he stored that question away with the others.

"Have you seen the exercise rooms?" Chris asked David, who nodded. "What kind of exercise do you like?"

"What? Oh, at the gym I use the treadmill, bicycle and universal gym, which I saw you have here."

"I'm sure you're welcome to use them. Just have Beth contact us so someone can let you in."

David thought this might be a good time to make up to Lisa Beth for some of his negative comments earlier, "Do you use the exercise room?" he asked her with a smile,

"I seldom come into the Preserve," she said. "Not that I couldn't. It's just that it takes extra effort."

"Jesse," David said. "I have a lot of questions and I really need someone to answer some of them. Can you do that?"

"I think your questions will be best answered by Michael," Jesse said. "He's the chairman of the board."

"What? You have a community of forty-five people and it's run by a board of directors?" he asked. "Is this a business?"

Lisa Beth's face scrunched up. "I'm sorry, David. I don't know how to answer your questions. You really need to talk to Michael."

"Fine," he said, folding his arms in front of him in a dismissive gesture. "We'll wait for Michael." He looked from Jesse to Chris to Lisa Beth to see if anyone would offer some answers.

"Don't be mad at me, David," she pleaded, apologetically.

"I haven't heard anyone say they care if I get answers to my questions," he said. He heard a sniffle and turned to see a tear on Lisa Beth's cheek. It broke through his shell and he reached an arm around her shoulders.

"I'm sorry, Lisa Beth. I'm trying to be patient, but I've been here for several days already and still have no idea where 'here' is, how I got here or how to get home. Do I need a pair of ruby slippers?"

Jesse had stepped away to use a radio and returned to see Lisa Beth's distress, "Is everything okay?" he asked.

"No, Jesse," Lisa Beth said, "It's not okay. David deserves to know what's going on. Can you contact Michael?"

"I was just going to tell you that Mike is ready to talk. Come with me. You, too, Lisa Beth. This affects you, too."

☢

Mike sat in a chair behind a desk, in what looked like an office, when the three of them entered. He looked like he was in his forties. He had a head full of dark hair with fringes of gray above his ears, and a smooth complexion. "Hi Lisa Beth, Jesse. Welcome David. How are you being treated?"

"Like a guest at a hotel, basically," David said. "I have some ques—"

"I'll answer all your questions," Mike interrupted, before David could complete his comment. "I apologize for leaving you in the dark for so long, but we had to know if you were the person we thought you were."

"What does—"

"Sorry, again," Mike interrupted. "That was too cryptic. Let me start over." Mike steepled his fingers and placed them to his lips, while he thought about how to proceed.

"My father, Amos Blund, and his partner, Terry Stephens—do those names mean anything to you? No? Okay. They foresaw a time when the world would suffer a major catastrophe, like another world war, so they built this preserve. It is totally self-sustaining. When that war occurred, seventeen years ago—" David had heard enough. He knew there had not been a world war since the 1940's, so this guy was blowing smoke or was crazy. He needed to interrupt.

"What war is that?" he asked, rather than saying what he wanted to say.

"There was a global thermonuclear war started by Al-Qaeda—" David was ready to interrupt again until he heard Mike's next words, "—in our world."

This was totally unexpected. He'd read enough science fiction to recognize the concept of parallel worlds, a world split into two timelines because of some traumatic event, but that was fiction, not real life.

"You want me to believe that we're in some parallel world and you've found a way to travel between the two?" David asked.

"He catches on quickly," Mike said to Jesse and Lisa Beth.

"So, you believe it?" Lisa Beth asked enthusiastically.

"I understand the concept," David said. "I didn't say I believe that's what's going on here."

"Maybe it would help if I tell you about myself," Jesse said, then paused.

"I'm listening," David said.

⊛

"Seventeen years ago, I was just out of residency, helping at the Huntsman Cancer facility in Salt Lake City. Single, in my late twenties, with five roommates, no assets and lots of debt, I was trying to work off student loans by treating cancer patients and helping with research into predicting the potential for cancer through genetics. Cancer had been cured, but there were still lots of people getting it and being treated for it. As fantastic as the cancer cures were, after a while, the work became routine, even boring. I felt like my life was going nowhere. I could do this every day for the rest of my life and never run out of patients, who needed one of a handful of treatments, that were becoming as predictable as basic math.

"Where was the thrill in life?" I asked myself frequently. "Should I just quit and find something else to do, like work in a fast-food restaurant? At least there, I might be able to meet girls that didn't have cancer, where the conversation wasn't going to be about their next treatment. I spent a lot of time sitting in my room, reading, or playing virtual reality games, by myself.

"One day, sitting in my room, I felt someone watching me. Looking around, I knew I was alone, but the feeling wouldn't go away.

"On this occasion, I walked out to the living room, where some of my roommates were sitting at the table, eating, studying or just talking, and asked if one of them wanted me for something. The only response I got was a sarcastic, 'You wish.'

"As I walked back to my room, I thought I noticed a difference in the lighting in the hallway. When I looked up, a strange stirring in the air seemed to block the doorway, which gave me pause, but only for a moment—I was accustomed to sudden bright lights, as part of the cancer treatments at the hospital—so I continued, thinking no more about it, and stepped through what looked like a doorway, where there wasn't a doorway, and into a clean, white room, with electronics on the wall and two men standing in front of me.

" 'Hi Jesse,' the older man said. 'I guess you're wondering where you are.'

" 'I'm in my dorm,' I said, although I must have had a confused look on my face, 'but something has changed. Who are you?'

" 'What's changed, Jesse,' the man said, 'is that you are no longer in your dorm. Hi, I'm Doctor Amos Blund.'

" 'What's going on?' I asked, still not thinking anything unusual had happened; but maybe I had died of a sudden heart attack and these were the angels sent to get me. Then I recognized the name. Amos Blund had been a close friend of President Gregory McCormick a few years earlier and had been given credit for finding the cure for radiation poisoning in people and in soil, water and air. I knew about him because his cure had been bigger news than the cancer cure, that had been discovered two years earlier.

"I've been here seventeen years, and I still have trouble understanding how I got here," Jesse said.

8

The Old World—The Preserve, seventeen years earlier

Mike sat in the lab, working the controls that maneuvered the Gemini gate around Salt Lake City in the old world. Most of the downtown buildings had suffered some, if not major, damage, and the homes were worse off than the commercial buildings. The Huntsman Medical Center was no better off and had been reconstructed before cancer research could resume. Mike didn't know what he was looking for, but after looking at the big picture for months, he had begun focusing on individuals, picking out one or another whom he could isolate from the crowd and follow for an hour or a day. It became a game to see how quickly he could figure out what that person thought was important—what was worth their time. He followed government leaders, medical professionals, businessmen, even housewives or children sometimes. He usually got bored after a while and broke it off without identifying their priorities.

He noticed when the military entered the Salt Lake Valley to begin reconstruction. Being an engineer, this interested him. He tried to predict what they would work on next. Having seen all of the technology when it was introduced by Doc Blund, from the twin world, Mike was already familiar with the capabilities, he just wanted to watch it all happen. He was not disappointed; being familiar with most of the utilities in the valley, he predicted those that the government would consider most important to get online first, and he was satisfied with the workmanship, generally. He thought the Corps of Engineers must be led by some pretty clever, intelligent, and competent people.

On this day, he focused on a medical professional at the Huntsman Cancer Center, Jesse Newman, who had reported some sort of problem to his supervisor and had been told to mind his own business, that the perceived problem wasn't his to worry about. He had stormed off and taken a break in the cafeteria. Mike expected Newman to quit the job, or at least to leave for the rest of the day. That's what he would have done. He was surprised and impressed when Newman finished his break and went back to work, as though nothing had happened. He followed him around for several more hours, until he felt like he knew him pretty well; knew his attitude, his habits, and his priorities. In all the time he watched, the man never met with anyone, like a friend, or scheduled to meet with anyone, like a date. He ate alone, watched television alone, played video games alone, and slept alone.

Of course, everything Mike observed in Salt Lake City, in the old world, had to be weighed against the extremely stressful conditions caused by the war.

☢

Doc had asked Mike to collect medical observations of different types of medical conditions into a database and load the data into the Observer, to see if the Observer could be used to diagnose medical conditions from simple observation—Artificial Intelligence, or AI, as he had called it. Mike had done as asked, loading about ten thousand observable facial and bodily reactions to different medical conditions. Then Mike watched to see if the Observer behaved differently, although he didn't see how just adding data would make a difference. To date, he had seen no unusual changes or further developments in the Observer. They were already able to use the gate to jump from one location to another and to look inside the human body to assess medical problems, and Doc had used it for both. Mike had seen nothing new, in the last two years, and had pushed the thought to the back of his mind.

A few days after Mike spent his day watching Jesse Newman at the medical center, he moved the gate around the University of Utah campus, looking at students moving between buildings, when the gate focused on a man and followed him, resisting Mike's attempts to move the gate or focus on anything else. Mike wondered why and studied the man, realizing that it was Newman. How curious! Doc's words returned, making him wonder if this was some new capability of the Observer and what, exactly, that capability was.

After watching Newman walk to the Huntsman center and check in for his shift, Mike turned the Observer off. He would have to think about this new development, maybe talk to Terry about it.

⊛

"What do you think it means?" Terry asked later that day, after Mike had explained his observations.

"We know the observer has memory, since we can jump to previously stored data points. Perhaps this is just another demonstration of its memory, remembering faces and focusing on them when seen again."

"Has it ever done this before?" Terry asked.

"Not in such an obvious way," Mike said.

"Is it possible that it's related to the AI data that Doc had you create and add to memory?" Terry asked. "Didn't he say he believed the Observer should be able to observe behaviors and correlate them to medical problems?"

"He did," Mike said, "Do you think, maybe this guy has a

medical problem which the Observer recognizes and is trying to communicate to us."

"That would be my guess," Terry said. "So, how did Doc say you would know what the problem would be?"

"The way I understand it, the Observer observes behaviors and facial expressions, compares them to the formulas in the database, and narrows down the problem to one or more likely medical conditions, then gives us a list of its findings, along with the list of potential medical conditions."

"How do you make it work?" Terry asked.

"I run the routine in the Observer and it spits out the list of potential problems, like this . . ." Mike said and typed an instruction on the control panel. In a few moments, a printout scrolled out of the Observer. The readout on the screen read: "Results: three; Elapsed time: 0.04 seconds."

"That was fast," Terry said. "What does the printout say?"

"It's a list. It says . . .

"Observations: emotional detachment, tiredness, restlessness, sweaty palms, poor diet.

"Problem: ulcers, probability fifty-six percent; sleep apnea, probability seventy-four percent; loneliness, probability ninety-four percent. Is loneliness a medical condition?"

"I suppose it is, Terry said, although I've never treated a patient for it. I don't think there's a medication to help. It's more of a behavioral thing."

"So, what do we do about it?"

"I don't know. There are a lot more serious problems out there. Perhaps it's not something we worry about."

"I'll ignore it in that case," Mike said. He tried to ignore Mr. Newman and focus on other people. Despite that, the observer continued to track Mr. Newman. Mike's observations confirmed

Mr. Newman's symptoms. Mike became convinced that the Observer had diagnosed his problem—loneliness—correctly. So what? Everyone had problems and this seemed like a minor one, unless it led to something more serious. Why had the Observer picked out Newman to focus on and what was Mike supposed to do about it? When he spoke with Terry about it again, Terry had no better idea than he did and suggested he avoid Newman and look elsewhere.

Two days later, after Mike had helped the Outcasts solve a plumbing problem in the cabin—Bryce had cross-threaded a pipe in the kitchen and it had sprung a leak, easy enough to fix with the correct tools—he went back to the lab to work with the Observer. When he turned it on, intending to look at people in downtown Salt Lake City again, the Observer immediately jumped to the university campus, found and followed Newman. Mike called Terry to show him the man and explain what had happened.

"But why would it automatically search for him?" Mike asked.

Terry had no answer, but had a suggestion.

"Perhaps we're supposed to do something about the man's problem" he said.

"But why?" Mike asked, "when there are probably thousands of people out there with more serious problems?"

"Maybe his problem is directly related to us," Terry said, "or something that we have the unique ability to solve."

"Are you attributing human reasoning skills to the Observer?" Mike asked. "If you are, I'm going to have to start worrying about you."

"No, Mike," Terry said with a chuckle. "I just wonder if there's something about the man that has triggered something that we built into the programming."

"Should I look at the programming?" Mike asked. "I wouldn't

know where to look or what to look for."

"Understood," Terry said. "Why don't you give it more time, to see if something develops."

Sydney and Rylee had moved out of the preserve, into Aspen Valley to be closer to Isaac and Zach, who were about their same age. The boys had come to the valley when Jason Carlsen had attempted to take over the Preserve. Jason had died in the battle for Aspen Valley, but the boys, and the other surviving invaders had been accepted and stayed. Kerri and Callie played chaperone to the four of them, Sydney, Rylee, Isaac and Zach, whenever they were together, which was most of the time. Lisa, who'd suffered from pneumonia, in addition to the radiation sickness that all of the Outcasts had developed, had moved into the Preserve in the twin world after her recovery. Doc continued to monitor her health and she stayed, moving into one of the unused bedrooms. She'd told Emily, the house manager, that she preferred sleeping in a soft bed, eating prepared meals in the dining room of the Preserve, over a sleeping bag on the ground, in the cabin in the valley, and preparing her own meals. In exchange, Lisa had agreed to be Doc's guinea pig, allowing him to use the Observer as a medical device, to check her lungs and other internal organs, skeleton, musculature, heart and brain. He was documenting his observations as part of his medical research for later publication.

Emily had observed that the more time Lisa spent alone in the hospital with Doc, the more familiar she became with him, even becoming infatuated with the good-looking doctor. Emily worried about it. As the house manager, with her mom and Doc living on the estate in the twin world, Emily tried to make sure everyone was happy and healthy, including the Outcasts in the valley. Lisa's move into the Preserve seemed to upset the balance that had been there before. When her mom paid one of her regular visits to the preserve in the old world, to check on the family, Emily explained her concern, that Lisa needed to be with people her own age, especially where there were unattached men that she could socialize with and maybe fall in love. That was something that was always on Emily's mind, love and marriage. In Lisa's present situation, she could have neither, and Emily could see the effect that Lisa's time with Doc was having on her.

"Emily," Lillie said, resting a hand on Emily's shoulder affectionately, "you're always so concerned about others. That's a great quality. However, in this case, I don't see that there's much you can do for Lisa. She has limited options. There are only three unattached men in the valley and they're all older and have been married before. The only other options would be to let Lisa leave the area or go to the twin world. Think about you and Matt. You met when you both had lots of choices. Lisa doesn't have that."

"That's only part of my concern, Mom," Emily said. "You need to go to the hospital to see for yourself what's happening."

When Lillie entered the hospital, Doc had the gate open somewhere inside Lisa, who lay quietly on the operating table in short shorts and a halter top, that left little to the imagination, and no shoes. Lillie cleared her throat to get Doc's attention, then suggested that they stop for the day, since she needed Doc. He looked at his watch and agreed.

"I didn't realize how late it was, Lillie," he said. "Thanks for checking on us. Why don't you take off, Lisa?"

"Do you want me back tomorrow morning at the same time?" she asked, maybe a little too enthusiastically.

"Let me get back to you on that," he said, seeing the look in Lillie's eye, which meant she wasn't happy. He didn't know why, but they needed to talk.

"Oh, alright," Lisa said, disappointed. She rolled off the table, slipped her sandals on her feet and slipped past Lillie to leave the room.

"You do realize that Lisa has a teenage style crush on you, right?" Lillie asked Doc, when Lisa was gone.

"No way!" Doc said, then paused when he noticed Lillie's expression.

"Look what she's wearing," Lillie said, exasperated.

"I told her she could wear whatever made her comfortable," he replied, innocently.

"So, if she wanted to be naked, that would be okay with you?" Lillie asked.

"Well, no," he said, beginning to see where Lillie was coming from.

"And what do you think is going through her head, knowing that you're looking all through her body. Just a little too personal, don't you think?" she asked.

"What do you mean. I'm her doctor and it's a medical exam, nothing more."

"But what does she think you're looking at? I think this needs to stop, Doc, at least for a while."

"Okay, honey," he said. "I'll tell her no more for a while."

❁

When Lillie and Doc left the hospital, Emily spoke to Lillie. "You're right, Mom. I hadn't thought of Lisa's problem that way. Is there any plan to let the outcasts leave? For that matter, maybe Rylee and Sydney would like more options."

"I'll talk to Doc and Mike about it," Lillie said. She had almost said "I'll talk to your dad," but Doc wasn't Emily's dad, although he was an identical copy of him from the twin world. Emily's dad, Amos, had died in the battle for Aspen Valley, three years earlier.

Doc didn't know what to do with himself, now that he'd been banned from the Observer and Lisa, so he wandered into the lab, where Mike and Terry were working. "How's your research going?" he asked Mike.

Mike told him about his unusual observation of Jesse Newman and asked what Doc thought.

"Heck if I know," Doc said. "Why don't you show me?"

Mike turned on the Observer and it jumped to a student dorm on the university campus, where four young men sat around a kitchen table and Jesse Newman sat alone, off to the side, The Observer zoomed in on Newman.

"That's him?" Doc asked. Mike nodded.

"Tell me about him," Doc said.

"He has a job at the cancer center," Mike explained. "No social life, in fact, any kind of life at all."

"Have you checked his background? Done any research on him at all?" Doc asked. Doc had set up an internet account for Mike in the twin world when they had first met and had been keeping it paid up so Mike could do research whenever he wanted to.

"I have. His name is Jesse Newman, from Salt Lake City. Twenty-eight years old, Bachelor's degree in psychology and an MD, completed his residency recently and went to work for the government helping with cancer research. No family in the area and no attachments."

"Meaning, I suppose," Doc said "that he has no girlfriend."

"Correct. I can't even tell if he has an interest in girls, since he never meets with anyone on a social basis."

"So, why is the Observer interested in him?" Doc asked.

"Terry thinks it might be some quirk that I introduced into the programming, but I can't imagine what that would be, or even where to begin looking. He also thought it might be focused on him because of something that's going on here in the Preserve, with one of us."

"So, you're giving it a human personality, Terry?" Doc asked.

"Not intentionally," Terry said, "but we have programmed a lot of information about human emotion into it. Maybe it's learning more than we intended."

"Has it shown any interest in anyone else?" Doc asked.

"I can't get it to go anywhere anymore," Mike said.

"Have you tried the twin world? Or here in the Preserve?"

With all the work Mike had done with the control panels for the gate over the last year, he was able jump between worlds without changing panels. He jumped the gate to Salt Lake City in the twin world, where the Observer wandered around for a while, then jumped, on its own to Newman, in his dorm room in the old world. Frustrated, Mike jumped the gate to Aspen Valley, in the old world, and moved the gate into the Outcasts' cabin. The gate wandered through the cabin, ignoring Mike's attempt to control it, and showed no interest in anyone. Suddenly, the gate jumped, again on its own, into the Preserve, where it focused on Lisa, lying on her bed, crying.

"Is the intercom turned off?" Doc asked.

Mike turned to the controls on the wall, to check. "The ones to her room are turned off."

"So, what's wrong with Lisa," he asked, suspecting that it had something to do with him and their recent exchange in the hospital.

"I have no idea," Mike said. "We'll have to ask Emily." Mike checked the cameras and found Emily and Lillie in the community center, sitting on a couch, talking. Doc opened the gate and stepped through into the community center, drawing their attention.

"Emily," he asked, "do you know what's wrong with Lisa?"

"What do you mean?" Emily asked.

"She's in her room, crying," he said.

"That's because of you," Lillie said. Doc frowned and shook his head, but suspected she was right. It confirmed his own suspicion.

"I asked her when she wanted to return to the cabin," Emily said, "and she said 'never'. According to Beth, Lisa was always outgoing and happy, before the hypothermia. It looked like she was regaining her old motivation, until I asked about the cabin. She said there is no future there for her. She gave no indication that she would be so upset about it. I'll talk to her later and let her know there's no hurry."

"Why are you asking?" Lillie asked, knowing Doc well enough to know that something was going on.

"I'm not sure yet," Doc said, with a twinkle in his eye. He stepped back through the gate into the lab, where Mike and Terry waited for him.

"What does it mean?" Mike asked, having heard the exchange with Emily and Lillie.

"I don't know, Mike, but I want to play a hunch. Lisa has been showing signs of loneliness, as well."

"What are you thinking?" Mike asked.

"Are you saying," Terry asked at the same time, "that the AI parameters Mike set up in the observer have found a solution to Newman's loneliness problem, and it's Lisa?"

"Is it possible?" Doc asked, "Has the Observer determined that she is the cure for Newman and Newman is the cure for her? Can we get Jesse Newman to come through the gate without explaining anything to him, so we can find out?"

"Doc, are you giving human characteristics to the Observer?" Terry asked, teasing Doc, who had just asked him the same question.

"It's just a hunch, Terry, but what if it works? What will it mean?"

"Okay," Mike said. "You know that Newman has to step through the gate. I can't force him through it by running it past him. Maybe, if we can get him alone, we can tempt his curiosity by putting the gate in front of him to see if he'll step through on his own."

"Okay, Mike. Try it."

Mike set the gate up in the hallway of Jesse's dorm and waited for him to step through, which he did, stepping directly into the lab, and facing Mike and Doc. His eyebrows went up in surprise.

"Hi Jesse," Doc said. "I guess you're wondering where you are."

"I'm in my dorm," he said, but he must have had doubts, from the confused look on his face. "but something has changed. Who are you and how did you get in here?"

"What's changed, Jesse," Doc said, "is that you are no longer in your dorm. Hi, I'm Doctor Amos Blund, and this is my son, Michael, and we've brought you to our lab."

"Right," Jesse said, "like that's possible, and the only Amos Blund I've ever heard of was a friend of President Gregory McCormick, several years ago, and you don't look anything like him."

"One and the same, Jesse," Doc said. "I just don't have on my suit and tie."

"So, if I'm not in my dorm," Jesse asked "where am I?"

"We'll get to that. First, will you tell me why you're so unhappy?"

"Who says I'm unhappy? Am I on *Candid Camera?*"

"You don't look happy, Jesse. You appear to have no friends, no girlfriend, and you go through your day just trying to get through it. There's no enjoyment in your life. Am I wrong?"

"Look, I like my job, well most of the time, when I'm not being bossed around by the nurses. I have roommates, so I don't need friends. Why do you care?"

"Our technology has singled you out as someone who needs our attention. We want to know why."

"I don't know why. I don't even know what you're talking about. What technology?"

"Never mind. I want you to meet somebody. Will you come with me?"

"What if I don't want to? What if I just want to be left alone?"

"Well, you're here now and you can't leave until we help you, so you may as well relax and try to enjoy it for a few minutes."

"I still don't know what you're talking about," Jesse said, but Doc had already turned and started to leave the lab, so Jesse, then Mike, followed. They went through the office and into a tunnel, that led to the community center. Jesse looked around at the rooms and hallways in confusion. "Where are we?" he asked again, but Doc didn't answer.

Lillie and Emily were still in the community center.

"What's going on?" Lillie asked when she saw Jesse.

"Would you go ask Lisa to come here?" Doc asked. "I want to introduce her to Jesse."

Lillie looked Jesse over; his worn jeans, torn t-shirt and unpolished shoes. She thought he might be handsome if he smiled and combed his unruly hair. She stood and turned toward him. "Hello Jesse," she said. "I'm Lillie and this is Emily. Welcome to our home" She turned and headed for the bedroom wing to get

Lisa, not trying to outguess Doc, who, just like her Amos before him, was always full of surprises and would explain himself when he was ready.

It took some coaxing to get Lisa out of her room, and Lillie had to encourage her to wash her face and comb her hair, but she finally arrived. "What do you need?" she asked Doc, possibly thinking he would ask her to return to the hospital to continue their sessions with the observer. Then she saw Jesse. "Who's he?"

"He's a visitor," Doc said. "His name is Jesse and I want you to show him around the Preserve. Will you do that, Lisa?"

"What does he want to see?" Lisa asked, totally at ease with the suggestion.

"Show him the library, the exercise rooms, the classrooms, the gardens and the kitchen for starters, okay?"

"Fine. Come on, Jesse," Lisa said, holding out her hand for him.

"Your home?" Jesse asked, still looking at Lillie. Although he had no idea what was going on or what to expect, he took Lisa's hand and followed her out of the room. As they headed into the tunnel, Lisa had already started explaining what they were going to see and he was asking questions. It may have been the first time in years that a woman about his age had shown any attention to him. It didn't hurt that she was good-looking and wearing short shorts, a halter top and sandals, that showed off most of her body. He didn't take his eyes off her the whole time they were within sight.

Lillie gave Doc a questioning look, inviting him to explain himself, but he just winked at her. "Let me know when they're back," he said, then returned to the lab, where Mike had turned on the cameras to watch and listen to them, as they strolled through the Preserve.

"I'm really impressed with the library," Jesse said. "Do you read a lot?"

"Some," Lisa said, flashing Jesse a beautiful smile.

"You're very pretty," he said, self-consciously, as they moved to the garden. He looked her in the eyes, then looked down, unable or unwilling to maintain eye contact. There were rows of green plants, in all stages of development. "This is amazing," he added. Lisa looked around, seeing what he was seeing. After a quick look around, Jesse focused his attention on her again, now oblivious of the plants.

"Thank you," Lisa said, "You're rather nice looking yourself. Where are you from?"

"Salt Lake City," he said. "I work at the Huntsman Cancer Center. Where are we?"

"Logan Canyon. How did you get here?"

"I don't know. I was in my dorm room, then I was in a room facing two men that I've never seen before. They said they brought me here, but I still don't know where 'here' is. Then they introduced me to you and I'm glad they did."

"Doc must have brought you through the gate. Did he tell you why you're here? And did he invite you to stay for dinner?"

"Is that the man's name who spoke with me? Doc?"

"Yes, Doc Blund, former advisor to the president of the United States."

"That's what he said. So, he brought me here using some super-secret military technology, is that what you're saying?"

"No, he invented it himself. He didn't tell you about it?"

"No, he didn't. Is he your father?"

"No. He's a leader in our community. Will you stay for dinner? I'm sure it would be alright."

"If you're sure it's okay," Jesse said, taking another quick look at her face.

"Let's go back now and I'll ask if it's alright," she said, leading him out of the garden and back to the community center. In the lab, Mike was ecstatic at the prospect that the observer had made this connection, that they had possibly understood its meaning, and had put Lisa and Jesse together correctly.

As they entered the community center, Lillie and Emily stopped talking and looked at them. "How was the tour?" Lillie asked.

"This is an amazing structure," Jesse said. "Who built it?"

"My husband, his partner, and my son, Michael," she said.

"Isn't Michael one of the men I met earlier?" he asked,

"He is, Jesse," Lillie said. "It's almost dinner time. Will you stay for dinner?"

Jesse looked at Lisa and smiled. She returned his smile, warmly. He hadn't felt this good in a long time, he thought. "I'd love to," he said. "if it's alright."

"We'd love for you to stay," Lillie said.

"Thank you."

At dinner, Jesse was introduced to the rest of the residents of the preserve, who sat around the long table in the dining room. Doc and Lillie had stayed at the Preserve, rather than going back to Logan, so Doc could make the introductions and deflect any questions. At the end of the meal, Lillie nudged Doc to get his attention and motioned toward Lisa and Jesse. Sitting together a few chairs down and across the table, they were glancing at each other surreptitiously, then looking away when caught at it. It was obvious to Lillie that they liked each other and that their relationship could get serious quickly if given opportunity. She determined to give them lots of opportunities, by putting them on the same work crews and giving them time to explore their feelings.

It made Doc smile, seeing that his hunch may have been correct. Or, it might have been a coincidence, but he didn't think so. He was sure that the AI had worked. The Observer was playing match-maker, not from a human emotion perspective, but from a logical, unhappy-people-need-each-other perspective. It had selected an unhappy, good-looking young man and found him an equally unhappy, pretty young woman.

Following dinner, Doc and Mike took Jesse and Lisa to the lab. He thought it best not to try to separate them.

"Would you like to see where you are?" Amos asked.

"Absolutely!" Jesse said.

Mike turned on the Observer, opened a small gate, and showed Jesse his dorm and his roommates.

"Can they hear us?" Jesse asked.

"They could if I had the speakers turned on," Mike said, "but I don't think we want to draw their attention to us."

"What would they see if they looked at us?"

"Right now, we have a small, one-inch diameter opening, near the ceiling. So. they wouldn't recognize you unless they came right up to the opening and put an eyeball up to it."

"That's weird! Can we see where I work?" Mike jumped the gate to the hospital, to the nurses' station on the floor where he'd worked.

"This is where you work," Mike said, "or at least where you worked until today."

"Do you have any questions, Jesse?" Doc asked.

"I remember seeing a shimmer in the hall by my bedroom just before I met you. Was that the gate?"

"It was," Doc said. "We couldn't force you to come to us, but you obliged us by stepping through the gate on your own. Are you ready to go back to your life?"

Jesse didn't answer right away—he seemed tongue-tied, unable to ask the questions that were on the tip of his tongue. He looked around the lab, at the door to the office, where they'd left Lisa, then back to the gate and its view of the hospital.

"If I go back," he finally asked, "Will I be able to see Lisa again?"

"Would you like to?" Doc asked. "I can bring you back another time . . . or . . . you can stay, if she's in agreement."

"Being with Lisa has been more enjoyable than anything I've done for a long time, but I don't know if she feels the same way about me."

"Would you like to ask her?"

"Would that be alright?" he asked reluctantly, unsure of himself, possibly afraid to hear her answer.

"Let's go ask her," Doc said.

Lisa had returned to the community center while they were looking at the hospital.

They found her sitting on a couch, talking quietly with Emily. Jesse sat on the couch next to her and spoke quietly. "Well?" Lisa asked, sitting next to Jesse on the couch, their knees just touching, "Did you get your questions answered?"

"Most of them," he said. "Doc showed me how the gate works and told me I could come back to see you again, or I could stay, if it's okay with you."

"Do you want to see me again?" Lisa asked shyly, lowering her head slightly so she didn't have to look at his face when he answered.

"What I'd really like," he said, taking both of her hands in his, "is to stay, so I can spend lots of time with you, every day. What do you think of that idea?"

"I'd love it," she said, looking up suddenly and looking into his eyes.

She looked at Emily, questioningly. Emily smiled reassuringly, as though they had just been discussing the possibility. Then Lisa turned her question to Doc.

"Can he?" she asked. "I mean, can he stay?"

"He can stay," Doc said, "if there's room for him and it's okay with you."

"We have room for him," Emily said.

"I want him to stay," Lisa said, immediately.

"Emily, you have a couple of spare rooms in the Preserve, can you make one of them up for Jesse?"

"I'd be delighted," Emily said, then waved to Lisa and Jesse to follow her.

9

The Old World—The Preserve, present day, 15 June

"So," David said, "you want me to believe that there was a global nuclear war in this world, and now you're kidnapping people to do what . . . repopulate this world?" He had thought he was upset when he didn't know what was going on. Now that he thought he knew; he was even more upset. What right did they have to uproot him from his life and bring him to a backward world . . . okay, simpler world, where he would do their bidding, whatever that was? Did they want him to marry Lisa Beth and make babies? Is that what they had in mind when they threw them together the day he arrived? Would that be so bad, he wondered? He really liked her, after all. But he wanted to know what this Doc Blund had in mind when he brought him here.

Jesse didn't know how to respond to David's unspoken frustration. Luckily, he was saved from any more stress when Doc appeared in the room, like magic.

"Hi Jesse, Lisa Beth, David," he said.

"Where am I?" David asked again, not satisfied with the previous answer.

"You're in Logan Canyon, David, in our Preserve," Doc said. He figured David was trying to make a point by not acknowledging that he'd already been told. He wasn't upset, just saddened that David was behaving this way.

"This is not the Logan Canyon I'm familiar with," David said.

"No, it's not," Jesse said, "but this *is* Logan Canyon."

"How can that be?" David asked. Jesse opened his mouth to

answer and David held up his hand to stop him. "I know. You're going to tell me we're in a parallel universe. But how?"

"Do you read science fiction?" Amos asked.

"Sometimes, but what—?"

"If you've read some of Robert Heinlein's stories, you know that he wrote about parallel universes, about events that trigger a division in the time stream to form two worlds that are nearly identical."

"You're not suggesting—?" David started to say, but couldn't get the rest out. He stared at Jesse, then Amos, incredulously.

"Would you prefer to think of this as living in a dream?" Jesse asked. "I sometimes find it easier to accept that way."

Amos smiled in amusement at Jesse's explanation. He hadn't realized that Jesse still had trouble accepting the truth after so many years living among them. "Thanks Jesse," he said. "I'll take it from here. David," Doc continued, "we invented a device to help with medical treatment, then discovered that it had other capabilities."

"Like kidnapping?" David asked angrily.

"Call it kidnapping if you want to," Doc said, "I'm not insulted. This device has done more for the peace and safety of the people in two worlds, than any other device created by man. You can't insult me."

David was impressed by Doc's cool, calm confidence. The realization caused him to calm down and listen. Doc could see the change when it happened.

"Would you like to know more about it, and what I'm talking about?"

"I would," David said, calmly. Lisa Beth smiled at him, likely noticing the change as well.

Doc explained the history of the Observer, its construction, their discoveries, and how it was used to exchange technology with a twin world to save millions of people in both worlds. Before Doc had finished, David was asking questions about the engineering that went into the discoveries and the technology. "You will get a better explanation of the technology from Mike," Doc said. "He's the engineer. The Preserve is his design and so is the construction of the Observer. Mike might appreciate talking to another engineer, someone who can understand him better than us doctors."

"I'd like that," David said. "When—?" he started to ask, but Amos interrupted.

"We'll set something up, but for now, we need to decide what to do with you."

"Why did you bring me here?" David asked politely.

"The reason we built the Observer was to diagnose medical problems non-intrusively. That means, no incisions, no swallowing cameras, you get the idea. With the Observer, we can look inside a body without any of those and diagnose problems, at a very early stage, if we know what to look for. A few years ago—"

"Seventeen, to be exact," Jesse interrupted.

"Yes, seventeen years ago, I asked Mike to see if he could program the Observer to diagnose some problems from observation of facial expression and body language. For example, sweating, tension, fidgeting, lack of appetite, and so on. Jesse was our first experiment. How do you think it worked out, Jesse?"

"The Observer not only diagnosed me correctly," Jesse said, "but found the cure for my problem, Lisa."

David looked at Lisa Beth curiously.

"Not me," she said, "Lisa. You've seen her, but haven't been introduced. I'm named after her and Dr. Beth Byron."

"We've been happily married for over sixteen years now," Jesse said, "and have two wonderful children."

"And Beth said Jesse was the best thing to happen to Lisa. He helped her regain her zest for life."

David looked relieved. "So, is Lisa Beth my cure?" he asked jokingly, taking her hand in his.

"Actually, she might be," Doc said. "This technology is new so we're not positive. The Observer made the same connection between you and Lisa Beth that it made between Jesse and Lisa. I can only conclude that the same thing applies to you two."

David lost the smile and turned a serious face to Lisa Beth. "Do you believe this?" he asked.

"I want to," she said. "I've been happier since you arrived than I can remember."

"I don't know," David said, apparently not hearing the pleading in Lisa Beth's voice. "This sounds like you're playing with our lives, like we don't have any say in our future. It's too easy. Where's the chase? Where's the struggle for self-identity? Do we just accept our fate because you say so?"

"Maybe it was a mistake to tell you all this," Doc said. "Okay, forget we had this conversation. We'll send you back and you can go figure life out for yourself. The Observer is just a machine; it's not intelligent."

"David?" Lisa Beth questioned, like she was asking him to believe in Doc's conclusion.

David looked at her, and patted her hand, which he was still holding. "I've heard enough for now," he said and stood. "I think Beth wanted to talk to me before bedtime."

No one said a word, but Lisa Beth cried quietly as they stood and turned toward the door.

"I'll get Beth to meet you at the door," Doc said.

"Not necessary," David said. "I think we can find our way out."

Lisa Beth followed him reluctantly, while the others stared after them.

"David, what does it all mean?" Lisa Beth asked, as David led her down unfamiliar tunnels, trying to remember which way to turn at each junction. When it appeared that he was lost, Lisa Beth took the lead and led him to the secondary exit. "Do you think they're telling the truth?" She asked him.

"You know them better than I do. What do you think?"

"I've known them all my life. Beth swears that they are as honest as the day is long. Doc is creative, a genius when it comes to technology, and a family man. He cares about people."

David stopped abruptly and studied her face, wiped a tear off her cheek. He was quiet as they stood before the exit door.

"What are you thinking, David?" she asked, standing close, holding his hand with both of hers.

"I think they still didn't answer my questions." he said.

"They told you how you got here and why." She sounded like she was pleading for him to believe. "What else did you want to know?" He thought about it a few moments, trying to decide what to say, decided on one that he thought she could answer. "What was the fallout in the air that you said is no longer there?"

"That was nuclear fallout from an explosion at an air force base north of Salt Lake City."

"Hill Air Force Base," he supplied the name for her.

"That sounds right," she said. "It caused an earthquake that destroyed large cities and displaced over a million people. A lot of them ended up in Bear Lake valley. That's where my parents encountered Jason Carlsen, who brought them here."

"Who's Jason Carlsen?"

"He lived here with his family until he couldn't stand the confinement and living under Amos's leadership and found a way to escape. When he couldn't convince the Outcasts to help him take over the Preserve, he brought back a small army and tried to fight his way inside. Jason was killed, but so was Amos."

"And Doc is the Amos from the other world, is that it?"

"Yes, the twin world. Doc was a special advisor to the president of the United States and had lots of scientists and doctors working for him. He and Amos's son, Michael, worked out a trade of information and technology. We've been cleaning the air, water and soil here in the valley ever since. They also cured the radiation sickness that the Outcasts suffered from."

"And the radiation sickness was from the nuclear fallout?"

"Yes. My mom was pregnant with me when they arrived, so they worried about me being born with the disease, but I was born immune."

"What disease?"

"A mutated form of Smallpox that escaped from the CDC in Atlanta when it was destroyed by the government. They were trying to destroy all the virus samples, but one escaped and the Outcasts brought it to the valley."

"This just gets more and more confusing," David said, trying to keep everything she'd said straight in his head and fill in the blanks.

"It was a difficult time for all of them. If not for Amos's brilliant mind, I don't think it would have turned out as well as it did.

"After I was born immune, then Matt Jr. after me, they stopped worrying about the babies, and everyone started having families. Now, Emily and Katie each have three, Rachel has two, I have two siblings—who I sleep with—Beth has one, Rylee and Sidney each have one, Callie and Kerri each have two and Lisa, who I'm named after, has one. That makes forty-three people living in the valley, plus Doc and Lillie, living in Logan.

"Did you have other questions?" she asked. They'd left the tunnel and were walking across the clearing, back toward the gardens.

"Not right now," he said. "You've given me a lot to think about."

"You seemed very upset in the lab, David. I hope you're not mad a me."

"No, Lisa Beth. I'm not mad at you. I'm just a little frustrated by their explanation that a machine decided we should be together, so here I am. I had a life before I came here. How can I pursue my career if I'm stuck here?"

Lisa Beth, who had been polite and caring until that point in time, suddenly showed that she had a limit and a temper. "So, you're stuck with me? Is that how you feel? Is that all I am to you, a burden? Maybe Doc will send you back where you came from."

David was taken aback at her display of emotion. Maybe he'd gone too far with his complaining. "No Lisa Beth, that's not—," he began, but he didn't get the rest out. Lisa Beth dropped his hand and stormed off, careful to step around the garden plants, and disappeared into her cabin. David could only watch in frustration, at her straight, stiff back. He debated going after her; he didn't know why he didn't, maybe his pride had been hurt. He tried to tell himself that it was her problem if she didn't understand. He didn't need her, did he? He'd been doing well enough on his own. Then he thought about the things Jesse had said, about his being unfulfilled in his career and his love life. Was Jesse right? Did he need Lisa Beth? Why was he here? Was it just a fluke? *Should* he go after her? He couldn't decide what was the right thing to do, so he would see how things played out.

He didn't go inside. He wasn't sure he could face Lisa Beth after hurting her feelings. He should probably apologize, but he was still upset, himself. He needed to cool off. He walked through the garden and orchard, checking lines and his earlier repairs. It began to rain and the rain soaked through his clothes, making him shiver. By the time he went in, he was soaked and shivering with the cold. Leaving his muddy shoes and socks by the door, he went inside, found Sheryl setting the dinner table and asked if a hot bath was allowed, since he understood that water was a precious commodity in the valley. She told him he only had a few minutes before dinner was ready and suggested he wash up in the sink to see if that would warm him. He was still cold when he came to dinner.

He was surprised when Matt Jr. and his family showed up from the Preserve for dinner. He'd been told that this happened sometimes, but he wasn't in the mood to be sociable. Matt's dad, Matt Sr. was a doctor and worked with Terry Stephens in the hospital. He'd already met Matt's mom, Emily, who was very friendly. She stood next to David and asked him lots of questions about how he was getting along. He answered in as few words as possible, wondering if he was being impolite, but she seemed to take no offense.

Matt Jr. selected a seat at the table next to Lisa Beth, who was already seated. Before sitting, he handed Lisa Beth a small bouquet of wildflowers and said something to her. She smiled up at him, took a quick look at David and frowned, then set the flowers carefully into her water glass. David was slow to sit and regretted when Dean sat on the other side of her. While he was contemplating what to do, everyone else sat, leaving him only one choice, between two young boys.

Almost immediately, the boy on his right, about five years old, with unruly hair and freckles, scraped his cooked green beans off his plate into David's lap. Trying to remain calm, David asked the boy's mother—sitting on the other side of the boy and oblivious to his actions as she talked to someone on the other side of the table—if she had a paper towel.

"We don't have paper towels anymore," she said, then pulled a rag out of her jeans pocket and handed it to him. He picked up the beans with the rag and set them on the table next to his plate, then used a corner of the rag to soak up the juice from the beans that had soaked into his clean jeans.

He had just cleaned up that mess, when the young boy on his left, about the same age, poked his bare arm with a fork.

"Ow," he said,

"Did that hurt?" the boy asked.

David looked at the mother, also oblivious, then at the boy again. "Not really," he said, then turned back to his lunch.

"Ow," he said again, when the boy poked him harder in the same place.

"Did *that* hurt?"

"More than the last time. Do you want it to hurt?" he asked with another look at the mother.

"I don't know," the boy said and David turned back to his lunch.

"Ow," he said again, when the fork poked his leg. "That one hurt," he said. Was the boy experimenting, testing his boundaries? David looked at the mother again, who had turned to see what the noise was about.

"Are you bothering David?" She asked her son while patting him on the head affectionately and smiling.

"No," the boy said and his mother turned away again.

David had had enough. He looked around to see if there was anyplace else to sit. Not seeing any, he decided to take his lunch to his room to finish.

He tried to figure out how to get away from the table. He was in the middle of a long bench pulled up to the table. He couldn't very well ask everyone to get up so he could get out. So, he tried to climb out, pulling one leg out from under the table and stepping over the bench. In the process, he became unbalanced and nearly fell over, the noise attracting the attention of everyone around him, including Lisa Beth and Matt Jr. Once he was upright again, he picked up his plate from the table and left the cabin, walking through the dark to the other cabin and to his room.

A few minutes later, sitting on his bed and holding his plate of food in one hand, he heard a knock at the bedroom door.

"Who is it?" He asked.

"It's me." came Lisa Beth's voice. "You left your glass of punch on the table. I thought you might want it."

His first thought was that this was an excuse to get with him and try to repair the damage he'd caused by his earlier behavior. She was giving him a chance to apologize.

"Thank you," he said. He had been about to get up and go to her, but when she opened the door to give him the water, he could see Matt Jr. behind her with his hands resting on her shoulders. Seeing Matt, he settled back on his bed. "you can set it there on the table by the door," he said, dismissing her.

"Are you alright?" she asked. She sounded genuinely concerned.

"I'm fine. Thanks." All except my ego, he thought.

Matt Jr. pulled on her shoulders, making her back up a step, then reached around her and pulled the door closed.

He stayed in his room, sulking, the rest of the evening, except for a short trip to the kitchen in the big cabin to drop of his dirty dishes. Everyone was in the yard for game night. He spotted Lisa Beth, with one leg tied to Matt Jr's leg in a three-legged race. He had an arm around her waist—hers was around him—and they were laughing. No one in the big house and he went out the back way to avoid being seen.

He felt left out and realized it was his own fault. Maybe he should go away. If he offered to help Mike with whatever he was doing with the gate, could he figure out how to operate it and return to his own life? It was worth a try. Then he thought about Lisa Beth coming to visit him before bed and decided he would wait until tomorrow before deciding what to do.

Lisa Beth didn't come to him that night, and he didn't sleep well, wondering where she was and what she was doing. Was she in her own bed, with her siblings? Was she with Matt, Jt., sleeping with him? Would he respect her the way David did, or take advantage of her innocence? The more he thought about that, the angrier he got, until he had to get out of bed and pace the room. He finally talked himself down by telling himself that it didn't matter to him what she did with Matt, he was going to leave, as soon as he could figure out the gate.

The next morning, after breakfast, with Matt's family still there—they must have spent the night—he raced through breakfast and left the cabin without talking to anyone, even when Lisa Beth tried to talk to him.

"David, are you . . ." she started to say, but he kept walking, not giving her a chance to finish what she was going to say,

Beth was approaching from the big cabin and called to him.

"David, can I talk to you about a little project I have?" She asked quickly.

"I really need to talk to Mike," he said. Do I need to call ahead, or can I just go in?

"Okay, David," Beth said, a little surprised by his abrupt manner. "I'll call Mike and tell him you're on your way."

❂

"Eve," the voice said. Kerri was sitting at breakfast with the rest of the household and stopped with a forkful of food halfway to her mouth.

"Kerri," Lisa said from her place a few chairs away.

"Did you hear it?" Kerri asked, turning to Lisa.

"That's spooky," Lisa said. "How often is that happening?"

"That's the second time in a week," Kerri said. "I've got to get him to leave me alone."

"Leave me alone," Kerri shared, "You're creeping me out."

"That's not my intent," Adam said. "I just want you to know I'm making progress. I just crossed over the border into Idaho. It won't be long now."

"Leave me alone. I don't want anything to do with you."

"You don't mean that," he said. "You're my Eve. Together, we're going to change the world. I'll be there soon and you'll see."

"I don't want to see, I have a life already and I'm happy with it, so leave me alone."

"Sorry you feel that way, Eve, but our followers are expecting you to come and take your rightful place at their head."

Kerri cut him off and looked over at Lisa again. She was staring, wide-eyed. She gulped a breath. "Kerri, you need to do something about him, before this gets out of control." Lisa said.

"I don't know what to do," Kerri said.

"At a minimum, you need to tell Mike or Doc. Didn't you say Doc was trying to get some information on him?"

Rick, hearing Lisa's comment, looked at Kerri with concern. "What now?" he asked.

"Adam's getting closer. He's in Idaho now." She decided not to tell him the rest; it would just worry him, and she could see nothing Rick could do to help.

"Well, I agree with Lisa. Let's tell Doc."

Kerri stood and backed away from the table. "Come with me," she begged Lisa, who stood and joined her.

They had to pull Doc away from his breakfast to tell him what

Adam had said.

"I'm sorry, Doc. Why don't you go ahead and finish your breakfast? We can wait." Kerri said apologetically.

"No," Doc said, "you're here, so let's take care of this now." He led them to the office so they could call President Jim Seymour. He found a voice message on his phone from Jim, that he'd missed the day before, since he'd spent the entire day with the family and hadn't checked voice mail. Doc called Jim instead.

"I sent you a file," Jim said immediately, when he answered Doc's call. I think you should avoid this guy.'

"Give me a quick summary," Doc said.

"The FBI used facial recognition to ID him. They got two 'possibles'. Since one of them has history in Montana, I took a wild guess and decided he's our man. You said he goes by Adam, right? His name is Aiden, Aiden Short. He's ex-marine, discharged for violent behavior. Witnesses said three guys, also marines, started teasing him about his last name. The report says he's only five foot three, so he's probably a little sensitive. Anyway, he killed one of them—blow to the head with a blunt object—and hospitalized the other two—broken limbs."

"I take it he was not discharged honorably," Doc said.

"The families wanted him to be court-martialed and tried for murder, but the Marine Corps said they didn't have enough evidence to prove it wasn't self-defense. Three-on-one. Anyway, after his discharge, he moved to Montana and joined a para-military organization, quickly rising to the top amid some questionable activities. It seems the head of the organization was ousted, his lieutenant died suspiciously, and Aiden was next in line."

"Cause of death?" Doc asked.

"No details. His latest activity is a little weird. He claims that he's a telepath and has actually advertised his intent to gather other telepaths and similarly-minded individuals and start a utopian society."

"When did this start?" Doc asked.

"About four years ago. He said he found his first follower, mourning the death of her best friend, in Wyoming and started communicating with her telepathically."

Doc had heard the story of Kerri hearing Lisa's voice in her head when they'd been in Wyoming, on their way to Utah, so he guessed that it was Kerri that Aiden Short had contacted, although Kerri hadn't said so. The Outcasts had been in the old world and Doc was from the twin world, so there were some things he hadn't been told.

"Any recent additions to the file?" Doc asked.

"You can see the last entry on page four. Eleven months ago, the husband of one of his followers died of head trauma after complaining that Short had seduced and raped his pregnant wife. Short disappeared, along with the woman and a bunch of other people, mostly the witnesses, during the investigation by the state police."

"Now he has his eyes on us," Doc said.

"How is this Aiden Short communicating with you? By telepathy? Really?"

"No lie," Doc said. "The next question is, 'Can he track us using his talent, or are we safe if we're not on I15 waiting for him?"

"Do you want me to do more?" Jim asked.

"You mean, like harass him?"

"That's a possibility. We could also send military in to disperse them. Hey, here's an idea. Why don't you loan us your gate to harass him?"

"Out of the question, Jim. If you do anything, I didn't ask you to," Doc said. Doc didn't want to be accused of being aggressive against Short, in case Short's intentions were benign, which he doubted.

"Understood, Doc," Jim said. "You didn't ask me to take aggressive action. Later."

❂

Mike met David at the outer door and invited him in.

"Is there something I can do to help you?" David asked, before they had even said hello.

"What did you have in mind?" Mike asked.

"I'd like to see the gate—how it works—and thought there might be something you were working on that I could help with. If nothing else, I'd like to see how the Observer selects someone for you to contact."

Mike smiled. "I'm kind of between projects right now, so this is a good time; I can show you how it works." They went to the lab and Mike turned on the Observer. He explained how they couldn't force anything or anyone to come through the gate, how they had to come through on their own power. He told David about their discovery, first with a rabbit, then with a mouse, and they were both laughing as Mike described chasing the mouse around the lab, trying to catch it and send it back.

David asked about the individual controls on the Observer and Mike showed him how each of them worked. It was easier to explain using the portable control board, because Terry had set it up so each dial or switch had a discrete function and operation. David was a quick student and Mike was impressed with his logical, engineering mind. They spent the day together. Mike showed him some of the details of the Preserve that had required Mike's engineering skills to build. Then they raided the kitchen for lunch. Mike was impressed with David's grasp of the skills involved. He encouraged Mike to talk about himself and all the things he had done.

Mike told him about his trips to the twin world, first getting beat up because he went through before they understood about the sinoatrial node's impact on the gate, his long recovery in the hospital, then his trip to meet Doc after his dad, Amos, had died. David asked him about the war, and Mike showed him some of the videos when David insisted. David asked about the technology that they had acquired from the twin world and recognized most of it, having been a child when it was introduced to both worlds.

David asked about the jumps that they had made, so Mike took him on a tour from the north end of Bear Lake to downtown Salt Lake City. Much of the destruction that had occurred to the Wasatch Front, from Brigham City to Ogden to Salt Lake had, by now, been cleaned up and many of the residents had returned to try to rebuild. Mike showed David his coordinate mapping system, with many of the locations written down, so Mike didn't have to figure them out again from GPS coordinates. When David expressed an interest in trying a jump, Mike thought there was no harm, so he let David set the coordinates, turn on the machine, and watch as the gate jumped to that location. They both cheered at his success.

When Mike told him that he had other things to do, David asked, "Can we do this again sometime?"

"Certainly," Mike said. "In fact, the next few days may be the best time, since I don't have anything pressing on my schedule. What does Beth have you doing?"

"She said she has something she wants me to look at," David said, "but I think she's just trying to find things for me to do, so I don't get bored."

"Are you bored?"

"This stuff certainly isn't boring. I'd like to learn more. Maybe you could show me your database of emotions, expressions and behaviors and explain it to me."

"Would you like that? You don't think it would be too boring?"

"I'm an engineer. Mike. I live on facts and details."

"Okay. Why don't you come back after breakfast tomorrow?"

"Okay. I can meet you here. How do I get into the Preserve?"

Mike debated the wisdom of giving David the combination for the outer door, then decided David was a safe gamble; he had shown his interest in the Preserve and the technology, and Mike would be here with him.

⊛

The next morning, David appeared at the door to the lab before Mike had even unlocked it.

"What did Beth need you for?" Mike asked right away.

"Nothing too dramatic," David said. "I repaired some damage to the sprinkling system and she wanted to know when we could turn it on again. I'll take care of it later today."

They spent the day reviewing and discussing the database and some of the recommendations the Observer had given them. Jesse had been the first attempt and the first success, having adjusted sufficiently to living in the Preserve. That experiment had been followed by three failures about two years apart. David asked about them, so Mike told him the story of Beau Harper, the first of the three; he had committed suicide after thinking he had been abducted by aliens.

10

The Twin World—fifteen years earlier

Beau Harper read science fiction, particularly stories about space aliens. As the assistant manager of the local GamePlace, he loved to show the teens that came into the store his favorite 'aliens' games. His favorite all-time movie was the old *Close Encounters of the Third Kind* and he envisioned himself being selected to go with the aliens and spending a few years with them. Single and twenty-four, he seemed happy with his life, until the Observer focused on him. The first time he noticed the little eye in his peripheral vision, he was afraid. But after a while, he began to think that aliens were watching him to see if he was a good candidate for abduction.

Approaching a potential customer one day in the store, he noticed a wavy pattern in the air. Thinking it was the aliens, he approached and studied it. He poked a finger in it, then an arm, then he stepped through, right into two men who were watching him from the other side.

"Where am I?" Beau asked. He was amazed at how closely the aliens had imitated the body structure of humans.

"Logan Canyon," the older man said.

"Great," Beau said. "When do we go to your spaceship?"

The two men looked from him to each other in confusion. Maybe they didn't have a good grasp of earth languages, so he waved his arms about, trying to imitate the motion he thought a spaceship would make, the way they moved in his favorite game. "You know," he said, "Your spaceship."

"I think you're confused," Terry said. "We're not aliens. We're humans, like you."

"Okay, if you want to have it that way. So, where are we going?"

"Right now," Mike said, "We're going to dinner and you're welcome to join us, if you're hungry."

"Do you eat earth-like food, or is it from your home world?"

Mike and Terry looked at each other again, wondering what they had brought into the Preserve, Terry led the way out of the lab, with Beau, then Mike following, through the tunnels, and into the dining room, where the rest of the residents sat at a long table down the middle of a long room. As they walked through the tunnels, Beau made a comment about tunneling insects, like those in the *Ender* series of stories. In the dining room, he asked if they had a reinforced ceiling to keep in the artificial atmosphere. They asked him to sit next to a beautiful young woman, who introduced herself as Kerri, and who began asking questions about him; Where do you live? Where do you work? What do you like to do? Do you like games? What kind of games? Do you like movies? What kind? Do you like to read? What genres? All of his answers included variations on space aliens.

By the time they'd finished dinner, Kerri was frustrated with him. She tried to think of something she could say or do that would elicit a response that didn't have to do with space aliens. She suggested they go for a walk outside.

"Do we have to put on space suits, or do you have another way for us to breathe outside."

"I don't think it will be a problem," she said, and led him through the tunnels to an outer door. When she opened the door, he cringed, like he thought he might be sucked out into space.

"This is Aspen Valley," she said, as she walked out of the tunnel into the fresh air. He followed, taking in great lungsful of air and coughing.

"You have near earth gravity and heavy air. That's wonderful. I feel right at home."

She took him by the upper arm and started walking toward the cabins.

"Your hand feels human. What is your exoskeleton made of?"

She had almost had it with Beau and they'd been together less than two hours. He was fixated on outer space and she didn't know if she could bring him down to earth. She knew that Terry and Mike had brought him here to see if he would make a good, compatible partner for her. Now she was thinking maybe that wasn't such a good idea.

"We call it skin." She finally said. "What do you call it?"

That stopped him. He looked at her for a few moments, then said, "That's good. Right answer," but the way he said it made her think he was complimenting her for knowing the human word for it as opposed to the alien word for it.

Finally, in frustration, she turned to him, grabbed his face in both hands and kissed him full on the lips. His face registered surprise, which she had expected, but something else also, which she couldn't place. "Did that taste like an alien or a human?" she asked.

He thought about it a moment, then his face lit up, like he had the answer to a quiz. "I don't know," he said, "I've never kissed an alien."

She thought he would follow up with the correct conclusion, which was that it tasted like a human. He surprised her by saying, "Then again, I've never tasted a human girl either."

Never been kissed! That was it. She took his arm and led him to the cabin, showed him furniture, the fireplace, beds, pillows, anything to try to make him understand that he was still on earth.

"Impressive recreation," he said. "You've gone to a lot of work."

"Don't you see that you're still on earth, not in outer space?"

She asked him.

"If you say so. Can we kiss again? That was kinda nice."

"What can I say or do to make you see that you're still on earth?" she asked.

"I don't know, but if you'll take off your skin and let me see what you really look like, I promise not to scream."

"I'd like to scream," she said. "You're impossible, and they expect me to give myself to you."

"That sounds weird," he said. "What would I do with you?"

"My thoughts exactly," she said. "You wouldn't know what to do with me. Let's go back and tell them." She took his arm and headed back to the Preserve.

Terry had been watching their interaction in the valley and their return—he could tell Kerri was upset, angry even—and met them part way. He took them immediately to the office, where Doc, Lillie and Mike were still talking. They stopped talking when the three entered.

"He thinks he's in outer space and that we're aliens," Kerri said. "I can't do anything to convince him otherwise."

"Why do you think you're in outer space, Beau?" Mike asked.

"Don't get me wrong. You've done an excellent job imitating life on earth, but I've known for a long time that aliens were coming for me, so when you showed up, I was ready for you."

"Ready for us?" Mike asked

"Yes. I expected you to try to fool me, but you can't, you see. I've read everything there is to read about aliens, your different forms and behaviors. I've seen every alien movie made, multiple times. You can't fool me."

"I think we've made a mistake bringing you here, Beau," Mike said. "I think we'll have to send you home."

"No. Don't do that. I've looked forward to this for years. I want to see how you live, I won't even mind if you run experiments on my brain. I expect that. Just don't send me back so soon."

"What do you think, Terry?" Mike asked. Should we keep him?

"You said you brought him here for me," Kerri interrupted, "but I don't want him. I told him you wanted me to give myself to him, but he admitted he wouldn't know what to do with me."

Lillie chuckled, which got the men chuckling.

"Tell me what you want me to do with her and I'll do it," Beau said. "Just don't send me back."

"I see the problem," Mike said. "He doesn't know what to do with her."

"Tell me," Beau said again. "I'll do it."

"It's not going to work, Beau," Terry said. "See that door over there? The round one? I want you to go through it. Then everything will be fine."

"I won't go," Beau said. "You can't make me. I want to stay."

"Mike, will you seat Beau in the office while we discuss this?" Doc asked. When Mike returned, Doc continued, "Options, anyone?"

"Send him back?" Terry asked.

"Send him to Area 51 in Nevada?" Mike asked. "Maybe the government has some aliens for him to make friends with."

"Give him more time to adjust here?" Doc asked.

"Do you think he would ever adjust?" Terry asked. "He seems too far gone, intellectually, to ever see reality. And who would we saddle with watching him? I don't think it's fair to Kerri to ask her to babysit him."

"What if we gave him one more day and see if he changes at all?" Kerri asked.

"Would you be willing to watch him?" Doc asked, "I won't ask it of you."

"From my experience with him so far," Kerri said, "I don't see that he will ever adjust. However, maybe I can recruit the others in the cabin to spend some time with him to see if that helps."

"Are you sure?" Doc asked. "I'm ready to send him back now if it will be too much of an inconvenience."

"I'd hate to be the one responsible for one of your experiments failing," Kerri said.

"Don't worry about that," Doc said. "I'm willing to accept that we made a mistake."

"It's okay. Let me show him around for a day, before you decide on a permanent solution." Kerri said.

"Oh Kerri," Lillie said, "are you sure you're ready to do that? That would be a real sacrifice for you. I'd hate to see you get hurt from this. You've already been through so much."

"I'm willing, Lillie," Kerri said reluctantly, "and we've all been through a lot. It's only a day out of a lifetime. I'll survive it." Although he might not.

"Alright," Mike said, "let's ask Beth to find a place for him to stay the night, that doesn't infringe too much on Kerri's space, and see where we are tomorrow at this time. Agreed?"

They all agreed and Kerri retrieved Beau while Mike called Beth. When Kerri and Beau arrived at the big cabin, Beth met them and took Beau off her hands. Kerri went to the girls' dorm and Beth took Beau to the boys' dorm. She asked Zach and Isaac to take care of him for the night, then Kerri would take him for the day.

The girls' and boys' dorms were two large rooms upstairs in the big cabin, filled with bunkbeds, where all the children and single adults slept. They each had a bed, a shared desk and a small wardrobe of their own. There was a bathroom for each dorm, located at the top of the stairs between the dorms.

Kerri had the top bunk, above Callie, who spoke to her as soon as she entered the room. "What's going on?" Callie asked. "What did Mike want?"

"He's brought a man through the gate for me, like he did for Lisa. His name is Beau. He's kind of cute. The only problem is that he's fixated on aliens and thinks he's been abducted. He thinks we're taking him to our world to run experiments on his brain."

"Is he scared?"

"No. That's the problem. He's looking forward to it. We tried to reassure him that we weren't aliens, but he wants us to be."

"How does he explain that everything here looks like earth?"

"He has an explanation for everything. He wants me to take off my skin to show him what I really look like."

"Did you agree?" Callie asked, laughing. "Are you going to?"

"That's sick," Kerri said. "He's a sick man."

"Did Mike tell him why he was here?" Callie asked.

"I told him I was supposed to give myself to him, but he said he didn't know what he'd do with me."

"A really, really sick man," Callie said, laughing harder. "So, what are you going to do?"

"I told Mike that I'd show Beau around for the day, tomorrow, then they're going to decide what to do with him."

"Sorry, Kerri. I wish I could do something to help."

"Feel free to spend some time with us tomorrow. I'd love to get your take on what to do with him."

Beth convinced two of the young boys to double up on a top bunk so Beau could have their lower bunk in the bed next to Zach.

"Where are you from? Zach asked Beau."

"Salt Lake City," Beau said. "Where are you from?"

"Garden City."

"Where's that?"

"By Bear Lake."

"I know where that is," Beau said. "I mean, originally? Where are your people from?"

"My grandfather came from England and my grandmother from Scotland," Zach said. "Isaac, here, is my cousin. His mom and my dad are brother and sister."

"Okay, so you've been here for several generations," Beau said, a little testily, not getting the answer he wanted. "But where are they from originally?"

"I don't know what you mean?" Zach said. "That's as far back as I know."

"Okay," Beau said, speaking as he would to a slow child, "Is your home planet in our solar system or somewhere else? Maybe Betelgeuse or Rigel?" he asked hopefully.

"What are you talking about?" Zach asked in surprise. "You think we're aliens?"

"Aren't you?" Beau asked.

"You're crazy, man. There's no such thing." Zach said and turned away from Beau, covering his head with his pillow.

"What makes you think we're aliens?" Isaac asked from the top bunk above Zach.

"It only makes sense," Beau said. "I've been expecting aliens to come for me and here you are. Your leader brought me here through a space warp, so I wouldn't know where I was, but I've read up on this stuff and knew immediately what was happening."

"You've got it all wrong, Beau. Sorry. The gate they bought you through is a gate between twin worlds. You've been reading the wrong science fiction writers."

Beau was confused. He knew adults lied all the time to get what they wanted and wasn't surprised to find that it was the same with alien adults, but young people had no reason to lie. Had he been wrong about these being aliens? He would have to be more careful tomorrow. They were ready to send him back if he didn't meet some expectation that they had for him. Maybe he would have to figure out what Kerri meant by giving herself to him.

⊛

They served breakfast at a long table, first to the children and singles, of which he was one, then to the adults, because there were so many 'people' living in the cabin. After a simple breakfast that he wasn't used to or familiar with—they said it was cooked wheat cereal, whole wheat bread and orange juice—the children were excused until lunchtime. Kerri caught up to him immediately and introduced him to her friend, Callie. They asked if he would like to go for a walk. They took jackets because, they said, it was chilly and there was a chance of rain. He tried to read a double meaning into everything they said but found it difficult; they sounded like average young adults—human young adults. When he didn't have an explanation, he just kept quiet.

Their hike took them uphill through the trees, all of which looked familiar to him, although he had no idea what any of them were called. He became winded long before either of the women did, which he thought was unusual, but maybe they were athletes, or maybe that confirmed that they were aliens, with a different metabolism. The day quickly warmed and they all began to perspire. Kerri tied her jacket around her waist and removed her top. She wore a sports bra underneath.

"Really?" Callie asked, with a sideways glance at Beau.

"He probably won't even notice," Kerri said quietly. He thinks we're aliens, so he'll just think this is part of the costume. A longer look at Beau confirmed that he seemed totally oblivious. So, Callie removed her top as well, and the rest of the walk was more comfortable for them. When Beau looked at them, he didn't comment.

Back at the cabin, they ate lunch, then Kerri asked Callie if she wanted to go to the pond, where they often went swimming—skinny-dipping if they didn't bother taking their swimsuits and weren't in mixed company. Callie suggested that she go ahead and she would join them later.

"Are you taking a suit?" Callie asked.

"Nah. We probably won't swim. Even if we do, I can go in my underwear. I could probably go naked and he wouldn't notice."

"Would you do that just to test him?"

"I don't think so. We'll see."

"What's next?" Beau asked, as he walked up to them. "I told Zach that I would show him the aliens game I brought with me, if he was interested."

"Is he?"

"Yes. So, what's the plan?"

"How much time do you need?"

"I could play forever—I never get tired of it—but he might get tired of it after an hour."

"Okay, I'll come and get you in an hour and we'll go to the pond."

"What do you do at the pond?"

"Mostly swim, or sit in the grass and talk."

"Doesn't sound too interesting, but I'll do whatever you want."

"That's sporting of you," she said, with a hint of sarcasm.

After an hour, Kerri went to the boys' dorm and stood in the partially open doorway, listening. She wanted to know if she could learn any more about Beau from his interaction with Zach.

"Isaac didn't like my questions last night," Beau said. "How do you like the game?"

"The game's fun. Isaac didn't like you calling him an alien."

"Does it offend you?" Beau asked.

"You didn't call me an alien. Why do you think we're aliens?"

"If you're not, how did I get here?"

"I think that question was already answered for you."

"But I don't believe it," Beau said. There's no such thing as gates in space. They're fiction.

"So, aliens are real, but gates in space are fiction? Because you say so? Who do you think you are and what makes you the authority on it?"

Beau wanted to explain all of his research on aliens, but realized he'd already done that with the adults and it hadn't gotten him anywhere. So, he chose not to answer. He stared at Zach until Kerri decided it was time to interrupt.

"Beau," she said. "Are you ready to go?"

"Ready," he said, standing, as he continued to stare down Zach.

"We're going to the pond, Zach. Do you want to go?"

"Nah."

"The weather's really nice. Are you sure?"

"Go ahead. Maybe I'll stop by later."

The pond was on the far side of the clearing at the end of a small stream that ran through the trees. It was shallow at one end and deeper at the other, deep enough to swim in. Kerri immediately took off her shoes and socks, rolled up her pant legs, and waded into the shallow end. Beau, still trying to show his willingness to cooperate, did the same.

"Brrr," he said. "It's cold."

"You get used to it after a few minutes, then you'll want to go swimming."

"I don't think so. Anyway, I don't have a swimsuit."

"You can strip down to your underwear," she teased. "Or, if

you're really brave, you can go naked."

"Have you gone naked before?" he asked.

"Several times. Not in mixed company, but there's always a first time," Kerri said, her voice dropping to a whisper.

A strange thought crowded into Beau's mind. Being an alien, was it possible that he could tell, if Kerri was naked? Would there be some kind of zipper or flap that showed how her skin came off?

"I have a question," he said. "Is there any way that you can prove to me that you're not an alien?"

She laughed. The question was absurd. "Like, what did you have in mind?"

"I don't know," he said. "If you had a removable skin, I suppose you'd have to have a zipper or other type of opening on your body to remove it."

"So, if I get naked and you don't see a zipper, then I'm not an alien? Is that what you mean?"

"Well, no. It might mean that you just have another way to achieve your normal appearance."

"Whew!" she said. "For a minute there, I thought you were going to ask me to get naked."

He stared at her as if considering what to say next, as if he *would* ask her to get naked. She heard voices and several of the others appeared, walking through the trees, including Callie, Zach and Isaac.

"Beau," Isaac said, "Zach told me about your 'aliens' game. Can I play it when we get back?"

"Sure," Beau said, but he continued staring at Kerri.

"What?" Kerri asked, trying to interpret the expression on Beau's face.

"Nothing," Beau said, "Just thinking about your comment that you were supposed to give yourself to me."

"Well, don't think too hard," she said sarcastically. "You don't want to strain your brain."

Everyone was taking off shoes and socks, rolling up pant legs and wading into the pond. The boys starting splashing water, so the girls got out and sat on the bank. Kerri sat next to Callie on the grass.

"What's happening?" Callie asked quietly.

"He's staring at me," Kerri said, whispering. I think he may be figuring it out.

"Let's hope he doesn't."

"I'm with you on that. I don't know if I could handle him if he did."

"He fits right in with the younger boys. Maybe he'll become sidetracked and forget what he's trying to figure out."

"I can only hope."

"Let's go on another hike," Beau said, wading over to Kerri and Callie and climbing up the bank. Kerri thought about what she had just said, trying to decide if she should be embarrassed by Beau overhearing it. She decided that he hadn't overheard, but why did he want to go on another hike. He'd barely survived the last one.

"Aren't you still tired from the last hike?" she asked.

"I've got my wind back, and you like to hike, so let's do it."

"Okay. Would you like to go anywhere in particular?"

"Can we get up there?" he asked, pointing toward the top of the cliff above the clearing.

"Yes, we can, but it's a difficult hike. Are you sure you wouldn't like to try something easier?"

"No. That's where I want to go, unless it's too difficult for you."

"I'm good for it," Kerri said. "Do you want to come along, Callie?"

"No. I'm good sitting here until the boys leave, then I may take a swim."

"Naked?" Beau asked. "There are bugs in there."

"I'm not afraid of bugs," Callie said. "Besides, I can take a shower afterward."

Beau stared at Callie for a few moments, then turned back to Kerri. "When can we go?" he asked.

"I think there's still time before it gets dark. Let's go now." Beau stuck out his hand and helped Kerri up. Kerri looked at Callie and made a face that said she was impressed that he had offered her a hand up.

The path to the top of the cliff was partway up the trail to the highway, then off the trail and into denser trees. Before long they were climbing over boulders and scrabbling up loose rock, holding onto tree limbs to keep from slipping backward or losing their balance altogether and falling down the mountain. Finally, they cleared the trees and came to an abrupt stop on the edge of the cliff. Kerri stopped three feet from the edge, but Beau stepped right up to the edge and looked straight down into the valley, a sixty-foot drop.

"Come here, Kerri," Beau said, holding out his hand to her.

"This is close enough, thank you," she said.

"It's okay," he said. "I won't let you fall." He motioned her forward with his hand.

She reached out and took his hand, then mincingly approached him. When she was close, he wrapped an arm around her waist and pulled her slowly to his side. It was then that she finally noticed how short he was, the top of his head stopping at her shoulder.

It was a beautiful view. They could see the entire valley, the field across the highway, the pond to the left through the trees and the cabins across the clearing ahead of them. Beau craned his neck to study the pond.

"Are the boys still at the pond," he asked.

"Only Callie," she said, able to see the pond better from her slightly different angle.

"Is she—?" He asked.

"It looks like it to me," she said. "Do you want to go back?"

Thinking that she was asking him if he wanted to go back to the pond, he said, "No, I don't think I'll take a swim tonight, but we can go back to the cabin and I'll show Isaac my game, if you're ready."

She had begun to think that he actually had a mature thought in his head, helping her stand at the pond, now offering protection on the cliff, then he spoiled it by showing preference to playing a video game with boys over spending the evening with her.

"Sure," she said, "Let's go back."

On the way down, he slipped on loose rock and slid about fifteen feet, tearing his jeans and scraping both palms, making them bleed. When he began to whine about the blood and pain, she pulled a clean rag from her pocket and wrapped it around the hand that was scraped the worst, then they held hands the rest of the way down, "so you won't fall and hurt yourself," he said.

Although she had a first aid kit in the cabin and was perfectly capable of doctoring his hands, she sent him to Beth. She'd had enough of him. As she walked away from him, toward the stairs at the back of the room, she heard him say, "You're not mad at me, are you?"

"No, Beau. I'm not mad."

The next morning, after breakfast, Beau cornered Kerri as she was leaving the cabin and asked where she was going. Kerri remembered that she was supposed to take Beau to Mike in the Preserve, later, but she didn't want to spend any more time with him. She turned to ask Beth to take him, but she was busy talking to Ben. She decided to handle it when she got back.

"For a walk," she said.

"Can I go with you?" he asked. "Where are you going on your walk?"

"I haven't decided," she said, then deciding it would be mean to exclude him, she said, "Where would you like to go?"

"Can we go where we can be alone? I think I figured out what I'm supposed to do with you."

"Oh?" she said. "What did you figure out?"

"When we saw Callie alone at the pond, naked—"

"You mean, when I saw her?" she interrupted.

"Okay, when you saw her, I remembered the website a friend showed me of men and women naked together. I think we're supposed to have sex," he said enthusiastically. "Am I right?"

"No, Beau, you're not right. We're supposed to fall in love. The only problem with that is that you're too immature for love. You need to be playing video games with other boys, until you're mature enough to know how to treat a woman and how to love, unconditionally. That's what will impress me."

"Teach me, Kerri," he pleaded. "I can learn."

"I know you 're capable of learning, Beau, but I'm the wrong person to teach you and it would take more time than I'm willing to invest."

"Why, Kerri? Why"

"Because you still think I'm an alien, and that's insulting," she said, not meaning to hurt him, but tired of dealing with him. She just wanted him to go away, and she didn't care how.

"Do you think Callie will teach me?" He asked.

"You can ask, but I think she feels the same way."

"Who can teach me?" he begged.

"Maybe if you talk to Beth, she'll have a suggestion. Maybe she'll send you to Mike."

"I don't want to go to Mike. He wants to send me back. I don't want to go back. I want to stay here. With you." He was in a full-scale adolescent meltdown now. "Please!" he begged.

Kerri rolled her eyes, then moved around him and left the cabin. When she glanced back, he was standing in the doorway, wringing his hands and looking back into the cabin. She kept walking.

Later that day, Kerri went to the pond, alone. Rylee was there with Zach and Sidney with Isaac, lying in the grass, hugging and kissing. They were inseparable most days and today was no different.

"Where's Beau?" Sidney asked, when she saw Kerri alone.

"I haven't a clue, she said. I haven't seen him since breakfast."

"We were just at the cabin and he wasn't there. Where else would he go?"

"He seemed intrigued with the cliff," Isaac said. "Do you know why?" He asked Kerri.

She didn't want to have to deal with him now that he thought he knew what to do with her—what he'd figured out after he thought he could see Callie skinny-dipping. Maybe he was up there now spying on the lovebirds, kissing in the grass. Involuntarily, she looked toward the cliff, imagining that she could see him up there, looking down at them.

Rylee must have noticed. "Do you think he's up there now, watching us?" she asked, looking in that direction, following Kerri's gaze.

"I don't see him," Kerri said, "but who knows. I don't care anymore. He needs to go away—to go back where he came from."

When Beau didn't show up for lunch, she spoke to Beth about

taking him back to the Preserve. Beth agreed, but didn't know where he was either.

Kerri didn't see Beau the rest of the day. Before dinner, Beth found Kerri and asked if she'd found Beau. "Mike wants to talk to him," she said.

"I don't know," Kerri said. "Maybe he's been abducted by aliens for real," she suggested.

Beth gave her a stern look and spoke into the radio that she had been holding against her leg, "We don't know where he is, Mike. Do you want us to look for him?"

"Okay," she said in response to something Mike said, "when we see him, we'll bring him to the Preserve."

Beau hadn't shown up by bedtime, so Kerri went to bed. The next morning, at breakfast, Zach asked Kerri where Beau had spent the night, raising his eyebrows at her. "He didn't come to bed last night," he said.

"I can't tell you," she said. "I haven't seen him since yesterday morning."

"Really?" he asked, then spoke loudly enough to get everyone's attention. "Has anyone seen Beau?" he asked.

No one spoke at first, then several spoke at once.

"Doesn't Kerri know"

"Where would he go, alone?"

"I saw him yesterday afternoon, up on the cliff."

"We need to find him," Kerri said, becoming concerned. She'd told Mike she would watch him for a day; now she had lost him. "Isaac," she said, "take some of the boys and spread out through the trees to the east. Zach, you take others and go across the highway. Callie, you go to the pond. I'll go to the cliff. Meet back here in an hour." She looked at her watch. "If we haven't found him, we'll get the rest of the adults involved."

It only took a few minutes for Kerri to find him. She thought she saw something unusual at the base of the cliff as she approached the trail that led to the top. She ran to it, certain of what she would find. It was Beau, in a crumpled heap. Whether he had fallen accidentally or jumped, she couldn't tell, nor could she tell how long he had been there. She ran back to the cabin in tears, thinking she had driven him to kill himself, and told Beth, who called Mike immediately. Within minutes, Mike, Terry, Doc and Lillie were there beside Kerri, Beth, Bryce and Sheryl, checking vital signs and discussing what might have happened.

Mike interviewed Kerri, then, based on what Kerri told him, Callie, Zach and Isaac. He asked if anyone else had spoken with Beau in the last twenty-four hours, but they didn't know of anyone. Mike had thought that someone might have information to help him discover what had happened and was disappointed that no one did. It was Lillie who reminded him of the discussion he'd had with Beau two days earlier, during which Beau had pleaded not to be sent back.

"But that was when he thought we were all aliens and going back would mean that he'd been rejected as a specimen. According to what everyone has told me today, I think he had realized that we weren't aliens."

"But he still didn't want to go back," Lillie said. "Kerri said he wanted her to teach him how to love her. I think her snub destroyed him, but we can't tell her that."

"I think she already believes she killed him," Mike said. "Should we make up an alternate reality to keep from hurting her feelings?"

"Your dad would," Lillie said.

"Alright," Mike said, thinking of a plausible explanation that didn't involve Kerri driving Beau to kill himself. "The scuff marks on the soles of his shoes convinced me that he slipped and fell accidentally."

"Thank you," Lillie said. "Now what do we do with his body? Cremate it like we did the invaders who died?"

"That would be the easiest solution for us," Mike said, "but they have a missing person case in Salt Lake now. Maybe we should send his body back."

"That would be the least painful for the parents," Lillie said. "At least they would have closure; but if he'd lived and we'd kept him, it would be no different. And if we send his body back, they'll have a suspicious death case instead, and will open an investigation."

"A lot of missing person cases are never solved," Doc said. "but I think sending his body back is the best plan."

⊛

"I think, if I were Beau's parents, I'd want to know what happened to him," David said after Mike had finished telling his story about Beau.

"I would too," Mike agreed. "I think anyone who loses a family member, wants to have that closure. However, in this situation, there was a risk that giving them that closure would reveal our existence."

"You mean the existence of aliens."

"It would be difficult to explain," Mike said, frowning at David's jibe. "You heard our options. What would you have done?"

"Doc is the genius. You're the chairman. One of you should have come up with something. Maybe you could have staged an accident somewhere close to Beau's regular hangouts. The investigation would still have been inconclusive, but his parents would have had his body."

"Good point, and I *did* think of it."

"So, what did you do with his body?" David asked.

"We arranged it so it looked like he'd jumped off his dorm roof. It was a three-story building, with easy access to the roof, where students could be found studying at odd times. We arranged his body in the bushes at the side of the building, with his Aliens video game nearby."

"What did the police think?" David asked.

"They concluded, from evidence at the scene and statements from his room-mates, that Beau had finally lost touch with reality and jumped."

"And what about Kerri?"

"She was upset that he'd committed suicide, and we're sure she still harbors thoughts that she had caused it, but she seems to have resigned herself to the fact that he had lost touch with reality and would probably never have had a normal life with normal relationships. She certainly didn't want to deal with his alternate reality or try to help him work it out. That could have been a lifetime exercise and she didn't have a psychology degree to help her understand how to help him."

11

The Present

"So, everything went back to normal, did it?" David asked, not sure whether to be amused or disgusted with how Mike handled Beau.

"Pretty much back to normal," Mike said. "Rick had been spending time with Kerri, whenever possible, and their friendship had deepened over the months. Then Beau showed up and we asked Kerri to show him around. I told Kerri and Beth later that the observer had selected Beau as a partner for Kerri, based on the AI database that Doc had asked me to collect and load into the Observer.

"Rick thought that he was in love with Kerri and was a little miffed that I would not only allow, but encourage Beau to get between them. He had no interaction with Beau and the only time he saw him, during meals, Rick was disgusted with Beau's obsession with aliens and his poor social skills. According to Kerri, Beau thought they were all aliens and had abducted him and taken him to their home planet in a distant solar system to conduct experiments on his brain. When anyone tried to make him see reason, he twisted their comments into something to justify his belief.

"I know Rick was glad he didn't have to deal with Beau, but felt badly for Kerri, thinking she had to work it out with Beau and eventually marry him. When Rick carefully broached the subject with Kerri one evening after supper, she told him she had finally had it with Beau and wanted nothing to do with him. Then Beau disappeared and a search of the places he frequented found him at the base of the cliff; an apparent suicide.

"Kerri was beside herself with guilt, in much the same way Rick had been when his wife and children had gotten sick and he could do nothing for them. His guilt was his inability to save them from the plague; her guilt was her inability to make Beau see reality.

"Rick had avoided Kerri, for the most part, when he'd understood that she was part of our experiment; but now that it appeared the experiment had failed, Rick felt justified stepping in to console her in her grief."

❂

"Kerri," he said after lunch the day she found Beau at the base of the cliff, "do you feel like working out in the gym?"

"No . . . yes," she said. "Absolutely. Let's go." They left immediately after clearing their dishes off the table and taking them to the kitchen. Kerri took him into the Preserve and through the tunnels to the gym. They exercised hard for an hour, working up a good sweat, then Kerri said she wanted to sit in the sauna for a while, to relax. They stripped out of their sweaty clothes in the locker room, wrapped towels around their bodies for modesty, and went to the sauna. They passed through the gate that Doc left in place for those in the valley to get between the gym in the old world and the Sauna and pool in the twin world. After the sauna, Kerri looked like she was starting to feel like herself again.

"Rick," she said, "this was exactly what I needed. Thanks for suggesting it."

"My pleasure," he said. "Do you want to swim some laps now?"

"Are you suggesting a swim because you know we didn't bring suits and you want to see me naked?" she asked.

"Do you want me to see you naked," he'd asked.

"Why did you answer my question with a question?" she'd asked.

"Because I want to hear your answer," he said.

"Then yes, I want you to see me naked. When I told Beau that Doc wanted me to give myself to him, Beau said he didn't know what to do with me. I bet you wouldn't have that problem."

"No, I wouldn't," he said. "Are you offering?"

"No, I'm not. Doc didn't tell me to offer myself to you, so you have to earn the privilege."

"What do I have to do to earn the privilege?"

"You have to court me like you would any girl, then marry me."

"Okay, I get it. Now, can we go swim naked?"

"Let's go," she said and led him and Callie down the hall to the pool, where they left their towels on a lounge chair and swam laps.

"And you know this all happened because?" David asked.

"Rick took great pleasure in telling me about it after my experiment failed," Mike said. "It proved to Rick that technology could never replace human nature. From that point on, Rick and Kerri's relationship evolved quickly toward marriage."

"After Beau's death, things settled down," Mike told David. "We still didn't have a solution for Kerri or Callie, until two years later, when we had our second failed experiment, but we weren't idle in the meantime. Doc and Terry were experimenting with the Observer as a medical device. They began regular physicals on everyone, systematically looking at their internal organs, joints, and muscles, keeping medical records on each person. Matt Sr. assisted.

"During their first round of exams, Doc caught Matt's kidney cancer while it was in the early stages and it was easier to cure.

It helped that he had questioned Matt about his family history before the examination.

"During the second round, Terry caught Sheryl's tubal pregnancy before it had a chance to rupture and cause more serious complications. She had been complaining about stomach pains for two days prior to her exam, thinking it might be her appendix. Terry asked if she also had shoulder pain in her left shoulder. When she acknowledged that she did, Terry immediately suspected a tubal pregnancy and checked her for it."

"So, what was everyone else doing while Doc was experimenting with the observer?" David asked.

"Doc asked me to determine what it would take to get the observer to see things farther away than Salt Lake City or Bear Lake. It took me, with help from Jesse, an entire year to figure it out, but when I found the solution, I was surprised that it was so simple. At first, I tried tweaking the existing programming, but it made little difference in the gate's ability to move farther away from the Preserve. I tried lots of things. One of them was to boost power to different parts of the program. Finally, one of my tries worked and sent the gate shooting out into the distance. I stopped the gate and found I was looking at the St. Louis Arch on the Missouri side of the Mississippi River. Not only could I see beyond Salt Lake, but the sight distance was nearly unlimited.

"I asked Doc to test it by taking it somewhere on the east coast, like Washington, D.C., that Doc was familiar with. He took it to Philadelphia, from where President Jim Seymour continued to run the country. Deciding that the only way to prove this test worked was to leave something on the president's desk that he could follow up on later, he thought frantically for something that he could use. He remembered that the president had attended his wedding to Lillie three years earlier and that they still had a few monogrammed napkins in a cupboard in the office. He placed one on a corner of the president's desk while the president was away, then closed the gate.

"Doc remembered that the president was concerned about the unrest in Brazil, so Doc went to Brazil to run a second test. He spied on General Ramos and the new president, who was the former vice-president."

"Did he find anything in Brazil that bothered him?"

"You mean, did he see corruption in government? Yes, he did. He listened to a conversation between the new president and a businessman named Oliveira that clearly showed the president had taken bribes in exchange for favors to Oliveira.

"For the third round of medical exams using the Observer, they checked intestines. Terry found two polyps in Doc's large intestine and removed them before they could become cancerous, and without a full colonoscopy."

David asked a few questions about the medical exams, most of which Mike was able to answer.

"That covers most of our activity. Are you ready for another story?" Mike asked David.

"Yes," David said and nodded.

"Chase Pedersen was twenty-eight years old, had graduated from medical school, and was a practicing family doctor. He came from a large family and had a relatively normal life, went to the gym three mornings a week before work, bowled on a league on Thursday evenings, owed a hundred and fifty thousand dollars in student loans, owned a twelve-year-old car with a hundred and eighty thousand miles on it, and had an on-again-off-again relationship with a woman two years his junior whom he saw most weekends."

"Before we approached Chase, we discussed why we thought

Beau hadn't worked out, decided it was because of his singular focus and interest, and concluded that we wouldn't, or shouldn't, have the same problem with Chase, because he had so many interests."

"Best of all, the Observer told us that Chase would be the solution to Callie's problem rather than Kerri's. By the time Doc realized that Chase was struggling and needed professional help—Doc had decided to take him to the twin world and turn him over to professionals—it was too late. He had overdosed on drugs he'd found in Doc's hospital."

12

The Twin World—thirteen years earlier

"Nice one Chase," his bowling partner said, as all the pins fell again. Chase was having his best start ever, with strikes in the first five frames, and he strutted a little on his way back to his seat. "Although you're only getting to roll half as many balls as the rest of us."

"Maybe I'll leave one pin standing at the end of the game, so you don't feel too badly," Chase joked. He was having the time of his life. Tonight, he didn't even mind the silly red and yellow jackets the league made them wear, with logos and team names embroidered front and back.

"Hey, isn't that Chelsea down about six lanes?" his good friend asked.

Chase looked, and sure enough, his supposed girlfriend was bowling on his league with a mixed foursome. She finished her turn, eight pins down, and turned to return to her seat, when the man who stepped up for his turn patted her bottom as she passed. He knew she didn't like people touching her—it was one of the arguments they had whenever he wanted to be affectionate—but instead of wagging her finger at him, or swatting his hand, she turned and gave him a peck on the cheek.

Chase was not prone to show emotion, but his face reddened and he balled his fists, considering whether to punch the guy's lights out or punch her lights out. She wasn't wearing the regulation red and yellow, so she must be filling in for someone who was sick, which meant that the guy had probably invited her . . . and she had accepted and let the guy get personal with her.

This rankled him. He knew his friends would come to the same conclusion he had—she was being unfaithful.

Chase's game deteriorated after that and he finished with a respectable 227 score, which was better than his average, but disappointing nonetheless. He tried to get to Chelsea after the match, but her team finished before his and she left quickly, arm-in-arm with her date.

In the lab, Mike watched the exchange, since the Observer had singled out Chase for attention. Mike got the impression from Chase's reaction that this was a surprise to him, which meant that the Observer had picked out Chase before Chase knew he had a problem. It told Mike that the Observer was still evolving, changing its abilities over time.

Over the next several days, the Observer followed Chase to and from work, the gym, the bowling alley, even church on Sunday. It showed him interacting with his parents, his friends, his associates at the hospital, even his neighbors and store clerks. To Mike, Chase seemed like a normal, healthy male, with normal male interests. When he showed Chase to Terry, then Doc, they agreed that everything looked normal. Doc got to watch as Chase arrived at Chelsea's home on Saturday. Chase went to the door, rang the bell, and Chelsea answered, wearing a halter top and shorts, carrying a light jacket over her arm. She slipped past Chase and walked toward his car, throwing a comment at him over her shoulder.

"What?" Chase asked. "No kiss? Don't I rate as high as your Thursday night date?"

At his question, Chelsea froze mid-step and turned to look at him. "What?" she asked.

"You bowled on my league Thursday night. You do remember that I bowl on a Thursday league, don't you?"

She looked pensive for a moment. "Of course, I remember," she said. "Was that your league?"

He nodded, afraid to say anything, in case it was the wrong thing.

"What did you see?" she asked, likely trying to remember what she had done with her date at the bowling alley.

"Enough," he said. "Are you sure you want to be with me today? Or, would you rather be with him?"

Chase held the car door open for Chelsea and she slid into the passenger seat without answering. Chase got in the driver's seat and started the car. As soon as his door closed, Mike could no longer hear their conversation. They drove away, but two minutes later, the car returned and pulled into the driveway. Chelsea's door flew open and she climbed out, not bothering to close the door, and stormed away toward her house. Chase's window powered down and he stuck his head out.

"Will you at least shut the door?" he called out the window.

Chelsea spun on her heels, returned to the car and slammed the door closed. Then she turned and walked away again. Chase powered up his window, peeled out in reverse and left, his tires squealing as he hurried away.

"Maybe he's not who we want, after all," Mike said to Doc and Terry. "What should I do?"

"What were you going to do before we saw that?" Doc asked.

"I was going to see if the Observer focused on someone in the valley," Mike said.

"Go ahead," Doc said. "Now I'm curious."

When Mike intentionally focused on Kerri, the Observer showed little interest in her, but jumped to focus on Callie when she entered the cabin and began speaking to Kerri. Doc tried to identify what problem the Observer believed they were the solution for, but it eluded him. Mike suggested that, from his observations, both Callie and Chase were approachable, affectionate, fun-loving, and unattached. He thought they would get along well and fill a need the other had.

Doc wondered if Chase was who Mike thought he was, originally, but agreed. Aside from the problem with Chelsea, Chase looked like a normal young adult male. Terry agreed, as did Lillie when they ran it past her, so Mike took the responsibility of finding a way to bring Chase across. It turned out to be almost as easy as it had been with Beau. Mike put the gate in Chase's path in the McKay-Dee hospital in Ogden, where he worked, and like a normal, busy doctor, he walked, head down, right into, and through, it into the lab, and came face-to-face with the three men.

"What are you doing in this wing," Chase asked absently, "visitors aren't allowed here."

"Sorry doctor, but where do you think we are?" Mike asked politely.

"In the surgery center," Chase said, finally stopping to look around. "What is this?" he continued, "I must have taken a wrong turn."

"I don't think so," Mike said. "I think you stepped out of your world and into ours."

"That's ridiculous," Chase said. "Do I know you?" he asked, taking a closer look at Mike, then Doc.

"I don't think so," Mike said, "but you may have heard of Doc, here. This is Doc Blund, former advisor to former president Buck McCormick."

"Yes, I have heard of you," Chase said to Doc. "What do you mean, my world and your world?"

"You just stepped through a gate that took you from your world and placed you in mine," Mike said

"There's no such thing as gates in space, but it doesn't matter, since my world and yours are the same."

"Not worth arguing," Doc said. "He's intelligent," he said to Mike. "He'll accept it when he sees it." He turned back to Mike and waited

"Let me show you some things," Mike said.

"I really don't have time," Chase said. "I'm expected . . ."

"You're here now," Mike said, interrupting. "You need to take a break."

"Fine. Do you want me to follow you?"

"Of course. This way please," Mike said and left the room, making sure Chase followed. They walked through tunnels into the community center. "This is our community center," Mike said.

"Where are we?" Chase asked.

"In an underground shelter in Logan Canyon," Mike said.

"How did I get here?"

"You stepped through a gate that brought you to us from the McKay-Dee hospital."

"What is the mechanism that made that move possible?"

Mike was impressed by the intelligent questions, thinking that Chase was accepting the things he was being told. "A machine that we created called the Observer, which punched a hole in the fabric of space and allowed you to move from one place to another, of our choosing, instantaneously."

"And what if I don't believe in holes in space and travel between worlds?" Chase asked.

"Then, how do you explain where you are right now and how you got here?"

"I think you drugged me and took me to a warehouse that you've decorated to look like this."

"To what purpose?"

"That's what I'd like to know. Why have you kidnapped me and brought me here?"

"First of all, we didn't kidnap you, we distracted you and secondly, to introduce you to someone."

"If it's money you want, be forewarned that I don't have any"

"We're aware of your student debt. We're also aware of your daily habits, your weekly schedule and your failing relationship with your girlfriend, Chelsea."

Chase bristled at the mention of Chelsea. "Have you been spying on me?" he asked.

"Actually, we have, for about a month" Mike said. We needed to know if you were a suitable candidate for our experiment.

"An experiment, you say? Tell me what you want me to do and I'll decide if I want to be involved with your experiment."

"I'll be honest with you, Chase. I wasn't going to share the details, because I was afraid you couldn't handle it, but after talking to you for a few minutes, unless you've been blowing smoke, I believe you are intelligent and curious enough that you *can* handle it. Our technology, which is artificial intelligence, has determined that you have a problem we can fix."

"And what problem is that?"

"You're lonely. You're a well-rounded, healthy, adult male, who hasn't found a compatible partner, someone besides Chelsea."

"And you're going to tell me you have a compatible partner for me, is that it?"

Mike turned to Doc, who had so far been sitting quietly, listening to their conversation, "I told you he was bright," he said. "Are Kerri and Callie still in the exercise room?"

"They are, Mike, Terry said. Do you want me to go get Callie?" Terry asked.

"No. I think I'll take Chase to them. Will you follow me,

Chase?"

Mike led, with Chase, Doc and Terry following, through more tunnels and into an exercise room, where two young women, dressed in tight exercise outfits, worked out on side-by-side exercise bikes. Both were tall and slender, one blond and one with dark hair, and both perspired from a hard workout. When the men entered, they stopped their bikes, wiped their faces with towels, and smiled broadly.

"Hello, Mike, Doc, Terry," the dark-haired lady said. "Who's your friend?"

"Kerri, Callie, this is Chase" Mike said. "We've invited him to join us to see what he thinks. What do you think, Chase?"

"I think this is a little awkward," Chase said quietly, hoping that only Mike could hear him.

"That's okay, Chase," Callie said. "You'll have to get used to Mike's lack of tact. He calls things as they are. Would you like to work out with us?"

"Maybe I should get back . . ." Chase started to say.

"Ahh . . ." Mike said. "Take a break."

"Okay. Sure. I'll join you, if it's okay." He looked at Mike to see what he would say.

"Go ahead," Mike said. "We'll catch you later." The men left.

"These scrubs aren't the best for exercising," Chase said.

"That's okay," Callie said. "There are sweats in that room over there." She pointed. "You can change in that room."

Chase went to the changing room and changed into sweats that were big on him, but would do. When he returned, Callie had moved over so Chase could use the bike between her and Kerri. He raced away, trying to keep pace with the women. In no time, he was perspiring right along with them.

"I'm ready for the sauna," Callie said after close to an hour of strenuous exercise.

"Sauna?" Chase asked. "Should I follow you?"

"Yes," Callie said. He followed them to the changing rooms, where they selected separate change booths and the women stripped out of their clothes. They wrapped large towels around their bodies and headed for the sauna. Chase, seeing what they had done, did the same and followed the women through a vague shimmer in the hallway. He saw a door in the hallway that had a small window. Looking through the window, he could see the women sitting on the top wooden bench, where it would be the hottest, with their legs tucked under them modestly. He opened the door and joined them.

"I noticed a shimmer in the hallway. What is that?"

"Doc set up a gate for us to get between the old world and the twin world, since the sauna and pool are only in the twin world."

"A gate?" Chase asked. "He told me he brought me here through a gate."

"Same thing," Callie said. "He has two of them. One he uses for his medical and travel experiments; the other he leaves here for us to use, since we use it so often."

"I'm going to take a few laps in the pool," Callie said eventually, sweating profusely.

"I don't have a suit," Chase said.

"We don't normally, either," Kerri said, "so we usually swim naked. Callie is the more modest among us, so I don't know what she'll do, but I'm going swimming. You can join us if you want to. If you're coming, the pool is to the left." Then Kerri got up and left.

"What are you going to do, Callie?" Chase asked. "I'll do whatever you do."

"Even swim naked in mixed company?" Callie asked.

"I went skinny-dipping once as a teenager and survived it. If I don't put too much significance on it, I think I'll be okay. It's just with you two, right?"

"I've never done gone skinny-dipping in mixed company," Callie said. "It sounds naughty."

"What if we do it together and don't analyze it too much?"

"I don't know if I can do it, but I'll go with you. The water is cool. It's a good way to end an exercise period."

He got up and she followed. An arrow pointed to the left that read 'pool'. He went through another door just in time to see Kerri drop her towel on a lounge chair, dive into the pool, naked, and start swimming the length of the pool. He stepped into the pool area and Callie followed.

He debated what to do. He decided that he really wanted Callie to be brave enough to do this with him, but he didn't want to push her or get in the pool without her, in case she decided not to do it. He was still fighting with himself when Kerri hopped up on the deck, wrapped her towel around herself, and headed back to the changing room.

"Too late," Callie said, following Kerri. Chase followed Callie.

"How often do you do this?" Chase asked, as they found their lockers and began changing back into their clothes.

"The exercise, the swim, or both?" Kerri asked from her change booth.

"Yes," he said, and laughed at his own joke.

"That's funny," Callie said and laughed with him. "You have a pleasant voice," she added.

"Thank you," Chase said.

"You're welcome. We exercise six days a week. The sauna and swim, usually three times a week, but it varies, depending on who's with us and what's going on with the others."

"The others?" he asked. "How many people are here?"

"In the Preserve," Callie said, "are seventeen people, with another fifteen people living in the cabins in the valley."

"And where do you two live?"

"In the big cabin," Callie said. "We're roommates, along with two little girls. It's more of a dorm than a bedroom, because of the shortage of space, but we don't mind. The girls behave themselves and give us privacy when we need it. Do you want to see the cabins?"

"Can I?" Chase asked, looking around to see if Mike was nearby. He was enjoying himself, but assumed Mike would have to decide what he could and couldn't do.

"Absolutely," Callie said. "We're headed there now. It's almost dinner time. You'll stay for dinner, right?"

"Sure, whatever you say," Chase said. "So, which world do you live in?" he asked.

"The old world," Callie said. At his questioning look, she added, "the one that went through a war a few years ago."

"Do you know which world I live in?" Chase asked.

"I'm almost positive it's the twin world," Callie said. "Doc does most of his research and experiments in the twin world."

"I'm afraid to ask what kind of experiments he does."

"It's no big deal," Kerri said, "His Observer observes people and diagnoses physical and emotional problems, then tries to solve them," Callie said.

"That's what he told me, but I thought he was jerking my chain. What kind of machine can do that?"

"He calls it AI," Callie said, with a laugh at Chase's confusion.

"Yeah, Artificial Intelligence." Chase said. "He said that, too. And you believe him?"

"Oh, Doc doesn't lie. He may withhold information if it's in the best interest of a person, like a good doctor with a patient, but he never lies, as far as I know."

"I see," Chase said. That was an analogy he understood all too well, since he had withheld information from patients on several occasions. It was his call what needed to be said and what withheld.

"So, Doc has the ability to kidnap a person from one world and place them in a different world. Is that correct?" Chase asked.

"I wouldn't say kidnap," Callie said. "I'd say . . ."

"Same difference, regardless of the name you put on it." Chase said, and started to shake. This was upsetting. If Doc could do this with impunity, he was trapped, a prisoner in Doc's experiment. "You said medical experiments. What kind of medical experiments?" He immediately thought of Frankenstein's monster. Why not? He wondered; what's to stop a mad scientist from experimenting on kidnapped victims . . . like me?

"Are you okay, Chase?" Callie asked. "I'm sorry I laughed at you. You're shaking. Here, put a towel around your shoulders." She stopped in the middle of dressing, opened Chase's locker room door, took his towel out of his hands and draped it over his shoulders. He did a double-take when he saw that she was still not dressed and tried to hide his reaction, turning away from her.

"Excuse me," Callie said, as a blush crept up her cheeks., seeing that he, too, was still not dressed. Callie straightened the towel and patted his shoulders to calm him, trying to keep her eyes on his face, to not look down at the rest of him.

"You asked about his medical experiments," Callie said, softly, backing out of his stall and trying to distract him. "They're really cool. His observer can look inside a body and diagnose diseases, find cancers, and other stuff like that."

"You mean like swallowing a camera to check the upper GI,

right?"

"Similar, but not the same. This machine just looks inside the body and can see things. You'll have to ask Doc for a better explanation. Being a doctor yourself, you'll understand when he explains it. Maybe he'll even give you a demonstration."

"I think I'd like that," Chase said, relaxing a little. A least he was no longer shaking. "Thanks for the suggestion. So, which world are we in now, and how do we get to your cabin?"

"We're in our world, the old world. Follow us."

Chase finished changing into his scrubs quickly, then followed the women along tunnels and through rooms until they reached the community center.

"I'll let Mike know where we're going," Kerri said and took off down a side corridor. She was back a few moments later to find Callie and Chase sitting together on a couch, with Chase's arm around Callie's shoulders. Callie had a hand on Chase's knee and she was leaning into him as though waiting for a kiss.

"Excuse me," Kerri said, as Callie and Chase moved apart. "Mike said he would call Beth and let her know what he wants her to do. Let's go to dinner."

Chase turned and looked at Kerri, wondering if that remark referred to what Mike wanted to do with him, as Doc's latest experiment.

They exited through the outer door that led into the valley. As they crossed the clearing, Callie lagged behind a couple of steps. Chase slowed until he was alongside her. "You're being really quiet, Callie," he said.

"That's normal," she said.

"You have a pretty voice. I bet you're a singer."

"She is," Kerri said. "I can't carry a tune, but wait until you hear Callie sing. She'll knock your socks off."

Beth seated Chase between Callie and Kerri at the dinner table and the three of them spoke quietly throughout the meal. Callie laughed at several things Chase said. After dinner, they helped cleanup, then Beth told them to go outside until bedtime, to get them out of her way, she said.

"Is she always telling you what to do?" Chase asked.

"No, this must be a special occasion," Kerri said. "We're getting special treatment."

"Maybe because of me, and Doc's call to her?" Chase asked.

"I don't know why Doc would care if we were inside or outside," Callie said.

"Maybe she wants you to sing for Chase," Kerri said.

"And Beth wants me outside so she doesn't have to listen? Is that what you mean?" Callie said and swatted Kerri on the arm.

"You know I think you have a beautiful voice, Callie" Kerri said. "Sing for us."

"Now you've put me on the spot," Callie said. "It will be a disaster."

"No way," Kerri said. "You'd have to try very hard to mess up."

"Excuse me," Chase said, "Callie, would you sing for me?"

Callie's demeanor changed instantly, from confrontational to shy.

"Do you really want me to?" she asked, looking down, "You're not just saying that to be polite?"

"Kerri has never lied to me," he joked. He hardly knew her. "So, I believe her when she says you have a beautiful voice."

The three of them sat in chairs on the porch. Then Callie sang *Amazing Grace,* beautifully. Chase encouraged her to continue, so she followed that with *Unchained Melody,* by the *Righteous Brothers.*

"Will you continue?" Chase asked when Callie stopped and looked toward the cabin door, as though expecting someone to come out and tell them it was time to come in.

"I think that's enough for now," she said. "Maybe another time."

"I'd like that," he said. "You *do* have a beautiful voice."

"Thank you," she said, as the blush colored her cheeks again.

"We should see what Beth has arranged for Chase for the night." Kerri said.

"You *will* spend the night, won't you?" Callie asked.

"I don't think I can leave without Mike's help."

"Great. Let's find Beth."

Beth introduced Chase to the other single men in the cabin; Isaac, Zach, and the two men from Garden City who had lost their families to the plague, Rick and Taylor. They all slept in the boys' dorm, along with two children, the infant sons of Beth and Ben and Bryce and Sheryl.

While everyone else settled into bed for the night, Callie invited Chase to sit with her in the swing in front of the fireplace. The evening was warm and the small fire cast shadows around the room. Callie snuggled against him. He wrapped his arm around her and pulled her to him. Her head tipped forward and she jerked awake, so Chase suggested that they go to bed. They walked slowly to the stairs leading to the loft and the dorms. They kissed at her door, then she entered and closed the door behind her, so he turned around and went to his own bed.

After breakfast the next morning, Callie remembered that Chase had wanted to see Doc's medical experiments, so she asked Beth to contact Doc to see if it was okay. They made an appointment and Doc met them at the outer door, escorting them to the hospital. He gave Chase a technical explanation of the technology, then offered to give a demonstration, if Callie was willing to be their guinea pig.

Doc opened a small gate, about a quarter inch in diameter, and entered Callie's neck, showing Chase her inner workings, things he knew were there, but had only seen with a scope through a patient's mouth. He took the gate through her head, showing Chase things he'd only seen on an MRI scan. When Chase said he'd participated in an elbow surgery, Doc took the gate to Callie's elbow and showed Chase what a normal, healthy elbow looked like.

Chase was overwhelmed. "Have you shared this technology with the medical world?" he asked. "The world needs to see this."

"I'll share it when the time is right," Doc said.

"The medical world needs this technology," Chase said emphatically. "You need to share it. You can't hide it in your personal medical center, where only you can have the benefit of it."

As Doc resisted each of Chase's arguments, Chase became more insistent, "It's selfish," he said, then, "You're being selfish." Doc was unmoved by Chase's threats and name-calling.

"Chase," Doc finally said, "the old world is so overwhelmed with problems that this technology would sit in someone's back office and not be used for years. The twin world, your world, has the technology. It's in the hands of someone I trust to reveal it to the world. What I'm doing is documenting all of my research for publication. I can't do any more than that." Should he give him more details, he wondered, then decided that Chase needed to believe him and accept the fact that he knew best.

When they were finished, Chase not gaining an inch of compromise from Doc, Callie led him toward the exercise room, telling him that she had arranged to meet Kerri.

"I need it," he said. She could tell he was upset, but didn't know if this was normal or a result of his discussion with Doc. "I need to work off my frustration. He's a difficult man."

"He has definite opinions," she said, trying to agree with him without demeaning Doc. I've never seen him change his mind once he makes a decision, and I'm told that the only person who can get him to change his mind is Lillie, his wife.

"Then I need to talk to Lillie," he said. "Can you arrange it?"

"Let's go exercise and I'll see what I can do."

After exercising, they spent some time in the sauna, then went to the pool.

"Are you okay with this?" Chase asked, as Callie dropped her towel on a lounge chair and moved to the edge of the pool, naked.

"I thought about your skinny-dipping comment and decided I could do this," Callie said. "We saw each other naked yesterday. So, as long as I don't think about it and just do it, I think I'll be fine."

"Well, not to embarrass you, but I think you're beautiful," he said as he moved to stand next to her at the edge of the pool.

"Now you *have* embarrassed me," Callie said. "I don't know if I can do this."

"Let's do it together," he said. Taking her hand, they jumped into the pool together, then swam their laps.

After dinner, Beth told Callie that she had arranged for Lillie to pay a visit to the cabin, to meet Chase and to see what he wanted. She would be there in a few minutes.

"Hello, Chase," Lillie said when they were introduced. "I understand that you want to speak with me."

Chase was impressed. Lillie was an elegant lady, with the bearing of a queen, who knows how important she is in her world.

"May I call you Lillie?" he asked, unsure of how to address Doc's queen.

"Of course," she said. "We try to be as informal as possible here."

"Thank you," he said. "You need to convince Doc to share his Observer technology with the medical world." Lillie listened patiently and intently to Chase's arguments about why Doc should make his invention known to the medical world, how the world would benefit from the technology, and how Doc would probably become rich beyond his wildest imagination.

"You told all this to Doc?" Lillie asked.

"All except the getting rich part," he said, "I just thought of that. Think of all the things he could do with the money he'd get from patenting the technology."

When Chase had talked himself out, without interruption from Lillie, she took a breath and told him what she thought. "Thank you, Chase, for your suggestions. I'm certain Doc will consider seriously everything you've said to him. However, please know that Doc is a brilliant scientist, as well as a knowledgeable statesman, with experience in national as well as global politics and diplomacy. He has given this technology to a respected doctor and scientist in your world, who will see that it is shared with the medical community, and when our old world has recovered enough for us to rejoin it, I'm sure he will share it with the old world. He *will do* what he thinks is best and it *will be* the best thing for us and for the country. If his decision doesn't match your expectation, I hope you will think about the reasons for his decision, before you judge him too harshly."

Not what Chase wanted to hear. He was sure that Callie, sitting next to him and holding his hand in both of hers, could sense his frustration.

"Come on Chase, let's go for a walk." Callie said, tugging on his arm.

He wanted to argue with Lillie, to convince her that he was right, but he could see that Lillie wouldn't budge; she was protective of her husband, and would defend him, even if he was wrong.

"Thank you for your time, Lillie," he said as he allowed Callie to drag him away. It was after dark, and he tripped over an exposed root in the path through the trees. Callie caught him before he went down, but he swore at the inconvenience of it. "Why didn't she see the benefit of getting rich by patenting his invention?" he asked.

"You have to understand Doc," she said. "He's earned enough money to buy this valley, build his preserve and his Observer, in two worlds. He called a president of the United States by first name, in two worlds. He gave away one of his most valuable inventions for free, in two worlds, just to protect his family and friends, of which I'm one and grateful for it. I would do anything for him."

"You make him sound pretty incredible, Callie. I would hope that someone could say such nice things about me some day." He sat down on a log and pulled her onto his lap. "What would I have to do to get you to say nice things about me?"

"I already think you're nice," she said.

"Oh, yeah, what's nice about me?"

She went still and quiet for a few moments, likely considering everything she had heard about him from Amos and Mike. She threw her arms around his neck and gave him a hug. "I hear you're a good doctor, one who cares about his patients."

"Someone just told you that. You don't know it's true."

"I trust the person who told me," she said. "Also, you're a good son and care about your parents and siblings."

"Hearsay evidence again," he said. "What do you know from personal experience?"

"You're good looking and friendly. You want to do what's right by other people. Is that enough?"

"You could say those things about a lot of people," he said. "Say something that's unique to me."

She got quiet again and looked down, frowning a little, as though she were having trouble coming up with something to say. Suddenly she looked up at him, making eye contact, and a huge grin split her face, "From personal experience," she said, "I can say that you have a cute bum."

He could feel his face heat up. He coughed into his elbow.

"Okay," he said, "I guess that's enough." He lifted her to her feet, stood and took her hand, then led her back to the cabin, without making eye contact again. As they walked, all he could think about was his frustration over his inability to get Doc to do what was right, for his family and for the nation and world.

He tossed and turned most of the night, unable to come to terms with his situation. Doc had an invention that would revolutionize the medical industry, but he refused to share it. He could save lives with early diagnosis of medical conditions, if he only would. Countries around the world would give him medals, knighthood, even sainthood, if they knew and had access to it. How could he be so short-sighted and selfish, and how could Callie not see it, and instead, idolize him so? Before morning, he had decided he would confront Doc and make him see his error.

13

The Old World—Philadelphia, Pennsylvania, present day

President Jim Seymour had trouble sleeping, worried about the unrest in Brazil. The Brazilian president had been accused by persons close to him of crimes against women, and the military had finally stepped in and taken control of the government. Brazil had long seen itself as a democracy, patterned after the United States, with a constitution, separation of powers in the federal government, and a freely elected president. Unfortunately, they periodically suffered from corruption in government, like most governments, and this time the military had decided that it needed to step in and stabilize the government before things got out of control. President Seymour wrestled with how he could help, worried that any instability in Brazil might lead to problems in other South American countries, many of which had long histories of political unrest, and could be easily influenced.

As he tossed and turned, he dreamt about Doc Blund and his Observer, with its gate, that allowed him to travel, not only between locations in one world, but between worlds. He imagined what he could do with a gate that allowed him to spy on and sneak up on enemies. He could solve all the world's problems, discover who was telling the truth and who lied.

He determined to talk Doc into giving him the Observer, with its gate. If he had to buy it, he would convince Congress to come up with the funding. Doc would agree. After all, the precedent had been set with the mini nuclear reactors, and Doc had admitted that he owed Jim a favor for his help with the wacko in Montana.

With that problem resolved in his mind, Jim turned over and fell into a peaceful, easy sleep.

14

The Twin World—thirteen years earlier

"What would you like to do today, Chase?" Callie asked as soon as she saw him. "We could go for a hike or a picnic, or we could go to the exercise room and pool." She was hoping he would say he wanted to go swimming, since that's what she wanted to do with him. She wanted to get to know him better before she committed herself to him for life, as Doc had in mind.

"I've got to talk to Doc," Chase said, instead. "I've got to make him understand."

Her face fell. She knew immediately that he was referring to the observer and the medical world. She was disappointed that he wouldn't rather spend time with her. "Chase, Doc knows how important his work is," she said. "You're not going to tell him anything he doesn't already know."

"Then, why doesn't he do something about it?"

"What do you want him to do, shout from the rooftops?"

"He needs to do more than he's doing," he said, agitated. "He needs to call a press conference, or something. If he knows government people, then he needs to tell them, and get the word out fast."

"Chase, your desire to see this technology available to the world is admirable, but you have to let Doc do it his way."

"Oh, you don't understand either. I've been in the operating room and seen the pain and suffering." He was shaking again, and she realized this time that it wasn't from being cold.

"So has Doc," she said.

"Maybe he's forgotten what it's like. I don't understand how you can be so indifferent and complacent about this."

"Chase, you're working yourself up unnecessarily. Calm down. Let's go exercise and swim some laps. How's your blood pressure?"

"My blood pressure is just fine," he said, defensively. "You go swim. I'm going to see Doc." He walked away from her, headed for the dining room.

He found Beth setting out breakfast. "Beth, I need to see Doc, right away," he said

"I'll find out when he'll be available and let you know," Beth said.

"Not good enough," he said testily. "I want to see him now."

"Okay, I'll tell him." She went to her room and called Doc on her radio. He answered on the fourth ring. "Doc," she said, "I'm sorry, but Chase said he needs to see you, right away."

"Did he say why?" Doc asked. "I'm in the middle of something."

"No. But he's quite worked up over whatever it is. He insisted that I tell you he needs to see you now."

"I think I know what it is, then. Tell him I'll meet him at the outer door in fifteen minutes."

"Thanks, Doc."

"Thank *you.*" Doc shoved the last bite of his breakfast omelet into his mouth, wiped his lips on a cloth napkin, and excused himself from the table.

"What is it?" Lillie asked, with concern in her voice.

"It's Chase. He's not happy that I'm keeping the Observer from the world. He's pretty worked up about it."

"But you're not keeping it from the world. You gave the technology to Terry Stephens. It will get out to the medical industry."

"We know that, but Chase doesn't think I'm doing enough. I better go."

Chase didn't even wait to get inside the Preserve before he started in on Doc. "You've got to tell the medical world about the Observer," he said when Doc opened the outer door.

"Hi Chase. I'm fine, thank you. How are you?"

"Don't try to humor me," Chase said. "You're keeping your technology a secret and that's not right."

"Chase, you're right. It is my technology, and I'll do with it what I want."

Chase was speechless. Doc had just admitted that he was selfish. But Doc wasn't through talking. "But just so you understand, I have already given the technology to someone in your world, and my world isn't ready for it. Chase, as a doctor, I need to know if you have high blood pressure and if you're taking anything for it."

"I do have slightly elevated blood pressure," he said, raising his voice. "but nothing to worry about. At least not for you to worry about. Don't change the subject on me."

"I *do* worry about you, just like I worry about everyone here. Maybe we should go to the hospital and check your heart. I'd hate to see you have a stroke or heart attack. When was your last physical and what was your last A1C score?"

"I'm pre-diabetic and have high cholesterol, okay? So, worry about me, but don't change the subject."

At the community center, Doc led him, not to the office and lab, but to the hospital. Chase didn't know any different until he saw the medical equipment. "You tricked me," he said. "I don't want a physical exam."

"Sit right up here," Doc said, patting an exam table. Chase obeyed, but kept talking, repeating all the reasons why Doc had to reveal his secret, including a couple he'd thought of in the middle of the night.

Doc took his blood pressure and pulse. "Blood pressure, one-eighty over ninety-eight," he said. "Pulse eighty-four."

"Give me five minutes to relax and take it again. You've got me worked up," Chase said.

Doc smiled indulgently and waited five minutes, "Take a deep breath and stretch your arms over your head," Doc said. Chase did, but he kept talking. If anything, he became more worked up.

"One ninety-five over one hundred one," Doc said. "I'm going to give you something to relax you." He unlocked a cabinet and searched until he found what he wanted, loaded up a syringe and shot it into Chase's arm.

"What did you just give me?" Chase asked.

"A mild sedative. It should help you relax almost immediately." Which it did. Within a few moments, Chase had trouble remembering why he was so worked up.

"Don't do that to me again," he said, "Now I can't remember the rest of my argument."

"It's okay Chase," Doc said, amused, "It wasn't that important anyway."

"It was, I mean, it is," Chase insisted, now frustrated with himself. "It's why I came to talk to you."

"Listen, Chase, I've done everything that's reasonable to do, from both a medical and a scientific perspective. I'll do more when it becomes apparent that my prior actions have failed to result in the correct actions by others."

"Okay," Chase said, acknowledging Doc's comment. "Send me back and I'll tell them."

"You think anyone would believe you?"

Chase had to think about that for a few moments, then his face scrunched up, he hung his head, and swore. "No one would believe me. In fact, I'd be lucky if I was able to keep my job and my medical credentials, but I'd be willing to risk it if I could reveal your technology. Please send me back."

"Sorry, Chase. Even if anyone believed you, they couldn't find me or the Observer. I can't let you do it. Anything you might say, would only lead to professional problems for you, confusion, and possible problems for me downstream. Now, I bet Callie is waiting to go to the gym with you, or go on a hike. You enjoy her company, don't you?"

"I do. Very much so."

"Good. She's good for you and you're good for her. Why don't you take off now?" Doc told him how to get back to the outer door and watched him leave. He went to the office, then couldn't remember locking the medicine cabinet and went back to the hospital. The cabinet was unlocked and he couldn't immediately see where he'd placed the bottle containing the sedative, but he locked the cabinet anyway and went back to the office.

"You look much calmer," Callie told Chase when she saw him crossing the clearing.

"Doc gave me something to calm me; I guess I was a little worked up. What do you want to do?"

"The weather's so nice, let's go for a hike," Callie said, and they did.

"I'm worried about Chase," Doc told Terry in the lab. He told him about their conversation and about Chase's blood pressure. "Maybe I need to send him home. What do you think?"

"Maybe you need to send him to a medical center to be checked over."

"I'm afraid that as soon as he opens his mouth, they'll send him to a psychiatric center, maybe even lock him up for a while."

Better than having him take the easy way out like Beau did.

"I would hope that Chase is a little more stable than Beau was, but you never know. Okay, Beth told me he's gone on a hike with Callie. Let's get him back here after that and decide what to do. Do you have the name of a good doctor that we can send him to?"

Terry looked up some names. Doc called Beth and asked her to send Chase back to the Preserve when she saw him. Beth called back a couple of hours later with bad news.

"Doc, Beth here. We've got a problem. Chase is laid out on the floor. He's alive, but non-responsive." They discussed his symptoms and Doc knew immediately what had happened. "I gave him a sedative earlier. When I went to lock it away later, I couldn't find it. He must have taken it."

Beth found the empty bottle and Doc said they should worry, because there was probably enough in the bottle to kill him if ingested orally. Doc opened a gate into the dorm room where Chase lay on the floor, unconscious, and carried him back through into the hospital. Callie, who had just left him a few minutes earlier, asked if she could go with them. Doc told her to wait until he had a chance to check Chase out. He called Terry and Matt to help him and they immediately checked his vital signs, started an IV drip and prepared medication to counter the effects of the sedative. A while later, Callie appeared at the hospital door.

"Can I see him," she asked Terry, who opened the door.

"Come in, Callie," Doc said, overhearing her. "Chase is currently aware of his surroundings and a visit might be good for him." She entered the hospital, where Chase had wires running from his body to a machine that beeped regularly, he had tubes running from both arms to IV stands and looked half asleep.

"Chase?" she asked quietly, coming up on one side of the table and taking one of his hands in hers. She leaned over and kissed him on the lips, then watched the heart monitor spike.

"Hi Callie," he said, his words slurred. "How are you?"

"Better than you," she said, then frowned at the insensitivity of her comment.

"Quite so," he laughed. "How am I doing, Doc?" he asked.

"I'm not happy about what you did or about your present condition," Doc said. Then turning toward Callie, added quietly, "He's in and out of consciousness and his condition is not improving."

"Will he be okay?" she asked

"TBD," he said, then noticed that Chase had lost consciousness again.

"We're losing him!" Matt said as Chase's heart monitor flatlined. Terry turned and brought a pair of heart defibrillator paddles from another table and set them against Chase's bare chest.

"Excuse us, Callie." Doc said. "Why don't you wait in the other room while we do this."

As soon as she closed the door, Terry said "Clear" and sent an electrical shock into Chase's chest, then again. Matt watched the heart monitor.

"He's back," Matt said as the monitor showed a weak heartbeat. They continued to work on him until he revived and began talking again.

"That felt strange," he said, "and my chest hurts. Where's Callie?" he asked. "Can I talk to her?"

Terry went to the door and looked out to see Callie sitting on a chair, her hands clasped between her knees and her head bowed, crying. He could see her lips moving, like she was praying. "Are you okay?" he asked.

"Yes," Callie said quietly, then wiped her eyes with her hands. She stood and walked slowly back into the hospital and took

Chase's hand, again, in both of hers. "How do you feel?" she asked.

"Like I just died and came back from somewhere else," he said and tried to chuckle, but it came out more like a croak. Then he started to cough.

"Don't try to talk," she said, then leaned over and kissed him on the lips, again. "You really scared me." She looked at Doc to get his reaction. He busied himself with his tool tray.

"I'm sorry," Chase said, sounding truly contrite. "Hey, let's go to the gym."

Doc immediately shook his head, "I'm afraid that will have to wait," he said.

"Is it the exercise you want, or the swim afterwards," she asked, ignoring Doc.

"I just want you to tell me I have a cute bum again," he said.

Doc's frown turned to a questioning expression, which Callie noticed and chose to ignore.

"You have a cute bum," she said and noticed that Terry was also giving her a questioning look, but Matt was amused.

"I love you," Chase said, then closed his eyes.

"I love you, too," she said, just as the heart monitor alarm went off again.

"Flatlined," Matt said and Terry asked her to leave the room again.

Terry used the defibrillator again, then tried CPR; but try as he night, could not get a heartbeat again. Chase was not going to be revived this time.

Doc peeled his surgical gloves off his hands and threw them angrily at the garbage can, watching them hit the side of the can and fall to the floor. "I feel like a failure," he told Terry, Lillie and Matt, who were all with him in the hospital.

"We did all we could," Terry said, trying to console Doc. "It was a stupid thing for him to do."

"He was so passionate about what he believed," Lillie said quietly.

"I've lost two people, two human lives, now, because I didn't understand human nature well enough. I didn't give either of them a way out of their crisis. Should we have sent them back before they reached crisis stage?"

"How do you know when they're at that stage?" Matt asked.

"Maybe we observe them more closely," Doc said.

"We had a pretty good idea when Chase had reached his limit," Lillie said.

"When was that?" Doc asked.

"When he tried to convince me to change your mind," she said with a look at the door Callie had just passed through to leave the hospital.

"He did that?" Doc asked.

"He did, and I didn't see it. Maybe if I'd told you, you would have drawn the correct conclusion."

"Hindsight is pretty good," Doc said.

"Maybe we gave him too much knowledge too quickly," Terry said. "Maybe we have to introduce our visitors to us more slowly."

"Poor Callie," Lillie said, still looking at the door. "Just when she found love."

"Was it love," Doc asked, "or Callie just trying to help him feel better about himself?"

"Believe me dear," Lillie said, "I know love when I see it."

"I don't doubt it, honey."

15

Interstate 15, Idaho, present day

"We have more coming from the west," Short said to his lieutenant, Bradley Caine, a grizzled, leathery-skinned, older, former Marine, who sat in the passenger seat of the Humvee, next to him. "Do they all have weapons?"

"They say they do," Caine said. "What are you going to do when you get to Utah and find Eve?"

"Good. That should double our number of soldiers and our weapons. We'll eliminate anyone who is keeping her from me, then set up headquarters wherever she's been hiding for the last few years."

"Didn't she say she didn't want to join us?"

"It doesn't matter what she said. After I spend a few hours alone with her, she'll be putty in my hands, and if my male charms don't convince her, we'll keep her restrained until she agrees to go along with me. I've convinced everyone that she is essential to our success as a utopian society, so we need her cooperation, willingly or unwillingly."

"It sounds like that should do it," Caine said, not looking at Short.

"If not, I could always keep her tied to our bed and encourage her several times a day. Maybe I'd even let you have a go at her to keep her wondering."

Caine didn't know how to respond to that. He'd never known Short to express doubts in his ability to convince people to his way of thinking. Then again, he didn't know how many people Short had killed because they didn't go along with him. He knew of at least one.

16

The Old World—The Preserve, present day, 15 June

"That was two in a row," David said, as Doc entered the lab and joined their conversation, "Beau, then Chase. Were you beginning to feel like a failure, Doc?"

"I was," Doc said. "We'd thought we'd found someone for Callie and Kerri, and both experiments had failed, miserably. Both women were mad at me, and Lillie was, too, although she won't admit it, even now."

"You said there was a third failed attempt," David said.

"There was," Doc said, "but not for some time. I told Mike that we were done for a while. We continued using the Observer to perform physicals on the family, documenting our findings and procedures, and prevented some serious problems. Terry diagnosed me with an enlarged prostate. We continued to monitor that until it got to the point where I needed surgery, which Terry performed. I found a polyp in Brittany's intestines and removed it. Terry found two more polyps in my intestines and removed them as well. We caught a thyroid problem with one of the men from Garden City, Taylor Sorenson, and started him on medication. He suffered an emotional roller coaster ride until we got the dosage worked out, but now he seems fine. He's Callie's husband now, by the way. He's sensitive and kind, just what Callie needed all along, we just didn't see it. Even the Observer got it wrong."

"So, what was your third failed experiment?" David asked, when it sounded like Doc had finished his explanation.

"The third experiment, an attorney named Debry Roberts,

actually went insane, unable to accept where he was and what had happened to him. I was able to transport him to the twin world, to a psychiatric hospital's front steps, where I left him to be discovered. I monitored him long enough to see that the doctors diagnosed him with a nervous breakdown and accepted him for treatment as a John Doe. Naturally, no one would believe his story about being kidnapped by Doc Blund and taken to another world through a gate in space."

"How long was this after Chase?" David asked.

"About four years," Doc said

"So, that was what, about ten years ago?"

"Yes. Mike claimed the Observer had found others, but I refused to do anything about it, until now. I think he said he found a professional golfer for Kerri, a basketball player for Callie, a school teacher or two. I know there were others, but those are the only ones I remember, mainly because I like golf and basketball."

"So, I'm the next experiment? Aren't you afraid I might commit suicide, too?"

"Does it bother you to be called an experiment?" Doc asked.

"Not at all," David said, although Doc could tell from David's posture and expression that it did. "Have you decided why some of your experiments have worked and some haven't?"

"I've thought about it a lot, actually," Mike said, "At first, I thought I was not understanding what the Observer was telling us. Then I thought better of that. The Observer is just a machine and doesn't *tell us* anything, *we* draw our own conclusions. Later, I thought the failures were caused by not allowing the men to acclimate properly before telling them the truth. But you and Jesse are exceptions to that. My current thinking is that it's all about personality types. You and Jesse are more grounded, emotionally."

"What do you mean, 'more grounded?"

“You’re more well balanced and sensible,” Mike said, “more emotionally mature, inquisitive, accepting of things at face value, deep thinking and intelligent. Each of our other experiments was lacking in some of those areas.”

David was flattered, but he had to agree with Mike’s assessment. He believed he was all of those things. “So, you had all of the women paired up except Kerri and Callie. What happened there?”

“Actually, it wasn’t until after the attorney’s breakdown that we looked at the big picture and realized that we had Kerri and Callie, but also Taylor Sorenson and Rick Bateman, the two previously married men from Garden City, that were single, because their wives had died.

“Knowing all four of them better over the years, we thought we knew they would match up pretty well, but we monitored them for a while, and the Observer agreed. Then. it was just a matter of getting them together in social situations and letting nature run its course. Kerri and Rick got engaged shortly after DeBry Roberts died, then Callie proposed to Taylor, since he was a little slower to respond, so they could marry on the same day. They’ve been married for about four years now.”

“Who performed the weddings?” David asked.

“That’s another long story,” Doc said. “When Amos set up the Preserve, he also set up a church, the Church of Aspen Valley, with him as the minister. He performed the ceremonies for his own children before he died. Lillie and I were married by a Supreme Court Justice. I don’t have the nerve to perform weddings. I don’t want to be a minister and don’t know if God would recognize a ceremony performed by me, so we needed another solution.

“We’ve tried to keep the existence of the Preserve a secret—not advertise that we’re here—so we looked at possible solutions that met that criteria and were still legal. I asked my security guard if he wanted to be a minister, but he declined. We finally found a real minister in Garden City, blind-folded him, and brought him through the gate to the preserve. It delayed the wedding by several months while we worked it out, but Kerri and Callie said it was worth the wait.

"So, with me here now, you have everyone paired up through Lisa Beth. The next on the list would be Matt Jr. and Dean, right?"

"That's true. Unless you commit suicide and we end up marrying Lisa Beth off to Matt Jr. He would like that, but I don't think she would."

"Would you force her to marry him?"

"Everything we've done so far has been for the good of the individuals, but has also helped the community. Would we put the community good ahead of the individual good? I can't imagine it, but who knows?"

David felt sorry for Lisa Beth, imagining her being married off to that jerk, Matt Jr., or having no one, but it wasn't any of his business if he was leaving.

He let himself out of the Preserve and returned to the cabin, not seeing Lisa Beth anywhere. He went to the big cabin and asked for Beth, to see what she wanted. It turned out that she just wanted to know what still needed to be done for the garden and orchard, so he referred her to Lisa Beth.

"Eve . . . Eve . . . Eve," Short said, then proceeded to explain when Kerri didn't answer. There was a better than average chance that she just chose not to respond. She'd been acting indifferently to him, a sure-fire way to get his attention. He didn't like being ignored "We just passed Pocatello. We'll be in Utah shortly, so we need more directions. Do we stay on the interstate or take one of these other roads, like highway 91 or 30? Take highway 91? Okay. I can't wait to see you. I've anticipated this for so long."

"How did he know to take highway 91?" Kerri asked Lisa, who sat across from her at the breakfast table. "I didn't share that with him."

"Did you think it?" Rick asked.

"I had just been looking at a map, so it was on my mind: but I didn't send it, like I normally have to," she replied angrily.

"Maybe you don't need to 'send it' to him. Maybe he's attuned to you and can read casual thoughts."

"Rick!" Kerri said angrily, "stop it."

"Don't be mad at me," he said. "I'm just trying to help."

"You're not helping!"

"I'm sorry. What do you want me to do?"

"Just go away!" She said.

"So I'm not in the way when your soul mate arrives?"

"No, Rick, I'm sorry. Give me a hug, then make him go away."

❁

"Hi Doc," Jim said when Doc answered the phone. "Do you want the latest on your stalker?"

"Go ahead, Jim. What's he up to?"

"We sent a helicopter from Mountain Home Air Force Base in Idaho, to see what would happen. Before they got close, Short stuck his arm out the window and waved them away. The pilot pretended not to know what he meant and went in close enough to kick up some dust. That's when Short pulled a handgun and shot at the helicopter. The pilot banked away, then noticed that the oil pressure was dropping. It appears that Short hit an engine oil line with one of his shots. They had to boogie back to

Mountain Home for repairs, which they weren't too happy about. What do you want me to do? Oh, by the way, he's now following highway 91 instead of the interstate, which will bring him right to Logan, and his convoy has expanded to about a hundred vehicles."

"Are the pilot and his crew safe?" Doc asked.

"The pilot said it was close, but she and her crew made it safely."

"Tell her I'm sorry and thank her for trying to help." Doc said, chagrinned at having assumed that the pilot would be male instead of possibly being a female.

"Will do," Jim said. "What are you going to do? You can't defend against a group that size, and the only options I've got left are: one—send in a team to take out the leader and hope that disperses them; or two—send in an armed force to take them all out."

"You know I don't like either of those options. Let me think on it for a day and get back to you."

"Fine, Doc. Hey, while I've got you, I have a favor to ask," Jim said. "Remember, you said you owed me?"

"What can I do for you Jim?"

"I'd like to use your gate to help resolve a political crisis in Brazil. Can I borrow it?"

"I don't think that's a good idea, Jim," Doc said. "I've already given you nuclear power. I don't think I can afford to let go of my gate."

"It would only be a loan, unless I can convince you to donate it to the country."

You mean the military. Knowing Jim's background, Doc suspected that if he let the Observer out of his hands, he'd never see it again.

"It doesn't have that range," Doc lied.

"But we both know you could fix that, don't we? Well, you think about it Doc. I'm willing to pay you five hundred million dollars for it."

"That's a lot of money, Jim!" Doc said. "Is that taxpayer money, or do you have that in your personal account?"

"Don't insult me Doc. The government would get that much use out of it. I don't need to add my paltry savings to sweeten the deal.

"I'll think about it," Doc said, *but not too seriously,* he added to himself.

☢

President James Seymour turned to his SECDEF, General Robert Peatross and the chairman of the Joint Chiefs, General Chris Ames.

"Is he going to do it?" Bob asked.

"He said he'll think about it," Jim said "but I'm sure that means 'no'."

"So, do we just give up?"

"No."

"Then what do we do?"

"We do what we do best, we go get it. Jim, put together a special op using the logistics I gave you."

"The layout is correct?" Bob asked.

Jim had been to Aspen Valley once, years ago on a Christmas Eve, when Doc and Lillie had married, had been given a tour of the valley and the Preserve, and figured he could find his way to the lab again and take it.

"It's been several years since I was there, but my notes were written shortly after the trip, so I'm pretty sure they're accurate. I even showed them to Greg and he agreed, although he wondered why I drew a map of the site."

"What did you tell him?"

"I don't recall exactly, but it was some lame excuse about memoirs for some future date. Bob, you'll be in charge. Just make sure it happens. We need that machine."

"Yes, sir. Consider it done."

17

The Old World—Aspen Valley, present day

"David, there's more damage to the garden," Beth said as soon as she saw him. "Come and see."

He followed, confused, since Beth had said she would talk to Matt Jr.'s mom. When they arrived at the orchard, it was apparent that someone had gone through the orchard and smashed several lengths of pipe.

"Beth, I don't think we have enough pipe to replace all the damaged pieces. Can you get more?"

"I'll have to ask Mike" she said.

"He can use the gate to go to the city and get more, can't he?"

"How do you know that?"

"It makes sense, since he has the gate and can go to Logan in either world."

"Where did you hear this?"

"Mike showed me how he does it. I'm going back in the morning. I'll make a list of parts and give it to him. Is there anything else you need?"

"No. I suppose that will do it," Beth said, a surprised look on her face that changed to concern before she left.

"Beth," he called, and she turned back to see what he wanted, "I thought you were going to talk to Emily about this."

"I did, David. She had a hard time believing he could be so upset, but said she would ask him about it. I haven't heard how that conversation went."

David took an inventory of the parts he would need, Then,

before it got too dark to see all the obstacles on the forest floor, he walked up to look at his car. There was no new damage, but the plants needed water, which he had anticipated. He had brought along a gallon jug. He checked the gas gauge, seeing that he had enough gas to go about twelve miles, more than enough to get to Stephani's, even enough to get to Garden City, but not enough to get back to the valley.

He went to bed, thinking about his plan to leave. Lisa Beth might be hurt that he left without saying goodbye. She might even want to commit suicide herself, he thought, flattering himself that she would miss him that much. Probably not. She would probably link up with Matt Jr. and live happily ever after. Before he fell asleep, he made a plan for how he would do it, what he would take, what he would say to Stefani, and how he would answer her questions. She would surely want to know where he had been and what he'd been doing. He decided he wouldn't say anything about Lisa Beth and his feelings for her; those would fade with time.

He was up early and at the door to the lab before Mike.

"Mike," he said right away, pleased with himself for his initiative. We need these parts for the orchard irrigation system and I told Beth I'd give you the list so you could go through the gate and get them.

"Why do you need them?" Mike asked.

"Someone smashed a bunch of pipe and it needs to be replaced."

"Who did?"

"I don't know, but I suspect it was Matt Jr. or Dean. This is the second time it's happened."

"And you think it's Matt because . . . ?" Mike asked.

"He's been harassing me and I think he's jealous of Lisa Beth's attention to me."

"I'll check into that," Mike said. "Why do you think I would use the gate to get this stuff?"

"Because you can and it's the easiest way."

"That may be, David, but we don't work that way. I can't just show up at a store with the gate and hand the parts through an open gate. I couldn't explain it."

"Oh," David said. He hadn't thought about that. "So, how do we get the parts?"

"I have to coordinate with Doc to handle it, discretely, from Logan, and bring the parts to us."

"So, you can do it today?"

"Or tomorrow. He isn't always available for me. He's trying to establish a medical practice in Logan and it takes a lot of his time."

"Sorry. I didn't know."

"That's alright David. There's no way you would know. I'm impressed to see that you're taking a personal responsibility for the orchard and garden. Are you ready to see what else the Observer can do?"

"Absolutely," David said and followed Mike into the lab.

Mike showed him the twin world. He was particularly interested in seeing where he'd lived and worked. He saw that someone was sitting at his workstation, someone he didn't recognize, and that it had been totally reconfigured. He asked Mike if they could watch and listen for a while, to see what was going on. It didn't take long for Ty Davis, and one of his other team members, to take a break. In the break room, the conversation went immediately to where David could be. It became clear that Evans had brought in a lead from another team to take David's place and get his work done.

"I heard Evans say that if David doesn't show up by the end of the week," Ty said, "he's firing him and giving his position to the new guy."

"Have you heard what you wanted to hear?" Mike asked. "It doesn't sound promising. But then, you knew Evans didn't like you, didn't you?"

David didn't answer. He was livid. How dare Evans give away his job to an outsider. He acknowledged that Evans had a right, if he didn't show up for work, but the least he could do was give the job to Ty, who was eminently qualified. It was a slap in the face for the whole team.

"I have to get back there," he said. "Mike, can I go back and straighten this out?"

"We've never let anyone go back before. I'd have to consult with Doc."

"Can we do that, please?"

Mike could see how stressed David was over this situation. One thing he didn't want to see was David hurting himself—committing suicide—over something that he could do something about. "I'll tell you what," Mike said. "You stay here and I'll go into the office and call him."

"Don't forget to ask him about the irrigation parts while you're at it," David said to Mike's retreating form.

As soon as Mike was out of the lab, David picked up the portable control panel and began turning dials. He had previously estimated the coordinates for Stefani's cabin and set the gate for those coordinates, then opened the gate. He was behind her cabin, about a quarter mile up the hill. There were no lights visible from the back of the cabin, so he moved the gate to the side of the cabin. Her car was in the driveway, so now would be a good time to go to her.

He heard Mike saying good-bye to Doc, so he shut down the gate, then spun a couple of dials, but he was still holding the control panel when Mike entered.

"Whacha' doin'," Mike asked, not appearing curious but rather concerned.

"Studying this control panel. It still amazes me that the Observer can do everything you showed me." He set it down and ignored it, although it took all of his willpower to do so. "What did Doc say?"

"He said that if he were to agree to anything, it would be to insert you into a different place—a totally different city, and let you work out your life from there."

"But that wouldn't fix the problem you created when you took me out of the timestream."

Mike was impressed with his use of the word 'timestream'. It told him that David understood what had happened and had, to some degree, accepted it, which David really had. He didn't think his going back would change anything, Evans would just fire him to his face.

"What about the irrigation pipe?" he asked instead.

"That he can do. He said he may have time to go get it later today and we could call him in the morning to arrange a pickup."

"Great," David said. "Anything else we can do today?"

"No. Why don't you take off and we'll talk again in the morning?"

⊛

"So, you were able to test the Observer changes for me?" Mike asked Doc.

"Yes, I took the gate to the president's office in Philadelphia and left him a surprise."

"What kind of surprise?"

"It was a napkin from our wedding reception three years ago. Along with our names and the date, the words 'Joining Two

Worlds' was embossed in gold in one corner. The president told me he's seen it and knew what it meant. That's why he wanted to borrow the gate, to spy on the Brazilian government. Then he really surprised me. He offered to pay me a large sum of money for it."

"How much?" Mike asked.

"Five hundred million dollars."

"Did you take it?"

"The gate is worth much more than that and he knows it. That was just a first bid, to see if he could tell where the market was."

"But would you sell it if the price was right?"

"No. I wouldn't. The fact is, it's not mine to sell."

"Whose is it?"

"It's owned by Terry and your mother, and I don't think either of them would agree to sell, let alone both of them. And that is what it would take."

"And it's Mom's because she inherited Dad's share of the partnership when he died?"

"Right."

"So, is that it then?" Mike asked.

"Not quite. I told the president that I had a suggestion for him. Without telling him that I'd already been to Brazil through the gate, I suggested he get in touch with General Ramos. Ramos, along with the rest of their high command, has stepped in to take control of the government in the wake of a scandal with their president. I know Ramos; He's an honest man. I told Jim to suggest that Ramos investigate a businessman named Oliveira who's a friend of the new president. When I took the gate to Brazil, I overheard a couple of discussions between Oliveira and the new president that convinced me that Oliveira is dirty. Oliveira hired the woman who instigated the charges against the old president, to lie under oath, in exchange for financial favors from the new president.

"I believe that the old president was removed from office on false charges and that the new president is more corrupt than the old one. We need to get him back in office. Jim guessed that I had used the gate to get the information, but I wouldn't confirm it. I believe if they investigate, they'll get enough information to fix the problem in Brazil."

David had been set on leaving that day, but he didn't think he had enough information to properly operate the gate. He needed to spend one more day with Mike in the lab. He was frustrated, wondering if they were intentionally dragging their feet to keep him here. He could see that it was beyond his control, so he'd be better off worrying about things he could control.

It was still morning, and since he wasn't going anywhere today, he still had a big chunk of the day ahead of him. He thought about what he wanted to do. He'd loved hiking in these mountains, when they were still *his* mountains; he wondered how he'd feel now that they were different.

Lisa Beth was in front of the cabin, by herself, when he arrived. "I'm going hiking," he said, "You're welcome to go with me if you want."

"Matt Jr. and I are going on a picnic," she said. "I'm just waiting for him now."

"Suit yourself," he said, disappointed, but not willing to beg. "I saw you at game night," he said, just to make conversation and give her a chance to change her mind.

"Were you there? I didn't see you."

So she looked for him. "I just passed by on my way to the

kitchen," he said. "You were tied to Matt Jr. in a three-legged race. It looked like you were enjoying yourself."

"I would have enjoyed it more if it had been you. I get tingly whenever we touch."

"So do I," he said, trying to understand what it meant.

"Why didn't you join us?" she asked.

He didn't have an answer that wouldn't be embarrassing, so he turned and went in to see if Sheryl had a snack and a bottle of water he could take. While she prepared him a sandwich to take, she asked if he'd done anything with Lisa Beth lately.

"I just invited her to go hiking with me, but she has a date with Matt Jr."

"That's too bad," Sheryl said. "I really wish she would go with you. This isn't good." she added, wiping and wringing her hands in her apron.

"What's the problem?" he asked.

"Beth told me that the Observer picked you to be with Lisa Beth, not Matt Jr."

"The Observer is just a machine," David said. "It can't make life decisions for people."

Sheryl handed David his sandwich and a bottle of water, then turned away, apparently dismissing him. Under his breath, David said, "Mike's going to have these people worshipping that machine if he's not careful." Then he walked away.

Sheryl followed him out of the cabin and found Lisa Beth still on the porch, waiting. "Lisa Beth, why don't you go with David on his hike?" she asked.

"I would," she said, "except that I already told Matt I'd go with him."

"Can't you put him off until tomorrow?" Sheryl asked.

"You know how he's been acting, Mom. I don't know what he'd

do when he found out. And . . . he made me promise."

"Alright, Dear," Sheryl said reluctantly. "I'll trust you on this; but maybe you need to plan something with David."

Lisa Beth looked toward David, perhaps considering what to do. She should tell him about the birthday party the next day. But David was already walking away. She would have to catch him later.

David hiked up the hill toward the Bear Lake overlook, not on the road, but over the hill through the trees. It was rough going and steep in places, but he felt invigorated by the clean air. H enjoyed listening to the birds and loved the smells of the forest. After hiking for a couple of hours, he found himself on top of a ridge, so he stopped to catch his breath and look around. He could see for miles in every direction Aspen Valley was below him, the field where he and Lisa Beth had picnicked was to the left and another large, flat valley lay to his right, in the direction he was headed.

He looked back at the field and could see Lisa Beth and Matt Jr. arrive with what looked like a picnic basket; it was too far away to be certain. As he watched, it looked like Lisa Beth laid out a tablecloth, as she had done for the picnic with him. Then, before she could sit down, Matt was on her, pushing her onto her back, and straddling her. Although it was a long way off, it appeared that she tried to push him off, but he pinned her arms above her head, lay down on top of her and tried to kiss her. He kept trying until he succeeded, then he let her up.

She stood up and took several steps back toward the valley, as though to leave, but he grabbed her arm and yanked her back, pulling her off-balance and onto the ground again. He was on her immediately, forcing her to face him with one hand holding her chin and kissing her several times.

David turned away, frustrated and angry. He felt badly for her, but he was too far away to do anything, and she had spurned him anyway. "She'll have to get herself out of this one," he said aloud, but the thought rankled him and he chastised himself immediately for his insensitivity. He really did care about her. She was so sweet and . . . 'chaste' was the best word to describe what he thought. Matt was a jerk and deserved to be punished for the way he treated her, but David didn't see any of the adults trying to correct him, or protect her. She was on her own.

He kept walking. It took him another two hours to reach the summit and the overlook. From there, he could look down and see all of Bear Lake Valley, as well as the back of Stefani's cabin. So, if he couldn't use the gate to get there, he could walk there in an afternoon. With that knowledge, he headed back. Lisa Beth and Matt Jr. had left the field by the time he got back to where he could see the field, so he continued on, enjoying the long hike back.

❂

"David," Sheryl said when he entered the cabin, having missed dinner, "Beth needs to talk to you, and so do I."

"What is it?"

"Lisa Beth came back from her picnic and I could tell she'd been crying, but she won't talk to me about it. I wondered if you would talk to her and make sure she's alright. I hope Matt Jr. didn't do anything to hurt her."

David felt like telling her what he'd seen, but wasn't positive that what he thought he'd seen was what had actually happened. He decided to talk to Lisa Beth first, to see if she would open up about it.

"Sure," he said. I'll go see what Beth wants first.

He walked to the big cabin and found Beth sitting on the swing in front of the fireplace, swinging back and forth, pushing the swing forcefully. It seemed to him that she was taking out some frustration on the swing.

"Hi Beth. I heard you were looking for me."

"Hi David. I've been waiting for you. I have a couple of questions for you. First: what can you do about the orchard?"

"Doc will buy new pipe for us and deliver it tomorrow to Mike, but someone needs to do something about whoever keeps breaking it."

"Thank you. That gets me to the second item. It seems that Matt Jr. is so mad at you that he's taking it out on Lisa Beth. She came home tonight in tears because he was physically abusive to her. She won't say anything to her mother because Sheryl and Emily are close friends, but she told me because I'm a doctor and she needed me to treat some cuts and bruises."

"What do you expect me to do about it?" David asked, defensively. "I'm the new guy here. Wouldn't Bryce or Mike be better positioned to punish him, if it's called for?"

"David, I don't think you appreciate the position you're in, here."

"What position is that?" he asked nonchalantly, but under the surface of his calm demeanor, he seethed that Matt Jr. could be so mean without being held accountable, and that the adults thought it was up to David to do something about it.

"You were invited here because the—"

"Stop right there!" David said. "If you're going to tell me that the Observer bought me here to marry her, I've already heard it and I don't put my faith in a machine to make life decisions for me." He realized he was breathing heavily and tried to calm himself. He shook his hands, which he'd been clenching since he'd started talking to Beth.

"David, It's not just the Observer. Haven't you noticed how comfortable she is around you?"

"Not lately," he said.

"She told me you had a misunderstanding. Those things happen, but since you arrived, she's come alive. I've never seen her so happy and full of life, and I've known her all her life. I delivered her, right here in this cabin, before it was completed. She needs you. You make her whole. I can take care of Matt Jr. I'll punch his lights out if he hurts her again, but you are the one she wants and needs."

"What if I don't need her?" he asked.

"But you do," she said. "I can see it in you, too. Before your unfortunate misunderstanding, you were just like her, alive and whole whenever you were together. Now, you drag around like you have nothing to live for. I wouldn't be surprised if you told me you'd asked Mike to send you back."

"I did, this morning."

"What did he say?" Beth asked, concern in her voice.

"No go. Doc would only agree to send me somewhere totally different, where I wasn't known and where I would have to make a life from scratch."

"Sounds like something Doc would say. He worries about contaminating the worlds."

"I don't know what that means, but please don't try to explain it to me. My brain is about to burst from everything I've heard in the last few days. Hey, I'll get the irrigation system working again in the next day or two, whatever it takes. Are we good with that?"

"Sure David. Thank you." Beth turned away, looking disappointed, and headed for the rear of the cabin, where she had her bedroom.

For some reason he couldn't articulate, even to himself, he put off looking for Lisa Beth until it was time for bed. When she didn't come to his room, he went to hers. She was lying in bed, turned facing the wall, with her two siblings lying in the bed with her, eyes closed and quiet, but he could see them wiggling under the covers. "Lisa Beth," he said quietly. The two younger children sat up and started laughing and playing. Lisa Beth turned her head toward the door. "What is it, David? I'm tired and I've had a bad day."

"I saw you from the top of the mountain. I'd like to talk to you about it if you're willing."

"I thought you wanted to go home, that you didn't want anything to do with me."

"I did . . . I mean, I thought I did . . . I'm not sure anymore. Can we talk? Please?"

"Alright, but not here." She climbed carefully over her siblings, threw on a robe over her pajamas, and went to the door. He backed out of the room and let her pass. She went to his room and he followed, sitting next to her on the bed.

"What did you see?" she asked.

"I was a long way up the mountain, so I can't be sure, but it looked like he pulled you down after you tried to leave. Is that when you got hurt?"

"That's when he realized that he'd gone too far and finally let me go."

"Did he hurt you?"

She showed him the scrapes on both hands. "These are from the fall," she said. "Also these." She turned her right hand over to show him that the whole back of her hand was bruised. Then she raised her pant legs to show him the scrapes on both shins and a bruise on her left foot. Then she raised her top to show him the scrape on the right side of her stomach. "I have a nice bruise on my backside, too, from landing on a rock. Do you want to see that, too?"

"That's okay," he said. "I get the idea. Did anyone talk to him about it?"

"His dad took him into the trees for a talk after Beth told Matt Sr. what Matt had done. I haven't seen either of them since, but they're staying in the other cabin, so they had no reason to come back here; and Beth came here, so I haven't been over there."

"I went there to talk to Beth, but didn't see him or his parents. Maybe he's still out in the trees, hanging from a high limb."

"We can only hope," she said, then scooted over closer to him, wincing in pain from the movement.

"I'm sorry, Lisa Beth. What do you need?"

"Thank you for the sympathy. I think I just need to sleep. Beth said that's what I need and that I'll feel better in the morning—or worse." She started scooting some more and David moved closer to the wall, so he didn't contribute to her suffering. When she was finished moving, she had placed herself where she could lay her head on his pillow. "Can I sleep here?" She asked. "I don't think I'll be able to sleep in my bed with two active children bumping me and keeping me awake."

"Absolutely!" David said. "I can sleep on the floor."

"I'd rather you lay by me to keep me warm," she said. "Will you put the covers over me?" She raised herself up off the bed, so he could pull the covers out from under her, then she laid down so he could cover her with them. He removed his shoes and socks, and laid down next to her, fully dressed, careful not to bump her where she hurt, which was pretty much everywhere. Then he covered himself with a throw that Lisa Beth had left at the foot of his bed. They both lay on their backs, staring up at the ceiling. He was afraid to move.

"Do you see the face in the texture of the ceiling?" he asked.

"You mean, the one with a bald head and big ears?"

"Yeah, that one. Does it look like anyone you know?"

"Not offhand. You?"

"I think it's an angel, here to watch over you."

Lisa Beth smiled at David. "Thank you for that thought," she said, then closed her eyes. She was asleep in moments, breathing evenly. David turned his head so he could see her profile and thought again how pretty she was and how much he liked her. Maybe he loved her. Beth's comments came back to him and he realized she was right; she made him feel whole. On that thought, he fell asleep, too.

"Eve . . . Eve . . . I just entered Utah at Lewiston, so we can be together in a couple of days. Give me a sign of how to find you." Short listened for an answer, but all he heard was singing, rock music, which he hated. "Eve, stop singing, so I can hear your thoughts," he said, but nothing changed.

Doc had come up with a plan, and the first step was to get Kerri to fill her head with music, hoping that Short couldn't read her mind or hear stray thoughts through the music. She had loaded her phone with rock music and played it loudly through her ear buds to distract herself. The second part required Terry and Mike, and Doc hoped it would frustrate Short and his followers enough that they would give up and go away.

Between Lewiston and Smithfield, Terry and Mike searched the highway for the perfect spot to ambush Short. When they found it, they parked the Gemini Gate and waited for Short to arrive. As Short and his army of followers approached at dusk, when they would have difficulty seeing the glimmer of the gate, Terry expanded the gate across the highway. Short and all of his followers drove through, transported to a remote area in Tooele County, west of Salt Lake City. Short, being the first one through the gate, became suspicious at the change in the road and eventually stopped to look around, wondering what had happened. He had felt a tingle to his nervous system, but had no clue what it meant or how it was related to his present situation. He looked back in time to see the long line of trucks and SUVs following him. He left his cab and walked back along the convoy. Other drivers exited their cabs to join him in the middle of the road to talk. Finally, one man said he thought he recognized where they were, between Tooele and Grantsville, in Tooele County. He recognized a racetrack that he'd been to sometime earlier to watch drag races.

With that man's help, Short's lieutenant, Caine, opened a map he'd been using to guide the group, and pointed out where they were and where they had to go to get back to Interstate 15. Several people complained about sudden nervous disorders, including Caine, Short and Caine had difficulty explaining to the frustrated group what they had to do. He tried to figure out what had happened to sidetrack them so far from where they needed to be and he didn't know of any technology the military had that could do that to him. He wondered if Eve had, in any way, been responsible, but couldn't imagine it. He would think about it; try to figure it out.

"Which way do we go to get back on track?" Short asked

Caine looked at his GPS and pointed to the right. "That's east," he said. "We have to go that way."

"What happened back there?" someone asked. "I suddenly developed a nervous twitch."

"Me too," someone else complained.

"I saw a shimmer in the air, then a tingling in my arms and legs," another said. "What could have caused that?"

Short looked at his watch. It had taken them so long to figure out where they were, and where they had to go, that it had gotten dark while they were searching.

"We need to stop for the night," he told Caine. "Any suggestions?"

"I saw a large parking lot back that direction," Caine said. Short made a U-turn on the road and headed for the parking lot. The others followed.

A police car cruised by the parking lot later and stopped at the first truck he came to, a Ford F150.

"Are you all together?" he asked the driver.

"We are. We got lost on our way to Logan and stopped here for the night."

"This is private property. You're not allowed to camp overnight." The policeman said. As he looked around at what looked like at least a hundred vehicles, with multiple occupants, many of them standing next to their trucks, cleaning guns and rifles, he had a vision of a massive confrontation, a western style OK Corral shootout. He could call for backup, but it would probably require calling out the national guard to control this large a group. Or, he could just ask them politely to leave early in the morning and not leave a mess that the owners would have to clean up. He looked back at his cruiser and saw his partner on the police radio talking to dispatch. As he considered his options, a man approached who looked like he might be in charge of this group.

"Hello officer," the man said. "My name is Adam and these are my friends. I can vouch for them. Is there a problem?"

The officer repeated what he'd told the first man, then added.

"I understand that you're trying to get to Logan. I can show you the best way to get there from here. If you'll leave first thing in the morning and leave no trace that you were here, I'll let it go and explain the situation to the owner tomorrow. Will that work for you and your people?"

Short agreed, got Caine to bring the map and get the directions from the officer. Then, he returned to his Hummer. The officer returned to his car, spoke to his partner for a minute, then drove away. The police drove by the parking lot two more times during the night to confirm that the group was not causing mischief.

The next morning, Short assigned two men to dig a trench to use as a latrine, then everyone ate whatever they'd brought with them and the caravan headed out to the northeast, eventually finding Interstate 215, which merged onto 15 north of Salt Lake City. Short thought they were a few vehicles short of what they'd had the day before.

They turned off Interstate 15 onto highway 89 and passed through Brigham City into Sardine Canyon. That's when they passed through another shimmering gate and ended up in a canyon west of Kemmerer, Wyoming. Mike had never taken the gate that far north before, but since he'd figured out how to extend its range, he'd jumped ahead to find a good place to send the convoy. When Short realized that he had been misdirected again, he stopped again to discuss it.

"I saw your Hummer disappear," the driver of the next truck in line commented. "You were leading us one moment, then the next moment you were gone. I tried to stop, but not in time, so I followed you through whatever it is we went through."

Other drivers approached Short, most of them complaining.

"What are we accomplishing?" one man asked.

"What are you going to do about the misdirection?" another

asked.

"Where are we?"

"We're wasting a lot of time. Is Eve worth all this?"

"I'm in serious pain," a man who'd complained about nervous twitches before, complained now.

"I want to go home," another complained. "This is a waste of time."

Short asked Caine if he thought they were losing vehicles. This was the second time they'd been misdirected and the second time he'd suspected that his caravan was shrinking.

The Preserve

"Some of them want to quit and go home," Terry said. He was in the lab, watching the interaction between Short and his followers, through the gate. Mike and Doc were also there, discussing what they could do if Short didn't give up.

"How can we encourage the dissention?" Mike asked.

"What if we just send some of them home at a time?" Doc asked.

"You mean, uncouple the caboose and send it down another track?" Terry asked.

"I like that analogy," Doc said. "Instead of placing the gate at the front of the train, let's place it near the caboose."

☢

Short tried to calm his followers while they figured out where they were.

"From the GPS coordinates," Caine said, "I'd say we're not in Utah. It looks like we're in Wyoming."

"Does anyone have a Wyoming map?" Short asked the drivers milling around him and complaining.

"I have one," one man said and hurried away toward his truck. When he returned, he handed the map to Caine, who took a few minutes to orient himself, then told Short they were near Kemmerer. They could take highway 30 west or 189 south to Interstate 80. As Short was giving directions, some of his followers, talking among themselves, threatened to leave. They had received phone calls from friends or family, asking them to give it up and come home.

Short realized that some of his followers were leaving anyway, but he hadn't noticed when they'd left; it must have been after dark. He didn't want to hear the complaining. He believed he needed this size group to ensure that Eve would follow him. He didn't know how large a group they would encounter and have to overcome to take her.

Short argued with them, that they had to find Eve, until it looked like he was losing them. Then drew his gun and threatened them. He was the leader and they would follow.

"Adam," one man said, pleadingly "What are we doing? Why are we here instead of looking for Eve?"

"We're looking for Eve, but someone or something is fighting us. I'll get to the bottom of it. In the meantime, get back in your truck and be ready to follow when we figure out where we need to go."

"I can't feel my left arm," One of his followers complained.

"I need to go to a hospital," another complained. "My nervous tick has turned into uncontrollable twitching." Her leg struck out and kicked Short in the shin. She got back in her car with her husband and drove off before Short could come up with a response.

"I'm not sure Eve is worth this," another said, holding a hand to his neck.

I heard voices to the east. One man said, pulling alongside Short in his truck. "We need to go that direction."

"We're going west," Short said, having confirmed it with Caine. "Load up and let's go."

"I've had enough," the follower said and drove away.

"Don't drive away from me," Short said, then drew his handgun and shot the man through the truck window. The truck crashed into a road barrier on the side of the road. Short could tell the man was dead from the contortion of his neck.

Several followers, close by the shooting, recoiled at the noise and the resulting collision and death. Short heard whispering behind his back and turned around, but the whispering stopped when he did.

"Everyone mount up," Short said. "We leave in five minutes."

Short thought he heard whispering after that, even negative comments about his decision on how to deal with dissenters. Caine mentioned it to him.

"So what?" Short said, sounding grumpy. "I'm the leader. They'll do what I say, or else."

Rather than argue, Caine looked up directions again and suggested they head west on 30 to the small town of Sage, then to Sage Creek Junction and on to Laketown at the south end of Bear Lake. It was the shortest way to get to Logan

Short got in the passenger seat and told Caine to drive. Short spent the time resting his head against the window and griping about stupid people who disagree with him. Caine kept quiet, but the twitch in his neck bothered him.

They stopped in Sage and bought food in a gas station. Some bought gas.

There was nowhere to camp overnight, so they drove into the night to get to Laketown. There was an RV campground at Rendezvous Beach, but it was full, so they pulled over and parked wherever they could find space on the sides off the road.

When Short checked his caravan in the morning he was surprised to find that about half of his followers were missing. He questioned the last driver in the line.

"Weren't there more vehicles behind you," Short asked.

"There were. I checked my rear-view mirror periodically, to make sure I was still being followed. Then one time I looked and no one was following. I even slowed down to give them a chance to catch up, but they never did. They were just gone."

"Did they turn off onto another highway?"

"I don't think so. We had just gone over a little rise in the road when I noticed them gone. There were no turnoffs on that stretch of road."

Short swore. Somebody was playing games with them. He tried to contact Eve again, but all he heard was her blasted rock music.

Short didn't understand why or how his followers had left him; but Terry and Mike had begun throwing up a gate suddenly in front of a few vehicles at a time, carving off the tail of the beast and sending small groups from the back of the convoy elsewhere. Every few miles, between Kemmerer and Laketown, they diverted up to a dozen vehicles at a time to places in Idaho where the drivers would recognize where they were and head back to Montana, or wherever they had come from.

Garden City

"Where are they going?" Short asked Caine. Caine was waiting to turn west onto highway 89, at the junction in Garden City, which was the way to get to Logan. Most of his followers passed him on the right and kept going straight north.

"The sign said Montpelier, Idaho is that direction," Caine replied.

Short powered down his window and waved at the line of car to get them to stop. Finally, one stopped, backing up the rest of the line.

"What are you doing?" Short asked.

"Goin' home," the man said. "We've had enough chasing around."

"You're going nowhere!" Short said angrily. He pulled his gun and pointed it at the man. "I'll shoot the next person to desert me."

"Are you going to shoot all of us?" the man asked

"If I have to," Short said, spittle shooting from his mouth as he spoke.

"What good are followers who don't trust you?" the man asked.

While Short was thinking about that, the man hit the gas and continued north. toward Idaho. The next truck tried to pass, so Short pointed his gun and shot the driver. The truck, along with the four people inside it, two men and two women, ran off the road and into a boarded-up ice cream stand called the Tasty Freeze. The truck hit it so hard that it crashed through the front wall and continued into the serving area. The demolished wall collapsed, along with the roof, burying the truck in construction material.

When Short looked behind his Hummer, there was no caravan--not one vehicle—behind them. He realized his plans were falling apart and the only thing he had left to live for was Eve. He could still find her, but he didn't know what he would encounter when he got to his destination. Would he have to fight for her, as some of his followers believed? How difficult would it be to convince her to go with him? Was he prepared to use lethal force?

Of course, he was.

"Let them go!" Short screamed. The group was well away, going in the wrong direction, and he wasn't about to chase after and beg them to turn around. "They'll come crawling back once I have Eve and we have our utopian society set up."

"What if we have to fight?" Caine asked. "We don't have any guns for backup now."

Short thought about that for a few minutes before speaking again. "I don't expect trouble from Eve, despite her protestations. She's mine and I'll convince her."

The Preserve

"Doc," Terry said, after watching Short's followers disappear up the road toward Idaho. He had been watching the caravan through the gate for the last hour or so. He saw Short kill four of his followers when they crashed into the Tasty Freeze—Zach and Isaac were going to be sad. "Now would be a good time to implement the final phase of the plan."

Doc had been dosing in a chair in the lab, with Lillie watching him from her chair. She loved this man. How had she been so lucky as to find two good men in her lifetime? It made it easier for her to accept, knowing that Doc was Amos from the twin world.

"Maybe we should let Short get to the valley and deal with him here," Terry said

"The last time we allowed invaders into the valley," Lillie said "Amos was shot in the head and died. There is no one in the valley that I would sacrifice, if it can be avoided."

"Okay," Doc said. "I have a Plan C. Can you get Kerri on the radio, Lillie?"

☢

"Adam," he heard in his head. It was Eve. "I'm still here. Are you coming, or did you decide to go home?"

"I'm coming, Eve. I'm in Garden City. Tell me how to find you."

"Wait, Adam," Caine said.

"Shush," Short told Caine. "Say that again, Eve."

"Turn west onto highway 89 and follow it up and over the view area," Kerri sent. "It will bring you right to me."

"Okay, we're already at the 89 turnoff. We're turning now."

Short told Caine what Eve had said.

"Something's wrong," Caine said.

"Why do you say that? I'm on the verge of meeting Eve."

"Why did she suddenly change her tune, from telling you to go away, to inviting you to go to her?"

Short thought about that for only a moment. "She's ready for me," he said.

"I say something's wrong," Caine said. "It might be a trap. We lose our backup, then she changes her tune. That's too much of a coincidence." Short saw the sign for the Bear Lake valley overlook. "We're on the right road," he told Caine.

"Eve," Short said. "I see a shimmer of light ahead. What is it?"

"That's where you'll find me . . . if you really want me," she said, knowing that Mike had been misdirecting Short by sending him through the gate for the last couple of days. She wondered where he was sending Short this time.

"Are you sure?" Short said, mirroring Kerri's thoughts. "I've been misdirected several times already. Will you be waiting for me?"

"I'm not going anywhere," she sent, "but you have to really want me."

Did he really want her? Was all of this crazy misdirection her effort to scare him off? Someone else's effort? Would he be misdirected again? What if he was. Did he want her badly enough to put up with it? Was it dangerous to keep trying to get to her? He thought about his plan to rule the world, with Eve by his side. He knew he still wanted that, badly enough to tolerate some misdirection. He was making progress. How much farther did he have to go?

Caine's comment made him pause. Was it a coincidence that she changed her mind right after he lost his followers? Was he in danger from her? No way. She may not go with him willingly, but she couldn't stop him. Was there someone with her who could stop him? He didn't believe it. He would be with her shortly and she would see.

Kerri didn't say more. Doc wanted to give Short a choice. He could go home to safety, or risk the unknown one more time, without his support group, by going through the gate again. Doc was pretty sure, thinking he knew Short's type, that he would not give up his quest to find his Eve. Only Terry, Mike and Doc knew where Short would be sent this time.

As Short drove his Humvee through the gate for the last time, Short, Caine, and their Humvee, were transported to a spot about ten feet above the middle of Bear Lake. With Caine's foot on the accelerator, the Hummer continued to move forward, as it dropped like a brick into the cold water of the lake and sank like a rock. Both men held their breaths as the Hummer quickly filled with water, then swam out of the open windows and surfaced after a few seconds. Short could see houses on the shore and began swimming in that direction, Caine followed.

Short didn't panic; He was a good swimmer. When he finally remembered to check on Caine, he was there, struggling to keep up. Their boots and heavy coats dragged them down and Caine went under, trying to remove them. He must have swallowed water, since he came up sputtering and choking, then went down again and didn't resurface. Short fared better, removing his boots and coat and letting them sink out of sight. He swam, keeping a steady pace, but he was cold and began to shiver. He faltered and went under. He resurfaced and continued swimming.

Short didn't know how far he'd gone—Doc estimated it was about half way—when his chin dipped below the surface and he had to breathe through his nose to keep from swallowing water. He was a strong swimmer and thought he could make it to the submerged trees, which seemed so close and which indicated shallower water. His arms ached, then his legs cramped. He went under, then bobbed back up, spitting water from his mouth.

Doc had moved the gate close to the side of Short's face so he could watch his expression. He noticed when Short began to fear that he wouldn't make it, then the panic in his eyes when he went under again. When Short bobbed back to the surface, he held one thigh, squeezing it as though trying to loosen a cramp. He resurfaced, then went under for a third time. He didn't resurface

Just to make sure it was over, Terry and Mike watched the site where they had last seen Short, for another half-hour, finally satisfied.

18

The Old World—Philadelphia, Pennsylvania, present day

"Jim," SECDEF Peatross said to get the president's attention. They were in the conference room in the capital in Philadelphia that they had designated for classified conversations. The president studied documents in front of him.

"What is it, Bob?" Jim asked without looking up. "The situation in Brazil is improving, but needs a boost. We need that observer machine from Doc."

"That's what I wanted to tell you," Bob said. "Our team is ready to move. I'm going to reposition to the Logan area."

"Let's think about that a minute. What are the chances we can set up in the Logan area without Doc becoming aware of us?"

"What do you mean?" Bob asked. "He's up in Logan Canyon, isn't he?"

"He has a five-acre estate on the west side of Logan in the other world. He may have property there in our world, as well. He also has a government-paid security guard that was trained by us. Don't underestimate Doc. He's clever. He may have surveillance set up around the area."

"Okay, but that changes things. I'll review our plans with that in mind and get back to you."

"Thanks, Bob."

The Old World—Aspen Valley

When David woke, Lisa Beth lay on her right side, facing him, her face inches from his. Her head rested on his left arm, which had gone to sleep. Her left leg was draped over his legs, so he couldn't move without disturbing her. Then he realized that her eyes were open. She was looking at him, a wide smile on her face.

He smiled. "How did you sleep?" he asked.

"Peaceful, dreamless sleep, like I slept with an angel watching over me." She glanced at the ceiling before refocusing on his face. "How did you sleep?"

"I woke a couple of times, when you cried out in your sleep, and realized that we were touching in places where you were injured. I had to move, so I wouldn't hurt you worse."

Her eyes moved, so she was looking at his lips, inches from hers, then moved into him and kissed him on the lips. When she backed away again, she said, "Thank you for caring."

"I do care," he said and leaned into her for another kiss. "I think I love you." Now why did he say that, if he was going to leave. Did he really mean it? He wasn't sure.

He carefully removed his arm from under her head, giving her another kiss in the process. She sat up slowly and sat on the edge of the bed. He sat next to her, trying to decide what to do next. She finally stood, collected her robe from a chair next to the bed, and struggled to get her arms in the sleeves. She winced as though the movement irritated her injuries.

"Let me help," David said, then held the robe so she could get her arms in the sleeves. She tied the sash and turned toward him.

"Thank you, again," she said, and gave him another kiss, this one longer and harder.

she left his room, returning a while later dressed in lightweight clothing.

"The scratches and scrapes have scabbed over," she said. "Now they itch. The bruises look worse but feel better."

"About what you expected, huh?" David asked.

"Yeah. I guess it will take a while to feel better."

They ate breakfast alone, being the last to arrive in the dining room. After breakfast, she followed him out to the orchard to check on the pipes. Matt Jr. and Dean were there. As David watched, Matt swung a hammer down on one of the pipes, shattering it after the second blow.

"Stop it!" David yelled as he started to run forward. Matt Jr. looked up only long enough to see who it was, then moved to the next pipe and did the same thing, shattering that pipe, too. David arrived and grabbed Matt Jr. by the right arm, the one holding the hammer, preventing him from swinging the hammer at the next pipe.

"Get away, or the next blow will be to your head," Matt Jr. said, switching the hammer to his other hand.

"That's enough," David said, Matt Jr stood and swung a fist at David's head, which he easily ducked under. Then David swung a fist into Matt Jr.'s stomach, knocking the wind out of him. Matt doubled over for a moment, then stood straight and swung the hammer at David's head. David backed up and the swing went wild. Before Matt could recover, David grabbed his extended arm and pulled him off balance, driving him to his knees in the dirt. Matt swung the hammer at David's foot, forcing David to back up again, then Matt was up again and moving to the next pipe.

"Stop it Matt," Lisa Beth said.

"Don't do it, Matt," David said at the same time, but Matt sneered at him and swung the hammer into the next pipe, which shattered on the first blow. David pictured Matt's head as the punching bag he had practiced on at the gym at school and swung a fist into his face. Matt's nose broke, blood running out of both nostrils and down his face, dripping off his chin. Matt staggered, but stayed upright, the sneer now giving an eerie look to his face.

He swung at the pipe again, perhaps not remembering that it had already broken, and his hammer embedded itself in the dirt a couple of inches. David took one more swing at Matt's head, a roundhouse that landed on his temple and dropped him where he knelt. His eyes rolled up in his head and he fell over, sideways. He didn't get up.

Bryce, Matt Sr., and a couple of others arrived just then to investigate the commotion. Matt Sr. looked at his son, a bloody, dirty mess, and turned on David angrily. Bryce moved in front of Matt Sr. and placed both hands on his chest.

"What have you done?" Matt Sr asked angrily, peering over Bryce's shoulder at the same time that Bryce said, "Hold on Matt. Let's give them a chance to explain what happened."

David looked at the men, then at Lisa Beth. Lisa Beth looked like she would cry and he didn't know if it was anger at him, sympathy for Matt, or something else. He shrugged, then walked away, leaving them to figure it out.

"Hey, don't walk away when we're talking to you," Matt Sr. called to him, but he kept walking. He had started walking to the cabin, then thought better of it. He didn't want to be trapped in a corner, where they could say or do what they wanted and where he couldn't escape. So, he turned and headed into the trees, walking toward his car. He would sit in his car until everyone settled down.

He heard Lisa Beth call his name, weakly, and considered going back to her; but he didn't want to get trapped by Matt Sr. or Bryce and have to explain himself. He kept walking and Lisa Beth didn't call him again.

After a while, several people came through the trees onto the trail, unhurriedly, and walked toward him, where he sat in his car. He thought it meant they just wanted to talk, but when he saw Matt Jr. with them, still wiping blood off his face with his shirt sleeve, he decided he didn't want to hear what they had to say. He was sure Matt Jr. had twisted the truth in his favor and that he would be the guilty party. Perhaps Lisa Beth had straightened out everything and there would be no repercussions. He didn't wait to find out.

He waited just long enough to see that Lisa Beth wasn't with them, then started the car, did a quick three-point turn and left the valley, driving slowly enough that he didn't damage the car on the rutted, muddy trail, but fast enough to stay ahead of them. It wasn't until he reached the highway that he realized he had no idea what he was doing or where he was going. He had enough gas to go about twelve miles, but then what?

He could see them in his rear-view mirror as he turned onto the highway and headed uphill toward the overlook. He gunned the engine and accelerated, leaving the valley behind. He'd had enough. He was going to go to Stefani's cabin and propose to her. The only problem with the plan was that he was in the wrong world.

The Old World—Philadelphia, Pennsylvania

General Peatross decided that their best approach would be to land the special ops team in southeastern Idaho, then travel by truck to Garden City and over the hill to the valley. The special ops team landed at the Bear Lake County Airport and transferred their gear from the military transport to their trucks and headed down the highway as fast as they could negotiate it. Their leader, General Ames, who had been a Colonel in the Prime bunker during the war and protected the president from Art Klemp, had the coordinates of the valley and a diagram to show him how to get into the Preserve and to the lab. He also had a sketch of what the Observer looked like.

Mike had been watching events unfold in the valley, from the lab, through the gate. He saw when David left in anger, rather than argue with the adults

"Very wise," he said to himself. "I wouldn't want to stand up to them if I were in his shoes." He watched as Lisa Beth defended David after he'd left.

"Who does he think he is?" Matt Sr. had said.

"He's the best thing to come out of Doc's experiments with the Observer, in years," Lisa Beth said, tears coming involuntarily to her eyes.

"What right did he have to pick on Matt Jr.?" his dad asked.

Lisa Beth choked on what she wanted to say, then collected herself and spoke boldly, staring at Matt Sr. "He built a beautiful irrigation system for the garden and orchard, which we needed desperately and which benefits all of us, including you; and Matt has nearly destroyed it out of spite. We should be thanking David, instead of chasing him off."

"Let's go get him," Beth said, "and thank him for his effort."

"Where do you think he's gone?" Bryce asked.

"His car is that direction," Lisa Beth said, "but he told me it was nearly out of gas."

"Would he walk all the way to Garden City?" Bryce asked.

"I don't know," Lisa Beth said, "but he's got a head start on us. We may not be able to find him if he gets too far away."

"Let's go!" Beth said, and hurried toward the trees where David had disappeared. "Are you coming?" she asked Lisa Beth, when she noticed that Lisa Beth held back.

"I don't think so," Lisa Beth said, with tears streaming down her face and a scowl aimed at Matt Sr. "I'm a mess and I ache all over. Just tell him thanks for me, too."

"I'm sure he'd rather hear it from your lips," Beth said. Then, when Lisa Beth shook her head and continued to cry, Beth turned and followed the others.

As Mike watched a few of them head into the trees, following after David, he recalled Beth's explanation from the previous evening, that Matt Jr. had attacked Lisa Beth on their picnic and the extent of her injuries. He had discussed the situation with Terry and Lillie, and they had agreed that they wouldn't blame David if he hurt Matt Jr. or decided he'd had enough. They were prepared to call this experiment a failure and send David back. Mike had even discussed it with Doc and Doc had reluctantly agreed. Later in the day, when Mike had been checking the gate, he'd noticed that David had been playing with the portable control while he was on the phone. One of the places that David had taken the gate was to a cabin just below the overlook on the Bear Lake side of the mountain. Mike had watched the cabin for a while, until he'd noticed the attractive woman who seemed to live there, who was about David's age. He recognized her as Stefani, David's girlfriend, whom Mike had seen when they were first observing David and considering bringing him across.

Now, in anger, David was headed toward the overlook. Was he trying to get to Stefani? Did he realize that he was in the wrong world? Of course, he did, or he would soon realize it. Mike was undecided about what he should do, if anything, about it. He called Terry and Lillie to join him in the lab, and help him decide.

"Maybe he's not trying to leave," Terry said. "Maybe he's just trying to calm down. He seems to like the fresh air up here, and he's level-headed enough to work through this, rationally."

"He doesn't have much gas, so he can't get far." Lillie said. "Let's just watch."

David pulled into the overlook parking lot with his engine chugging, almost out of gas. He turned off the engine and sat in the car for a long time, just looking out at the scenery. Then he got out of the car and walked around for a long time.

"See," Lillie said, "He's just trying to calm down before returning. He has nowhere to go."

"Maybe you're right, Lillie," Terry said. "He seems lost and unsure of what to do. Should we push him one way or another? I mean, should we open the gate and give him the option to stay or go?"

"Yes," Mike said. "Let's allow him to make his own decision. I'll open the gate near him and we can watch him decide whether to stay or go to the twin world."

"You think that's wise?" Lillie asked. He'll know the walk back to Logan is a long one.

"No," Mike said. "If he decides to go to Logan, he can hitch-hike. If he wants to go to Stefani, he can walk across the hillside. We already agreed to send him back, if necessary. What's the difference?"

"I think you're right, Mike," Lillie said.

"Are we agreed, then?" Mike asked.

Lillie nodded her head and Terry said, "Go ahead. Do it."

Mike opened the gate a few feet away from David, small at first, then larger until it was an oval shape large enough for him to step through. David didn't notice it at first, so Mike moved it around a little, until he was sure David had seen it. David stopped walking and stared at the opening, leaning against the side of his car, as if trying to decide what to do. Finally, David opened the rear, passenger side door.

"What's he doing?" Terry asked, getting no answer until David stood back up with two potted plants in his arms.

"Is he planning to take the plants to Stefani?" Lillie asked. "That's what he was planning originally, wasn't it, when we sidetracked him?"

"I think you're right, Mom. Should I stop him by shutting down the gate?"

"I don't think so," Terry said, "Let's watch and see how this plays out."

They watched David step through the gate and begin his slow progress across the hillside, trying to keep from slipping on the steep hillside and keep the plants from falling out of his arms. It was slow progress and they realized that he was committed to this plan of action, just as he was committed to each plan, once he decided on it. That was one of the things they liked about him, his commitment.

He finally arrived at the back of the cabin and set the potted plants down on a planter that already stood by the back door. There were a variety of colorful flowers all around the cabin, in pots on shelves and in a small greenhouse. David shook his arms, likely trying to get his circulation back, then went to the back door.

Garden City Overlook

David saw the gate wink out of sight as he walked away from his car. That avenue was now closed to him. He couldn't go back to the old world if he wanted to.

When he reached the cabin, he looked through the window in the back door. He shook his arms to get the blood circulating again. His left hand had gone numb; but he had arrived with the two plants intact and the wedding ring and other jewelry in his pocket. He debated going back for the other plants now or waiting; she might want to walk with him to get them. Then he realized that wouldn't happen. She didn't like to walk or hike. Why she had a cabin on a hillside in a small community baffled him. Besides, the gate was closed.

What he saw in the window confused him at first. He could see Stefani in the living room, on the other side of the kitchen, walking around the room, straightening things. She did that a lot, doing two things at once; but what confused him was that she seemed to be talking to someone else in the room. As far as he knew, she didn't know her neighbors in this sparsely populated community, the nearest one of which lived a quarter mile away. She also didn't have many friends, as far as he knew, since she had only lived in Utah for a couple of years and worked from her home office. Besides there was only one car in the driveway—hers.

He tried to see who she was talking to, but couldn't get the right angle. Then she turned and started climbing the staircase that stood between the kitchen and living room. He tried the doorknob, finding the door unlocked, and eased it open. It made no noise--he knew it wouldn't--because he had lubricated the hinges himself. He slipped into the kitchen and closed the door behind him. Wouldn't she be surprised when she came back down and found him there.

He remembered the plants and brought them inside, setting them on the kitchen table. He heard her footsteps and pictured her walking along the upper hallway toward the staircase. He backed away from the table where she wouldn't automatically see him when she came down the stairs, unless she turned into the kitchen, but she didn't even look in his direction. When she reached the bottom of the stairs, she turned back into the living room.

She laughed out loud, and went over and sat on the couch, patting the cushion next to her. Suddenly he could see who she spoke to. a man about ten years her senior moved into view and sat next to her—very close. An uncle? He wondered. Her boss? The man stared into her eyes, his attention totally focused on her. When she took his hand and placed it on her thigh, leaving hers on top of it to make sure it didn't get away, David realized that this must be a new boyfriend. When he placed his arms around her and kissed her hard and long, David was convinced, and wondered what he should do.

He could confront them and ask what was going on, but it was obvious what was going on. He could leave and come back, making more noise, so she would have time to make up an excuse, but he didn't want excuses; he wanted the truth and thought he already knew the truth. She had moved past him in the few days he had been gone. Had someone—the police—contacted her, asking where he was, telling her he had disappeared? Did she think he had moved on, found someone else, moved away suddenly, died in an accident? Any of those things were possible. He had no idea what she would think. In any event, there was no future for him here.

He suddenly realized that he was relieved instead of upset. All of the things that had bothered him about her, not wanting to go walking or hiking with him, not wanting to socialize with his friends, not wanting a pet dog or cat, or fish, suddenly came to mind.

What should he do? What did he want to do? Lisa Beth's face suddenly blossomed in his mind. He saw her with a smudge of dirt on her face from digging in the garden, he saw her in her nightgown, sitting on his bed, touching his hand. He saw scratches, scrapes and bruises. Did he feel sympathy because she was hurt, or did he love her because of the way she made him feel?

He knew what he wanted to do. He found a pad and pencil right where he expected to find them, on a stand next to the wall phone. "Stefani," he wrote, "These plants are for you. There are several more in the car at the overlook parking lot." Then he scratched that line out when he remembered that the car was in the old world, so she wouldn't be able to get to it unless the gate were reopened. He doubted Mike would allow that.

He considered setting the jewelry and ring next to them, but decided she wouldn't want them from him, so they stayed in his pocket. He couldn't think of anything else to say. In the end, he didn't even say 'I love you' or 'good luck'. He just signed the note, 'me', shoved his car keys into his pocket and left.

He snuck out the kitchen door and considered his next steps. He couldn't take his car, since it didn't have any juice left in it and the gate was closed. Maybe he could hike down to Garden City, where he could get lift back to Logan. It would probably take him two or three hours, but it was still early afternoon, and it would give him time to think and plan.

What he really wanted was Lisa Beth, but how could he get back to her? Then he remembered Mike telling him there were monitors set up around the valley to alert him to intruders. Would Mike notice him if he walked to the valley and open a gate for him? If not, Lisa Beth was lost to him and he would have to find his own way in the world from another location, as Doc had said. He had to assume that he could get back to Lisa Beth.

As he walked away from the cabin, he regretted losing his brand-new car—his baby—but it only bothered him for a moment. If he could have Lisa Beth, it would be worth the sacrifice. The car was just a thing, and things come and go.

Would Lisa Beth be happy to see him, or angry at his sudden departure? He could apologize, but would that be enough to make up for the way he'd acted? Beth had said that he was good for her and she was good for him. Well, he certainly knew that the second part was true, but he might be apologizing for a long time. He absentmindedly picked flowers from Stefani's greenhouse. They were beautiful, and he thought Lisa Beth would like them. He arrived at the overlook, confirmed that the gate was still closed, so he couldn't even see his car—it was in the old world. He would have to walk, and hope that he could find a way to contact Mike, to open a gate for him to return to the old world.

Sometime later, Stefani went to her kitchen for a drink of water and saw the flowers and the note. David was here? He was! Why didn't he say anything? Then she realized why he hadn't stayed, or made himself known. She thought he might still be within sight, so she stepped around the muddy footprints on the floor, opened the back door and looked out, but she couldn't see him anywhere. The police had told her that he had disappeared and that they couldn't even find his car. His work associates had told them the last place he had been seen was in the canyon, so they wondered if he'd run off the road into the river, or crashed into a tree, but he'd said that the car was here. What did it mean that he had scratched that sentence? Did it mean the car had been here, but that he'd decided to take it somewhere else?

Where had he been? She had no idea and had moved on when she met Peter at a dance club. Looking absently around her back yard, she noticed that the greenhouse door was slightly ajar. Looking inside, she could see that some of her prize-winning flowers had been plucked off their stems and swore at David's insensitivity. But maybe the plants he'd left for her would make up for it. They were some of her favorite flowers. How had David known? Had she misjudged him all along? She walked back into the kitchen, threw the note in the garbage, and sauntered back into the living room, a huge smile on her face.

The Old World—The Preserve

David took one last look at the view from the empty parking lot, then started walking back to the valley in the twin world. He straggled into the valley late in the day. He stopped on the road into the valley and waved his arms back and forth, jumping up and down, hoping to get Mike's attention if he were in the lab. When nothing happened, he decided not to become discouraged, He took the shortest route to the cabin, walking through the trees.

Mike was alerted to David's presence as soon as he entered the valley, by one of the sensors. He saw David jumping and waving and had a good laugh. When David gave up and headed through the trees in the direction of the cabins, Mike opened a gate a short distance from David, where he would see it. David paused, looked at the gate for a moment, as if considering one last time what he really wanted, then stepped through. Mike noticed David shaking his head as if considering and discarding ideas, before making up his mind and stepping through.

David continued walking through the trees, to the big cabin. No one was outside, so he removed his muddy shoes and socks and slipped quietly into the cabin, only to be met by some type of noisy party in progress. Not only were all the Outcasts and their children present, but all those from the Preserve had joined them. Even Doc and Lillie had come from Logan to be there. Mike seemed to be the only one missing.

Doc was in the process of telling an amusing story, but when someone saw David, a hush spread through the room and everyone turned to look at him.

"Don't let me interrupt and spoil the fun" David said, with a forced smile plastered on his face. "Go back to what you were doing."

Doc slowly continued his story and about half of the people turned back to him to listen, while the other half continued to watch David.

As he studied the crowd, and they studied him, it looked like Lisa Beth was the center of attention, with a homemade crown on her head. A cake adorned with lighted candles sat in front of her at the far end of the table. The small children wore homemade party hats. When Doc finished his story to a meager response, everyone's attention returned to David.

"Is it someone's birthday?" David asked no one in particular.

"It's mine," Lisa Beth said excitedly, putting her hands together in front of her. "I meant to tell you yesterday, but things got pretty crazy and I missed my chance. I just turned eighteen." She stood from the end of the table and walked toward him, slowly. She picked up a cloth napkin, licked the corner of it, and used it to wipe a smudge of dirt off his cheek. "Where have you been?" she asked. "I didn't want them to start until you got here, but we couldn't find you and it was getting late."

He remembered the flowers he'd brought and showed them to her, "For you," he said. "Happy birthday."

"Thank you," she said. "They're beautiful."

"I'm sorry I'm late," he said. "I didn't know, but I wouldn't have missed it for anything."

"Not true!" a voice shouted from the back of the crowd. Matt Jr. stepped forward and confronted David. His face was swollen, he had a band aid across his nose and his arm was in a sling. "We saw you get in your car and drive away. You left us. You quit. You gave up. You're a quitter. You don't belong here. Go away."

Lisa Beth took David's hands in hers and looked deeply into

his eyes, "Those are some serious accusations, David, but I don't believe them. Do you?" She asked him.

What could he say to make this right?

"Lisa Beth," he finally said, nearly choking on his words, "I'm not perfect. I have lots of flaws and make lots of mistakes, but I know I love you, and I want to stay with you forever, if you'll have me."

There wasn't a sound in the room, as if no one wanted to miss her response. Lisa Beth stared into his eyes for a few more seconds, then smiled, threw her arms around his neck and gave him a big kiss, oblivious of all the eyes on them.

"I accept!" she called, looking around the room triumphantly and making eye contact with Beth, then her mother. She looked up at the ceiling, and called in her loudest voice. "I'm eighteen, I can make my own decisions. I love him, and I accept him." Then she grabbed him by both wrists and dragged him toward the big cake at the other end of the table.

Epilogue

The Old World—Aspen Valley

The special ops team found the turnoff to Aspen Valley, in the old world, and turned onto the rutted dirt trail. As the first truck turned in, Mike was alerted by a monitor on the wall and sent the gate to collect Doc and Terry at the birthday celebration in the cabin. The three of them stood in the lab, in the old world, looking through the gate as the soldiers spread out, some sneaking through the trees, while others stayed in the vehicles and drove into the valley, right up to the rock face.

"As I suspected," Doc said. "Let's finish the evacuation."

Doc had wondered whether or not Jim would be desperate enough to get the Observer that he would attack the Preserve. He gave it a low probability, since he had given Jim the information he needed to resolve the Brazil crisis; but, true to his nature, he planned for the possibility. Almost everything of importance had already been moved through the gate to the preserve in the twin world. All that was left were the people and what they could carry in their arms.

Mike called Beth and gave her final instructions. With the portable control in her hand, it took only minutes to have everyone out of the cabin and through the gate, along with the cake, the other food, the party decorations and the rest of their personal property. Being the last one through the gate, she just missed the soldiers who crashed the cabin door and entered.

General Ames approached the larger cabin, where there was smoke curling up from the chimney, likely thinking that was a clue to where the residents were. His men were already gathered on the porch.

"Corporal," Ames said to one soldier standing nearby, "take three soldiers and circle the cabin. Look for anyone hiding or running away. Also, secure any other exits. You four, come with me. The rest of you follow Captain Espey to the other cabin and search it."

Ames pushed open the front door—it was unlocked—and entered a large common room, where a fire burned in a fireplace to the right. The room was otherwise empty, with no place a person could hide.

"You two," he said, pointing, "take the stairs and check the upper rooms. You two check the downstairs rooms. Bring me anyone or anything you find."

A few moments later, a soldier stuck his head out of an upstairs doorway.

"Sir, do you want us to bring furniture or bedding?" He asked.

"Of course not," Ames said firmly.

"Sorry sir. Not trying to be flippant. But that's all that's here. Not even a toothbrush or comb."

"Impossible!"

"I even looked under the beds, sir. Not even cobwebs."

Ames stormed towards the back of the cabin and was met by another soldier coming from that direction.

"Nothing sir," the soldier said. "Not even dirty dishes in the sink."

Ames turned and headed for the front door, followed by his soldiers, all with their heads bowed, as though the failure to please their general was their fault. On the front porch, he was met by Captain Espey, just coming from the second cabin.

"Nothing there, sir," Espey said. "It looks abandoned. Cleaned and abandoned."

"Unbe-flippin-lievable!" Ames said. He looked across the clearing and could see the other half of his special ops team standing around the location where there was supposed to be a hidden door in the rock wall. He started walking, determinedly, in that direction, passing through a well-cared-for orchard. He paused long enough to pluck a large, ripe peach and take a large, juicy bite. Then he continued on, commenting to Espey on how good the peach tasted.

Doc heard the explosion that meant the special ops team had blown the outer door and would be charging into the room any minute. He took one last look around, picked up the portable control panel off the desk and slipped through the gate after Terry and Mike. Ames sent his team in all directions, following a plan they had practiced beforehand, having laid out the Preserve in a warehouse on base. They found nothing of a personal nature and very little that was portable.

Mike was glad Doc had suggested they do a trial run a few days earlier. They had learned that everyone was fuzzy about what to move ahead of time and what to keep with them. Riley had left her favorite hand lotion and Ben's five-year-old son, the one who had dumped his beans in David's lap at dinner one night, had left his favorite toy, a hand-carved gun that his dad had helped him carve. He was proud of it because, his dad said, it looked just like the one his dad had used to help protect the valley during the battle with Jason's army.

Since they'd run the trial evacuation, everyone knew what to expect, and nothing of value was left behind. Mike watched the mad search of the buildings and the preserve, by the soldiers, through the gate, a satisfied smile on his face.

Mike, Doc and Terry were watching through the gate as General Ames called General Peatross with his report. Doc recognized Peatross's voice.

⊛

"They're gone," General Ames said into his radio.

"What do you mean, 'gone'?" General Peatross asked, from his position at the Bear Lake County airport.

"Just what I said. We've searched the Preserve and the cabins and no one is here."

"Then bring the Observer and get back as quickly as you can. Bring anything else that you . . ."

"Sir?" Ames interrupted. "The Observer is missing, too. The lab and office are empty, even the closets and the pictures off the walls."

Peatross was speechless. When he finally found his voice, all he could think of to ask was, "Did you pass them on the way? Did you search the valley?"

"They're not in the valley, sir. They're just gone."

Knowing the timing of the attack, Bob had the president on another line, so he could report the team's progress. "Sir," Bob said to the president, then didn't know how to explain. He had failed, after promising to succeed.

"They're gone," Jim said, "aren't they?"

"Yes, sir. I don't know how. We didn't . . ."

"I was afraid of this," Jim said. "The observer links two worlds. All they had to do was step through the gate into the other world."

"But there's no way he knew we were coming."

"One of the things I learned, working with Amos and President McCormick all those years, is that Amos thought everything through, thoroughly. I suspected Doc would be the same way. If he had any inkling that we would come after the Observer, he would have been prepared to evacuate within minutes. It appears that's what he's done."

"So, what do we do?"

"You can try to find out if he has property in Logan, but when I was there, there wasn't much left of the city. Besides, he's probably three steps ahead of us. Just come home."

☢

In the lab of the Preserve in the twin world, Mike, Doc, and Terry set the Observer on the table.

"Does it feel like we're running away?" Mike asked, "like they're going to keep trying to find us?"

"It kinda does," Terry said. "What do you think, Doc? Are we going to have to keep hiding?"

"The alternative is to rejoin society and try to answer where we've been for several years," Doc said.

"Why would we have to answer any questions?" Mike asked. "Couldn't we just stay in Aspen Valley and only venture out when we need something?"

"You mean, like credit cards, bank accounts, Social Security numbers, groceries and building materials? That sort of thing?" Doc asked.

They thought for a few minutes about how complex life had become in the twenty-first century.

"Maybe the board needs to tackle this," Mike finally said. "Maybe we can integrate into society in stages. I'll take that on as my next task."

"That's good, Mike." Doc said. "I don't know if I'll live long enough for you to figure it out. I think I'll get your mother and go hide in Logan."

☢

In the community center of the Preserve in the twin world, Beth had organized everyone into teams to play games. Beth looked up as the men entered, and smiled. They returned the smile as they looked around at the most important people in the world, their extended family.

"Thanks, Beth," Mike said. "It looks like everyone is fine."

"They're more than fine," Beth said, looking around the room at the happy faces. "They're wonderful."

David took Lisa Beth by the hand and led her quietly out of the room. She protested about leaving her birthday party until David pulled her close, gave her a hug and kiss and whispered in her ear. After that, she followed him willingly, holding tightly to his arm and eventually dragging him along in her hurry to reach their destination. Beth, watching the birthday girl leave the party, debated calling them back, then decided to leave them alone for a while. Reaching the library, David grabbed a chair and carried it to a dark corner, between bookshelves and sat, easing her onto his lap, where they resumed their kissing, oblivious of the party taking place a few yards away in the community center.

After a while, David lifted her off his lap long enough to reach in his pocket and remove a small box. He let her take his place on the chair, then knelt in front of her. He opened the box to show her the diamond ring inside, the one he had intended to give to Stefani. He had wondered if it would bother him, or Lisa Beth, to have it, then decided it didn't matter.

"I love you," he said. "Will you marry me?"

"I wondered how long it would take you to ask," she said, as he slipped the ring on her finger. Then they kissed again.

Author's note

The Heritage of Aspen Valley marks the end of the *Gemini Gate* series. However, I still have a couple of stories in me, so I'm going to continue writing. Watch for my stories on Amazon.

About the Story

The Gemini Gate series combines real-world geopolitics, including a detailed, behind-the-scenes look at the White House and the possibility of a global thermonuclear Armageddon, with a fictional technological discovery that just might hold the secret to saving the human race. It takes a component of science fiction—a hypothetical, fictional technology—and embeds it in a realistic, present-day world.

The premise of the Gemini Gate series is that: faced with the prospect of nuclear weapons in the hands of madmen—what we see in today's headlines would have us believe that there are radical ideologies in the world that would welcome another world war—the U.S. government feels compelled to confront the perpetrators and defend itself; while the people of the world suffer as a result of global political decisions, with the exception of a few, like the Blunds and Stephens's, who anticipate and prepare in advance, to survive the chaos.

When the idea for the story came to me, Aspen Valley existed, but only in my mind. Having travelled extensively throughout Utah over the years, visiting the beautiful and unique natural treasures of Utah's State and National Parks and forests, I tried for years to match up what was in my head with a specific location. Driving up Logan Canyon to a family vacation at Bear Lake a few years ago, I realized that we were in the right canyon. I just needed to find Aspen Valley. It's there, a little different than I've described it in the story, but close enough to recognize it. If you're ever in Logan Canyon and spot it, send me an email to let me know.

I've been to and loved many of the places I've written about in the series. Many of my characters are reflections of people I know and care about; I hope you see yourself in one of them.

One of my goals in writing this story was to give each character a unique and believable personality. So, many of the characters in the series are patterned after people that I know or have known. Just to be sure that I don't offend anyone, let's just say that if you identify with one of the characters, he or she was meant to resemble you—except for Jason, who is a composite of all the bad character traits I could think of.

This story is a work of fiction. All of the characters in the book are from the author's imagination and any resemblance to known persons is purely coincidental. Location names, government organizations and functions and the effects of man-caused and natural disasters mentioned in the story are accurate to the best of my ability to determine.

About the Author

I grew up in Salt Lake City and graduated from the University of Utah in Civil Engineering. My life revolves around my family and most of my spare time is spent with them. Together we enjoy camping, hiking, travel and get-togethers with extended family. In my quiet time, I enjoy gardening, family history, emergency preparedness, home remodeling, reading and now, writing.

I've traveled to six continents, either for pleasure or business. I survived two floods in Rio de Janeiro and a drenching rain forest in Costa Rica. I've been stung by a Ray on a California beach, I managed the construction of a graphite composite America's Cup race boat and watched it compete and win off the coast of San Diego. I managed the construction of a graphite composite prototype of the V-22 Tiltrotor aircraft. I managed the construction of five large steel wind turbines, which were installed in Washington, Wyoming and California. I managed and coached project managers in the U.S. and Canada and helped several of them earn their Project Management Professional certification.

Like many people, I had a story in me that wanted to be told, but life got in the way of actually writing the story until recently. My career as an engineer and project manager has led me through multiple industries and specialties, including electric utilities, nuclear power plant construction, water management, global mining and aerospace. Each of those experiences contributed to the broad perspective needed and the interest to research and write about the potential effects of global thermonuclear war on the infrastructure, on people and on the world, itself.

The premise of this story is that, faced with the prospect of nuclear weapons in the hands of madmen, the U.S. government chooses to confront the perpetrators and fight back, rather than sit idly and be abused. Like you, I hope we never see nuclear war. However, what we see in today's headlines led me to speculate on the ability—or inability—of government leaders to control the radical ideologies that threaten to engulf us in world war.

Feel free to contact me with questions and suggestions.

This story about a door between two worlds is meant to entertain. I hope you enjoyed it. Thank you.

Steven E. Wilde
Facebook: StevenEWilde_GG
Email: StevenEWilde@gmail.com
Website: www.stevenewilde.com

www.ingramcontent.com/pod-product-compliance
Lightning Source LLC
Chambersburg PA
CBHW020303030826
48979CB00027B/2035/J
* 9 7 8 1 7 7 3 4 2 1 1 1 7 *